DELETED!

DELETED!

A Sam and Vera Sloan Mystery

ROBERT L. WISE

A
JANET
THOMA
BOOK

THOMAS NELSON PUBLISHERS®
Nashville

A Division of Thomas Nelson, Inc.
www.ThomasNelson.com

Published in Nashville, Tennessee, by Thomas Nelson, Inc.

Scripture quotations are from THE NEW KING JAMES VERSION. Copyright © 1979, 1980, 1982, Thomas Nelson, Inc., Publishers.

Publisher's Note: This novel is a work of fiction. All characters, plot, and events are the product of the author's imagination. All characters are fictional, and any resemblance to persons living or dead is strictly coincidental.

Library of Congress Cataloging-in-Publication Data

Wise, Robert L.
    Deleted! : a Sam and Vera Sloan mystery / Robert L. Wise.
      p. cm.
    ISBN 0-7852-6697-6 (pbk.)
    1. Sloan, Sam (Fictitious character)—Fiction. 2. Sloan, Vera
(Fictitious character)—Fiction. 3. Computer theft—Fiction. I. Title.
PS3573.I797 D45 2003

Printed in the United States of America

03 04 05 06 07 PHX 6 5 4 3 2 1

For
MITCHELL C. BRANTLEY, SR.

my buddy, my friend,
my father-in-law

a man of excellence

Why the word "hacker" came to refer to a computer criminal, instead of the intelligent and curious is quite simple: For nearly two decades, people who don't have the intelligence to be real hackers have tried to lay claim to that mystical title by substituting bravado for creativity, and by substituting breaking the law for seeing beyond the confines of the ruts in our minds.

—CAROLYN P. MINEL, *The Happy Hacker*

Prologue

BLOCKS AWAY FROM THE CENTER OF AMMAN, THE BULLHORN on top of a worn white mosque completed the midday Muslim call to prayer. The faithful finished their prayers, but no intercessions came from the large, darkened, two-story stucco house on Al Abdullah Street, several blocks from the entry to the University of Jordan. Although the spring weather had not yet reached the fierce temperatures that would boil over in a couple of months, intense sunlight beat down on the flat roof of the Natshes' house. Yakoub Natshe paid no attention to the changing weather. Every ounce of his energy remained singularly focused on his reckless pursuit. Yakoub had almost completed an invention that could make him an exceedingly rich man.

The door to Yakoub's office slowly cracked open. His father scolded, "When will you make a finish of it?"

Yakoub peered over his shoulder at his father's face framed in the doorway. "I don't know," he snapped.

"Your constant, endless tinkering disrupts the schedule of the entire household!" The father's growl pushed an irritating twist into every syllable. "Come on! Get this thing done. I need to use the office myself."

"*Ay-wa abb,*" Yakoub answered hesitantly and promptly tuned out the noise. "*Na-am,*" he affirmed a second time and then fastened his attention again solely on his Celeron processor's screen.

Abu Natshe slammed the office door with an unusually forceful bang. Yakoub's younger brother and sister were never allowed to enter the office when he was working. Kawlah, his mother, never came in anyway, so no other interference would come from the family. The twenty-one-year-old Arab zeroed in on his work with the intensity of a laser beam cutting through a piece of steel.

Yakoub Natshe's unusual capacities with a computer came by hard work and application. For five years he had been one of the top math students at the University of Jordan. Obtaining a job at a local Internet café had allowed him the unlimited use of a computer. Countless hours of pounding the keyboard had proved exceptionally valuable, turning him into a master of the Internet.

"Not yet," Yakoub mumbled to himself, "but almost. Almost . . . I can't be far away." He kept pressing the plastic keys. "Got to find *exactly* the right combination," he murmured.

Algorithms had become Yakoub's choice of subjects at the university, opening up the field of encoding and decoding encrypted messages. Yakoub was studying what could be done by applying algorithm techniques to opening and closing secret passwords and hidden messages used by large companies' computers. In time, he began to understand how his exceptional ability with a computer might lead into a world that could make him wealthy.

"Got it!" Yakoub suddenly shouted. "I found the pattern!" He pounded the table with his fist. "I've done it! I've broken the system! I'm in!"

———

Ten days later, on the other side of the world in Encino, California, Paul Miller sat at his computer station at the Motion Picture Association of America offices, staring at a blue screen and checking the chat rooms as he did every day of the week. The young man had completed graduate work in computer science at the University of California at Davis before signing on to become one of the association's monitors for possible copyright violations. It wasn't really what he'd wanted, but then again Paul wasn't that highly motivated to leave California. Disney, Sony, Paramount, Universal, Warner, and Twentieth Century Fox kept the association running with people like Miller paid to keep their backsides covered.

"What in the world?" Paul whispered to himself. He leaned closer to the screen. "Can't be."

"What'd you say?" the woman in the next cubicle asked.

"Come here!" Miller demanded. "Oh, man! Look at this!"

An attractive woman in her late twenties sauntered in. "Whatcha got, Paulie boy? Been takin' short trips into those forbidden, naughty Web sites again?"

"Don't be cute, Sandra. Look at what's just come in over the Internet."

Sandra leaned over Miller's shoulder. "Hmm, a message from Amman, Jordan. Now *that is* far out." She traced along the line with her index finger. "A sixty-kilobyte software . . . why, that's hardly a heartbeat on a computer." She stopped talking and her mouth dropped partly open.

"I told you this was something to see."

"Some geek's finally done it! He's cracked our system."

Paul Miller immediately began typing in instructions for the computer to print out the screen's message. "The boys upstairs are going to be shocked out of their minds over this one."

"Boys upstairs?" The woman cursed. "Blew my mind and I don't even have a twit to do with finances around this place."

The printer spit out the copy of the Internet message, and Miller hurried out of his small cubicle. "Keep it under your hat," he called over his shoulder. "This is all on the q.t. Got me?"

Sandra nodded and shrugged. "I don't want *anything* to do with this one."

Miller trotted up a flight of stairs and marched into the executive vice president's office. He nodded to the secretary but didn't break his stride.

"Wait a minute!" The woman stood to try to stop Paul. "You can't just walk in there!"

"Sure I can." Paul opened the vice president's door and quickly shut it behind him.

G. Boone Jones looked up from his desk with surprise written across his face. "Miller? I believe your name is Miller?"

Paul sat down in front of the desk. "Yes, sir. Paul Miller. Please excuse me for breaking in unannounced, Mr. Jones, but I thought you'd want this information immediately. I just pulled this off the Internet moments ago." He laid the printed copy in front of Jones.

Jones quickly scanned the copy and then stopped. He reread the entire page carefully. The vice president slowly lowered the paper. "You think this Internet message is for real?"

Miller nodded. "I have no reason to doubt this report. These people have been consistently right in the past."

Jones cursed. "Hollywood has no defense against such an invention. Why, every DVD in the world is now up on the auction block!"

Paul Miller shrank back in his chair. "Yes, sir. Digital Versatile Discs are blown wide open. Any movie can be illegally copied!"

G. Boone Jones stared at Paul Miller as if they might have suddenly become intimate friends. "Last year over sixty-four million dollars' worth of those DVDs were sold all over the world. You realize what this discovery in Amman could do to those figures? What these people could steal from us?"

"Yes, sir."

Jones wiped his mouth nervously. "Every dime could now go down the drain tomorrow morning. *Sixty-four million dollars!*"

1

"LOOKS LIKE MURDER'S IN THE WIND," SAM SLOAN SAID, driving his unmarked police car along the curb on Sierra Madre Street, four blocks from Colorado Springs's City Hall. Buildings from fifty to a hundred years old lined the deserted street. At seven o'clock in the morning, only two other cars were parked on the entire block. The air was quiet but tense. "You boys got your guns loaded?"

Detective Dick Simmons reached under his arm and released the safety on the pistol in his shoulder holster. "Yeah, I'm set."

"Absolutely," Basil Abbas said from the backseat.

"There's the building where our snitches say the murder is supposed to happen." Sam Sloan pointed to a two-story, dilapidated warehouse. The word *Warehouse* had been painted across the bricks decades earlier. Now the name had faded and looked worn. A black front door appeared to be the only functioning part of the brick structure, built before the turn of the twenti-eth century. "My understanding is that the men we're chasing will walk into that place and attempt to shoot Ralph Oliver."

Detective Abbas shook his head. "You Americans certainly do these murders in a crude sort of way."

"Oh, really?" Simmons raised an eyebrow and looked over his shoulder. "You Arabs over there in Jordan have a more gentle means of wiping people out? I don't think so."

Sloan flipped open his laptop computer and hooked the car's remote telephone line into the machine. "Let's get ready to move. Pay attention to what comes up."

"You studied computers in college once, right?" Simmons asked Sloan.

"Used to work in the business," Sam said. "Turned out not to be my favorite field." He typed directions. "Dissatisfaction is how I got into police work, but I know how to use one of these things when I need to."

"There's a car pulling up to the side of the warehouse." Simmons pointed to the back of the two-story building that lined Monument Creek. "Looks like a woman's getting out."

An attractive woman in a fitted red sweater slipped out of a green 2000 Oldsmobile and walked with a long, easy stride to the front door. She put a key in the lock, turned it, went in, and closed the door behind her.

"Okay," Dick observed. "We've got our first player on the court. Oliver's girlfriend is on the scene."

Sam located the Web site. "Here's the face that we're look-ing for." He pointed at the screen. "If the information we received is correct, this Charlie Boyles creep will be one of the hit men. Look carefully at his picture. He's tall, skinny, and probably will have brown hair pulled back in a ponytail. We're going to need to identify him quickly and move immediately."

Detective Abbas leaned over into the front seat. "Hmmm. As the great North African bishop Commodianus once recognized, 'If men do not abandon the wickedness and blindness of the world, they will come to the ways of death.'"

Simmons glanced at Sloan. "What does *that* have to do with this Boyles character?"

"Who knows?" Sam quipped. "Basil simply enjoys driving us crazy by quoting the early church fathers at every opportunity. It's one of his peculiarities."

Ignoring their criticisms, Abbas leaned farther over the seat and stared at the man's face. "Anyone else we should be looking for today?"

Sam punched the button and several more profiles flew past on the small screen. "Here we are. Alfred Harris is the other guy. Notice that he's got a fat face and is nearly bald. The man should be easier to identify than Boyles will be."

"I saw a movie the other night on television," Simmons said, "called *Six Degrees of Separation* or some title of that order. The idea was that we're only separated from anybody else in the world by six people." Dick pointed at the screen. "If we knew the right six people, we'd find this Harris creep immediately."

"Interesting idea," Abbas said. "Only six people away from the pope, the U.S. president, anyone?"

Sloan held the mouse to his laptop computer in the air. "I'd say that idea is now obsolete. We're only about six clicks from anyone in the world. That's the difference computers make."

Sam glanced in the rearview mirror to make sure no one was coming up behind them. He looked virtually as he did every day of the week: he had a boyish face, thinning brown hair, and he wore plain clothing. Dick Simmons was different. He always dressed like a business executive with the most expensive suits. Some of the cops even referred to him occasionally as "Pretty Boy," which made him angry, but he was a world away from Basil Abbas. Basil had a strand of long black hair that always hung down in his eyes, giving him a slightly unkempt appearance. Sam thought that they made a strange trio, sitting idly on an isolated side street watching a building that probably had only one person inside.

"Here comes the number one target!" Simmons pointed to a red 1999 Cadillac that pulled up next to the woman's car. "Isn't that Ralph Oliver? The character who operates our local extortion racket?"

"You got him," Sam said. "I think Boyles and Harris want to put him out of business with the help of a few well-placed bullets."

"Again," Basil Abbas said, "as Commodianus recognized around A.D. 200, 'An evil mind ends up in terrible punishment.'"

"Abbas," Simmons said as he turned around in the seat, "could you refrain from laying those endless lines on me?"

"Look!" Sam pointed up the street. "That brown car stopped up where Sierra Madre and Kiowa Streets meet." He grabbed a small pair of binoculars. "Sure enough. There's Alfred Harris's lovely bald head. Guess who the tall, skinny guy with the ponytail next to him is?"

The detectives watched the two gunmen walk half a block and then dart into an empty space where a building had once stood.

"They're going down the alley!" Sam immediately closed

his computer. "We've got to outflank them before they have a chance to pop Oliver . . . even though he's probably got it coming." He pushed the car door open and stood up. "I'll take the front door. You two double to the back side of the building. Remember, you don't grab Boyles and Harris until we've got the evidence of their intention to shoot Oliver."

He hurried across the street. Simmons and Abbas disappeared around the side of the large old warehouse.

Sam walked to the black front door where the woman and Ralph Oliver had entered. He tried to turn the handle but it was locked. Sam knocked hard on the door. No one came. He knocked again, harder.

Sloan could hear the sound of a person turning the lock from the inside. The door opened slightly and the woman in the red sweater looked out.

"Good morning," Sam said politely.

"Yeah?" she said.

"I'm here to see Mr. Oliver."

The woman frowned and looked at Sam out of the corner of her eye. "Do I know you?"

"No." Sloan jutted his chin out. "Ralph Oliver will."

"Hmm." She held the door open. "Come in."

"You're . . . ?" Sam asked.

"Mr. Oliver's secretary," the woman snapped. "Follow me."

Sam glanced around the large, open area. The building smelled musty. Heavy, exposed timbers ran along the ceiling, and the wood looked like it might have been cut with hand axes. Grates and boxes littered the downstairs floor. To the left of the open area overhead, Sam could see what looked like a second floor. It appeared to run back through the rest of the building.

"Mr. Oliver's *not* expecting you." The woman looked defiantly at Sam. "Who'd you say you—"

"An old friend," Sam cut her off.

She kept walking but obviously didn't like his answer.

At the end of the corridor a door was partially open, and light from a single bulb beamed into the dim hallway. The woman pushed the door open and stopped. "Someone here to see you."

"Who?" Ralph Oliver growled.

"Me." Sam stepped in front of her. "Need to talk to you."

Ralph Oliver's fat jaw dropped. "Sam Sloan! As I live and breathe!" He cursed. "What are you doing down here? You got a search warrant?"

The woman looked surprised and stared at Sam. She started backing out of the office.

"Don't do that," Sam told her. "Sit down in that chair over there."

"What?" The woman scowled.

"Look, Sloan, you can't come barging in here and tell my people what to do." Oliver stood up. "You may be the police but you're not God Almighty."

The woman cursed at Sloan and started to shake her fist. At that moment Sam heard a noise above him like someone walking quietly on the ceiling. "Can that upstairs be entered from a window, an outside door, anything?" Sloan demanded.

"You gone nuts?" Oliver barked. "I ain't tellin' you nothin', Sloan. You've got no business barging in here."

Sam flattened against the doorjamb and pulled out a snubnosed .38 revolver. "Be quiet!"

"Hey!" Oliver held his hands up. "Don't be pointing that gun at me."

The secretary threw her arms around her chest, fell into the chair, and doubled up in a ball.

"I mean it, Sloan," Oliver warned. "We ain't done nothin'."

Suddenly a burst of gunfire exploded through the ceiling as a machine gun sprayed the room with bullets. Sam leaped through the door and saw Alfred Harris standing on the building joists, firing down into Oliver's office. Sam instantly shot back and Harris dropped out of sight. From somewhere behind Harris another person started shooting at him. Dick Simmons appeared and started blasting at the second story. Sam jumped behind a steel grid and kept shooting. The gunfire continued for several seconds and then abruptly stopped. Sam could hear a man running.

"Careful!" Sam yelled at Dick. "The other man may still be up there with that machine gun."

Simmons inched toward back steps that led to the second floor. His steps creaked on the old wood. He peeked over the top. "One man's up here . . . holding a machine gun . . . but he's dead!" Dick shouted. "There's an open doorway down there at the other end."

"Be careful!" Sam yelled back. "Abbas could be out there somewhere. Go get that other jerk!"

Dick took off across the second floor toward the back door. "I'll see if I can run Boyles down."

The sound of shots opened up from outside the building and Sam could hear someone running. Other gunshots echoed back. For a moment Sam heard only the sound of shooting, then a distant car started up and sped away.

Sloan inched back into the office. Ralph Oliver lay crumpled over his desk with at least six shots through his body. He was obviously dead. The woman in the red sweater lay in a corner whimpering.

"You get hit?" Sloan asked her.

"No," she muttered. "Don't think so."

Sam got down on one knee to look her in the eye. "You're more than Oliver's secretary, aren't you?"

She barely nodded.

"Thought so." Sam heard the back door open. "Stay where you are and you'll be safe."

Abbas started calling his name.

"I'm in here," Sam yelled.

"He got away!" Abbas huffed. "Flat went around us. Got in the car. Took off."

Sloan shook his head. "We might have been more observant of where he went."

"I guess I should have stayed between the building and his car."

Sam nodded. "Okay, call for a couple of ambulances and report the runaway car to headquarters unless Simmons has already done so. Unfortunately, we didn't do Oliver much good."

"At least we got one guy," Basil said.

"Really?" Sam sounded cynical. "That's not much when you let the other man escape."

"But we did get Harris."

Sam flinched. "Sure. Harris is deleted."

2

THE DAY AFTER THE SHOOTING ON SIERRA MADRE STREET, Sam Sloan sat at his desk in the Colorado Springs Police Station, staring at the dull white wall. Usually the well-known detective was running hard to keep up with the demands of solving a gruesome murder or a big-bucks bank robbery, but this morning he was lost in his thoughts.

Although he tended to maintain a tough exterior, Sam loved people. A shoot-out with people like Charlie Boyles or Alfred Harris came with the job, but killing deeply troubled Sam. While it wasn't clear who shot Harris, Sam was certain that he had. Long ago he'd faced the fact that killing would happen in police work, and Sam knew that his own life was always on the line. Harris could have shot him with that machine gun as easily as not. Still, he didn't like the fact that some man had to die.

Oliver's death wasn't encouraging either. The police chief had been quite upset that Boyles escaped.

Sloan looked out the window at the gorgeous blue sky above the mountains and thought about what a wonderful spring day it was. The usual pressure of getting business done had slacked off during the first months of spring. Tourists were walking up and down the streets. It was just the right time to go fishing, he mused, which would truly help his attitude this morning . . . if there were any way he could slip out the back door without getting caught.

"You busy, Sam?" Basil Abbas asked from the doorway.

Sam jumped. "Abbas? Where'd you come from?"

"Looks like I startled you."

Sam studied his dark-complexioned Arab friend, who enjoyed sneaking up on people. Sam's job was to make sure that Basil, who was on loan to the Colorado Springs police force from Amman, Jordan, knew every technical aspect of American police work. With his usual strand of black hair hanging down in his eyes, the tall Arab had an innocent look. He wore the same clothes he'd worn the day before. The half glasses on his large nose added to a scholarly appearance, making Basil look more like a professor than a cop.

"Didn't mean to frighten you," Abbas said.

"I was absorbed in thought."

"An excellent pursuit!" Abbas raised his finger like a scholar making a point. "Socrates taught us that to think is to know ourselves. A most excellent pursuit."

"I don't want to get off on one of those long-winded dia-tribes, Basil. I was only reflecting on the beautiful day," Sam said.

Abbas nodded his head. "Certainly. Mind if I sit down?"

He immediately dropped into a chair before Sam could answer—another of Basil's tricks. "Quite an experience yesterday. Wasn't it?"

"Uh-huh." Sam kept looking out the window. "What do you need?"

"I was thinking I'm going to need your help on a case that's come up. You're obviously a master with a computer."

Sam nodded. "I know a little."

"More than a little!" Abbas raised his eyebrows. "Much more. A few minutes ago I was given a strange case to solve. Some local is using the Internet to extort money by manipulating people's credit card numbers. Been taking home a bundle through the back door."

"Oh?" Sloan scooted closer to the desk. "We're talking major money here?"

"Size is relative, but enough has been going down the drain that we need to stop this character quickly. May turn out to be some kids, but someone has taken in more than thirty thousand dollars in the last few months."

"I'd say this one is worth your time, Basil. What can I do to assist?"

"I need you to help me explore how these people broke into the computer system to steal the credit card information."

Sloan shrugged. "Sure. Shouldn't be too difficult. You do know how to use a computer?"

"Vaguely. I've got Windows 98 on my laptop back in my office."

"Okay. That's a starting place. The secret to hacking into any on-line service is in your MS-DOS component. That's where the Internet tools are hidden."

Basil stared as a frown slowly crossed his face. "I'm not sure I understand. I'm a real neophyte."

"My point is that you've got to learn how to run several Internet and network applications simultaneously. Got me?"

Abbas shook his head. "No. I don't think so."

Sam glowered and started to say something caustic but then held his tongue. "I'd say you need to move away from those antiquarians you quote all the time and get into the twenty-first century. Go get your machine," he said. "I'll show you what to do."

"Excellent!" Abbas hopped out of the chair. "I'll be back in a moment."

Exactly what he wanted me to say, Sam thought dismally. *Goodbye, fishing.*

———

Sam and Vera Sloan's seventeen-year-old daughter sat at her pine desk in her bedroom, staring at the blank screen on her Ascentia computer. Beanie Babies, dolls, stuffed animals, trinkets, and other memorabilia lay carefully placed around her bedroom, giving it a homey, warm feel. As of late, Cara's desk had changed from the place where a little girl played to the desk of a student almost on her way to college. Reference books, computer discs, and printer paper lined the desktop.

Since her father had always been a virtuoso on the plastic keys, Cara had learned how to use her laptop like a pro years ago. She saw a faint outline of herself in the blank screen. The long hair, the adult face, the shape of a woman meant that Cara's time with her parents was soon coming to an end. Before long she'd be out on her own, and that thought left Cara feeling ambivalent.

On the simple wooden desk, a school assignment stared Cara in the face, so she didn't have much time to get this computer task done. Her boyfriend, Jack Brown, would be coming over soon. Thinking of Jack reminded Cara of how much she wanted to be out from under the set of rules her parents imposed on her comings and goings. At the same time, she loved her parents and respected their ideas. Cara wouldn't admit it out loud, but most of what they asked of her was reasonable. They hadn't been hard, mean, or unfair. In fact, her relationship with her mother had dramatically improved in the last couple of years; they'd become more like close friends.

Since Vera had become a private investigator, Cara thought, everything had changed for the best. At first she found her mother's switch from a full-time homemaker to a full-time professional detective rather disconcerting, but the evolution had released a new dimension in her mother's personality. Vera and Sam spent more time together talking and even had solved a number of murder cases together.

No matter what she wanted, Cara knew that it wouldn't be long before she'd be on her way to college, and that would settle matters. She'd be a full-fledged adult, like it or not. And the rules would be ones of her making, not her parents'.

Cara reached down and turned on her computer. Immediately it started humming. The screen changed from gray to blue and clicked through its start-up process.

As she watched the screen, Cara mused some more . . . She didn't want to share these tugs on her heart with anyone. They felt too personal and close. Certainly she didn't want her boyfriend to be in on this emotionally difficult matter. Jack had become a warm, dear part of her high school life, but she wasn't ready to expose her deepest heart—to tell him how torn she felt about growing up.

Cara took a deep breath and watched the computer screen fill with the icons and images that ran her various programs. What did all of these symbols mean, anyway? The computer world seemed to be filled with the strangest implications and possibilities. Cara wondered what her mother thought about the powerful tool of the Internet, but she would have to ask later. Right now she needed to check out what was happening on the Web and take care of her schoolwork. Cara clicked on the icon and Columbia On-Line came up on the screen.

Mom will be home shortly, she thought. *Maybe we can have another one of our private talks. I have a lot to ask her.*

3

BASIL ABBAS PLACED HIS LAPTOP COMPUTER ON SAM'S DESK and hooked it up to the telephone line. "I think we're ready to go. I just don't know how to operate the internal process you described."

Sam raised an eyebrow but didn't say anything.

"I'm sure you have your own way of starting this crazy machine up." Basil leaned back. "I'll watch how you do the job."

Without adding any comment, Sloan started the computer and watched the screen.

Basil studied Sloan's face as he intently stared at the screen. Sam had to be in his early forties; his thinning hair added a bit to his age, but he still looked much younger. Sam's gentle appearance often deceived suspects, a quality he shared with Basil. They both kept a low profile that usually threw criminals a curve.

"We're going to do a bit of port surfing, Basil. A port is a way of hooking up with an Internet host computer."

Basil didn't want to sound stupid, but he had no idea what Sam was talking about. Best just to listen. "Fine," he said.

"Here we go." Sam began typing in numbers. "We'll see if we can get at some source of information that might help us get a lead on who these people are."

Basil nodded and watched as the type buzzed across the screen. "You think we can get inside information, huh?"

"Don't know. We are sort of . . . going fishing." Sam smiled mischievously. "We're going to trace the route that a message takes as it hops around to the Columbia On-Line domain server computer," Sam explained. "I want to see if we can pick up some hints about where your people were coming from when they started picking up those credit card numbers."

Basil nodded but was totally lost. *Sam's so far ahead of me that I won't ever catch up*, he thought. *Most amazing man I've ever met! There isn't anything that this man can't do.*

Sam stopped and rubbed his chin. "Hmm, I may be on to something." He typed: *Tracing route to dns-aol.fu.net [999.83.210.28] over a maximum of 30 hops.* He kept hitting the keys and following the responses with more commands. The code that appeared on the screen seemed to be a jumble of meaningless letters and punctuation.

"Think we're getting there?" Basil asked.

"Getting *somewhere*." Sam kept typing. "Sometimes, to arrive where we want to, we have to take some steps that are quasi-legal or even illegal for the average citizen." He typed in several more commands and then leaned back with a satisfied look on his face. "I think maybe I've come up with data for you to run down, Basil. Watch the screen."

Abbas leaned closer but wasn't sure of what he was seeing.

"I sometimes use the code *http://www.ipsubnets* to more than scan ports. In fact, you can map an entire subnet with that one."

"Yes," Basil said commandingly, feeling like an idiot.

"Ah!" Sam grinned. "Here come a couple of names that might prove interesting to you." He hit the key to start the printer.

Basil's mouth dropped slightly. He couldn't believe what he was seeing in such a short time.

"Nothing to it once you get the hang of things," Sam said. "Just got to fool around a bit."

"Of course." Basil nodded his head authoritatively but his mouth hung open slightly and his eyes widened.

"Don't forget that we're still hunting Charlie Boyles, the man who escaped yesterday. Right?"

Abbas nodded mechanically, swooped up his computer, and hurried back to his office.

———

An hour had passed since Cara started working, and she had completed the school assignment in a way that ought to impress the teacher. Cara anticipated she would knock down another A on her task. The doorbell rang and she hurried out of her room.

She opened the front door. "Jack! I didn't expect you this soon."

Jack grinned and leaned against the doorjamb. "How could I stay away from my favorite girl?"

Cara pulled him inside. "What can I say—except that you have great taste?" They laughed and hugged.

"Whatcha been doing, kid?" Jack asked.

"Just finished my schoolwork and was getting ready to talk to my mother. Come on in the kitchen and join the conversation."

"Sure." Jack followed Cara into the kitchen where Vera was preparing supper. "How are you, Mrs. Sloan?"

"Why, hello, Jack." Vera turned away from the kitchen sink. "Didn't know you were here." Vera was a petite woman whose naturally reddish hair dangled attractively around her shoulders. "Nice to see you."

"I dropped by to say hello." Jack sat down at the kitchen table. He glanced around at the kitchen's knotty-pine cabinets, which gave the room a rustic look. Little tourist magnets held pieces of paper against the refrigerator door. An inviting smell of food cooking hung in the air. "Looks like you're hard at work."

Vera smiled and her blue eyes conveyed a special warmth for the young man. "The big boss will be home soon, and it's time to set the dishes on the table." She kept moving around the kitchen. "I'm sure Cara came in just to *help* me."

"To *talk* to you," Cara corrected. "That was my actual interest, I believe."

"Hmm." Vera looked askance at her daughter. "Sounds like we're trying a little end-around play to avoid getting our hands dirty."

"No, no!" Cara shook her head. "I truly wanted to ask you some serious questions." She glanced at Jack, though, and quickly decided not to pursue anything on the personal level. She'd stick to more mundane topics. "Mom, I've been working on my computer, doing an involved problem for school. Of course, everyone uses computers these days, and I want to ask you a question about them."

Vera stopped and looked at her daughter. "Computers? Well, I can use one. But that's about all I know about them."

Cara sat down next to Jack. "This is a strange question, but

I want to know how you place computers in the order of things. I mean, do you see them as good or bad?"

"Good or bad?" Vera frowned. "I guess it all depends on how they are used. They're only machines."

"I'm thinking about how fast they are and the amazing capacities that they have given us to run down information, data, ideas. Sometimes I wonder if the world isn't venturing out into a no-man's-land where evil could happen before we even see it coming."

Jack nodded. "Couldn't computers conceivably get folks into a significant amount of trouble, Mrs. Sloan?"

Vera pushed a casserole into the oven and shut the door. "Only teenagers could come up with questions like yours," she said. "Sounds like what you're asking me is the meaning of knowledge. Something like that?" She moved to the kitchen sink and picked up a vegetable peeler.

Cara nodded. "I don't want to make this too complicated. It's just that the world seems to be run increasingly by machines. They've become our new race of slaves that save us a lot of time. I'm wondering—is that good?"

Vera sat down opposite Cara and Jack at the kitchen table and laid her peeler down. "Interesting question, Cara. Christians have often thought about the meaning of knowledge and truth. I'm no theologian, but I think most of our ministers and Christian thinkers would tell you that our heavenly Father has given us a partnership in which He has endowed us with great capacities to develop wonderful inventions. Computers are simply one of the creations God equipped us to discover and develop."

Cara leaned back in her chair and crossed her arms over her

chest. "I see," she replied. "But couldn't computers get us in a heap of trouble?"

"Sure," Jack intervened. "But so can cars or airplanes. It's all in how we drive them."

"That's my point," Vera added. "When we come up with these new ideas, we must also be prepared to make sure that our inventions are used for the best purposes. But there is never anything wrong with seeking new truth.

"I could put the matter another way. Your father taught me something that I live by. In his reading he discovered that the Christian theologian Saint Augustine taught that the closer people come to truth, the closer they come to God. We don't have to be afraid of new ideas."

Cara beamed. "That's a twist I would not have thought of all year. Very helpful, Mom."

"The Bible says in Psalm 51 that God desires truth in our innermost being," Vera continued. "You also might check out the book of James in the New Testament. I believe that book tells us that if we lack wisdom, we should ask God for this gift. The Scriptures paint a picture of God blessing the pursuit of truth."

"Bright people are closer to the Lord?" Jack asked.

"I'm not saying that smart people are closer to God, or that technologically advanced societies are more holy," Vera explained. "What I'm saying is that we don't need to stop and worry over whether some new discovery is going to wreck our relationship with God. He honors our heartfelt pursuit of truth. Okay?"

"You bet," Cara said.

Vera pushed the carrot peeler across the table. "Good. Now

do something really significant: help me finish preparing the salad."

Cara looked at Jack. "I guess we walked into that one." She pushed the carrot peeler to him. "Want to help?"

"Only if it makes me more intelligent," Jack replied.

4

MONDAY MORNING BROUGHT ANOTHER BRILLIANT SPRING day as Sam strolled into the Nevada Street police station. The air seemed filled with the vigor of the approaching summer. On Saturday night more than the usual number of drunks had been arrested and a few burglaries had cropped up, but there was nothing big or demanding for Sam Sloan to run down. No one had turned up any leads on Charlie Boyles, leaving Sam feeling restless. *Boyles still ought to be around town and some cop should see him,* he thought.

"Sam?" a familiar voice said from the doorway. "Got a minute?"

Basil Abbas is about to attack, Sam thought and nodded.

"I wanted you to know that I'm making significant progress on that computer case you helped me with last Friday. We have isolated two men who give every indication of being prime suspects. We're going to seek a ruling from a local judge today to tap their phones, and I hope we'll be able to shut them down. If not this week, we ought to be able to nab them shortly. Your contribution really sped up the discovery."

"Good news, Basil."

"Some of the pieces in the puzzle are starting to fit together."

Sam smiled as he turned back to his desk. "Yell if you need more help." He kept his eyes locked on a pile of papers before him.

Basil stood awkwardly in front of Sloan's desk, shifting his weight from one foot to the other. "Sure." He started backing out of the room. "See you later." Abbas disappeared down the hall. "Call you after a while."

Sam glanced up to make sure Basil was gone and then turned to a number of files waiting on the corner of his desk. He had paperwork to do and knew Abbas would enjoy chewing on this situation all morning.

Thirty minutes later Sloan had completed the reports on several cases; he wanted to be caught up and ready for developments on the Boyles case. He reached for another stack of papers just as the phone rang.

"Sloan here."

"Dad, it's me."

"Cara! My goodness. To what do I owe the honor of this surprise call?"

"I need to tell you something." Cara stopped and cleared her throat nervously. "You always told me to bring any unexpected detail or problem to your attention. Right? I mean . . . particularly if it might be police business."

"Sure, dear. Shoot."

"Well, I don't know if this situation would really be of interest to you, but then again it could be a big deal. Know what I mean?"

"Cara, I'm always interested in anything that you think is important."

"I just got through logging on to a computer chat room to kill time in my computer lab. I discovered the most amazing message. The hot gossip is that some guy in Jordan has discovered a DeCSS device—a descrambler for DVDs. In other words, this guy has figured out how to copy movies straight off of discs bought from the store shelf. His discovery could be worth millions."

"Where'd you get this information?"

"Dad, I know you won't like this, but I've been sort of listening in on a conversation between computer hackers."

"Cara! I can't think of a better way to spend the next five years—in the can."

"I know, I know, but I don't do any of that bad stuff. I only read what they say in their chat room and on their Web site. Anyway, I logged into the MoRE group, which stands for Masters of Reverse Engineering, and this hacker network is buzzing over the discovery."

Sam thought for a moment.

"You there?" Cara asked.

"Sure. Waiting for you to tell me more."

"This DeCSS—everything about it is illegal."

"Cara, I appreciate your calling me, but I'm not sure this is a problem that I can work on. I'll have to check it out with my superiors."

"I think you need to talk with the chief, Dad. This device could really wreak havoc all over the place. It's the big key to unlock the box office."

"Yes. Yes, you're right." Sam thought for a moment. "You could have stumbled onto a very important discovery."

"I'm telling you that the guy who came up with this is going to become the center of all kinds of problems. We're talking millions of dollars on the line."

"Okay, Cara. I'll talk to the chief and see what the big man thinks. Your calling me was important. Let me see what I find out and I'll tell you this evening."

"Great, Dad! Sounds good. I'll look forward to what you bring home tonight."

"See you then, dear."

Sam hung up the phone. *Don't think this fits our local bill of fare, but who knows?* He stood up. *Let's see what Chief Harrison has to say on this one. Maybe it's more locally significant than I think.*

Sam walked down the hall to Dorothy Waltz's office. The chief's secretary was typing on her computer. "Excuse me, Dorothy."

"Yeep!" The secretary jumped. "Good heavens! I didn't hear you."

"I need to talk to the chief," Sam said. "I might have something that will interest him."

"Okay," Dorothy said slowly, "let me check and—"

"Dorothy!" Police Chief Al Harrison suddenly appeared in the doorway. His hair looked ruffled and the once-crisp police shirt was already wrinkled. "I need you to—oh! Hello, Sloan."

"Chief, I hate to interrupt you, but I've got something that might be important."

Harrison scratched his head and glanced at his watch. "We've got a couple of big problems coming down this morning. By the way, you found that Boyles character yet?"

Sam cringed. "No, sir."

The chief sighed. "What is it, then?"

"It's a matter that may involve millions of dollars."

Harrison's eyebrows raised. "Millions!" he said and frowned. "In that case, come on in."

5

AT 4:40 ON MONDAY AFTERNOON, SAM SLOAN AND BASIL Abbas pulled into the Sloans' driveway, and Sam turned off the police car. "Ready?" Sam asked his friend.

Basil nodded his head. "Your daughter's expecting us?"

"Yes. After I talked to the police chief this morning, I called Cara at school and told her to meet me here at about this time. Everything should be fine."

Abbas opened the car door. "Let's see what Cara says."

"She will get a bang out of being the center of attention," Sam said, chuckling, as they walked toward the back door. "Cara loves to talk."

"She sure is a smart girl, Sam. Can't believe she's only seventeen."

"Thanks, Basil. Cara's always been precocious, and she's done extremely well in school."

"Must take after her mother's side of the family," Basil joked.

"Yeah," Sam quipped, as he opened the door and let Basil in.

The two men found Cara sitting at her desk in her bedroom, working on an after-school assignment. She seemed completely occupied and didn't hear them walk in.

"Don't jump," Sam warned softly.

"Daddy!" Cara whirled around in her chair. "Glad you're home."

"Basil and I need to talk with you," Sam said. "Can we sit down in here?"

"You sit on the bed, Mr. Abbas." Cara pointed at the bed. "Daddy can sit here next to me."

"Good." Sam pulled one of his daughter's chairs closer to Cara's desk. "The police chief was highly interested in your chat-room discovery when he and I discussed it this morning."

Cara beamed. "See? I told you this stuff was important."

"Basil's been working on a computer fraud case here in Colorado Springs," Sam continued. "That's why I brought him along with me."

"What can I do for you gentlemen?" Cara leaned back in her chair and said in a voice like her mother's, "Always glad to help the local police."

Sam laughed. "Thanks, Vera. Let's go back over what we talked about this morning. Tell both of us everything that you've picked up on the Internet."

"Dad, lots of people like to play with the Internet as sort of an intellectual challenge. That's how I got interested in what this MoRE group was doing. Those Masters of Reverse Engineering tinker around and usually know the latest discovery long before the computer companies are advertising their finds. That's the main reason I check out what they're saying and doing."

Sam nodded. "What you were telling me was that some man in Jordan had come up with a software device that makes copying DVDs a snap. Right?"

"There's no telling how much a device like that is worth," Cara said. "Apparently, it's very small and could be used with any computer. The interesting thing is that the invention was created outside of the United States. That little twist in the rope is going to give the executives in the movie business some genuine headaches."

"The inventor lives in Amman, Jordan?" Basil asked.

"That's what the MoRE report said."

Sam looked at Basil with an eyebrow raised. "Sounds like this is happening in your backyard. You shouldn't have too much trouble finding him."

"The Web site was pretty vague about many aspects of this invention, and I didn't get the guy's name," Cara added. "Maybe I could trace it through the Internet. I'm sure this will be a hot topic for a long time, since everyone wants to get his hands on a copy of this discovery."

Sloan crossed his arms over his chest. "That's part of why we need your help. The police chief made me aware of some problems bubbling up in Colorado Springs and across the state of Colorado. Apparently we've had more crimes involving the misuse of computers than I would have thought—like the one Basil's working on right now."

"People stealing credit card names and numbers," Basil explained. "Your father's been helping me run these guys down."

"We'll catch them quickly," Sam said. "Cara, tell us more about this invention."

"The MoRE Engineers are calling it a DeCSS because it

reverses what a content scrambling system does to make disc movies nonreproducible. I'm sure that Hollywood will have the FBI, the CIA, and Scotland Yard running up and down the streets, trying to prohibit the release of these gadgets. If our Jordanian inventor starts selling this product in the USA, he'll make a mint."

Sam nodded. "That's what Chief Harrison is concerned about, Cara. We're close to the front of the line on this project, and at the least it is a crime because it violates copyright laws. Since I've worked with the CIA previously, I may well end up trying to stop this device from hitting the streets. I need you to give me any details you can come up with."

"That's an exciting thought," Cara said. "Nothing like the police coming to your backdoor asking for help!"

"That's not quite what your father means," Basil said. "I think—"

"Cara knows what I mean," Sloan said, cutting off Abbas. "She understands the confidentiality policy of the police department. We're walking on a fine line on this project, Cara. I want you to research every bit of data you can find and print it up for me this afternoon. Okay?"

"Absolutely! I'll hit the chat rooms and even do a little hacking around the edges. Who knows what I might turn up?"

"Can you work on this through the evening if necessary?"

"Sure, Dad. I'll get you a copy of everything that's out there."

———

The next morning Sam walked into Dorothy Waltz's office with a typed report in hand. "I think the chief will want to talk with me."

Dorothy looked up from her desk. "Yes, Al has been expecting you. Go on in."

Sam opened the door and walked in. "Morning, Chief. I have an initial report for you."

Harrison tended to look like he'd been in a wrestling match, but at this early hour his shirt still looked good. He nodded at Sam when he walked in.

"You wanted me to check this DeCSS device that's been discovered for duplication through a computer."

Harrison nodded again. "Find out anything?"

Sam laid the report on his desk. "Here are several pages of explanation about what's humming across the Internet today. I think my report will answer many of your questions."

"Excellent." The chief picked up the report and swiftly read through a couple of pages while Sam waited. "You never cease to amaze me, Sam." He laid the report down. "I've been doing a little homework myself."

"I guessed you'd come up with something for me to do," Sam said dryly. "Isn't that the way it usually works?"

Harrison chuckled. "That's what we pay you for. Earlier this morning I received a copy of a report that came through the Washington offices of the CIA, but that originated with the Motion Picture Association in California. The matter that you brought to my attention is burning a hole through the floor out there in movie America."

"That's about what I gathered from the Internet. By the way, my daughter, Cara, garnered all of the information in that report."

"My, my, violating the child labor laws, Sam?"

"She's seventeen."

"The calendar won't save your hide," Harrison said out of the side of his mouth. "We'll both keep her involvement filed in the Forget Bin. Okay, let's get down to business. People in the CIA know you from the case you worked on with the investment bank shooting several years ago. I spoke with them this morning. Remember when that Alexander character was murdered?"

Sam nodded. "Sure."

"These computer crimes have a bunch of Washington folks upset, and they want the business stopped immediately. I guess there's a significant concern about the country becoming afraid of doing business over the Internet. You get the picture?"

"The way that I'd say it is that someone out there in the Motion Picture Association has financial and political ties to Washington. They've yanked the chain hard and now everyone is jumping. You want me to hop too."

Harrison grinned. "Either way you say it, the results are the same. They want you to help work on finding this decoding device business, and they see Basil Abbas working as your partner because he came from Jordan."

"Dick Simmons has usually worked with me in the past," Sam noted.

"Mr. Pretty Boy can help you if you need him, but I'd put Basil in the front seat with you."

Sam chuckled. "Okay. Whatever you say. How are we going to pay for this investigation? We'll probably do some flying around the country, and those trips can get expensive."

Harrison scratched his head. "We actually haven't gotten that far yet, but I'll discuss this with the CIA people. They've probably got a budget big enough to swallow ours in a single gulp." He leaned back in his chair. "Talk to Abbas about this and let Simmons know that you'll call him if he's needed."

"What about finding Charlie Boyles?"

"Who?"

"You know, the guy who escaped in our raid at the Oliver warehouse last week."

"Give him to Simmons to find. That'll keep him happy."

Sam walked toward the door. "I think you've taken care of my time for the next several weeks."

"Weeks?" Harrison raised an eyebrow. "You may be walking down the computer trail with a magnifying glass in your hand for months, Sam."

6

IMMEDIATELY AFTER SCHOOL ON TUESDAY AFTERNOON, Cara drove home and unlocked the house with her key. "Mom, I'm home!" she shouted from the entryway. "You here? Anyone here? Nobody?"

She must still be down at her office, Cara thought. *Dad is probably still at the police station.* She closed the door behind her.

Cara strolled into the kitchen and took a couple of cookies out of a large ceramic jar, then walked back to her bedroom. She sat down in front of her computer and reflected on her father's assignment the previous evening.

Helping her dad gather information on the descrambling device had been exciting. He had treated her like an equal, and that made her feel more confident about handling some of the growing-up and leaving-home changes she was facing.

She switched on her computer. After several seconds the

screen filled with images. Cara clicked the Columbia On-Line icon and quickly navigated to the homepage.

"Let's see what my ol' buddies at the Reverse Engineering Corporation are up to this afternoon." She scrolled through a list of e-mail messages. Abruptly the words *Warning! Warning!* flashed across her screen.

"What's this?" Cara said aloud. She watched the admonition pop up on her monitor: *An emergency message from Amman, Jordan.* "I can't believe my eyes!" The message read: *Yakoub calling for help. A copy of the sixty-kilobyte device I invented for copying DVDs has been stolen from me. ATTENTION! An American thief is working through the Internet. Great caution advised.*

Cara immediately typed in a response: *Colorado Springs to Yakoub with concern about your theft problem. We will try to help.* She sat back and stared at the screen, wondering if anything would follow. To her surprise, a response quickly appeared. *Thank you.*

Yakoub, Cara typed, *can you tell me more about what occurred?*

The computer response continued. *An American tried to buy my invention. I would not sell and he became difficult. Only a few hours ago I discovered he had stolen one of my discs. I am angry.*

Can you tell me more? Cara quickly pecked out on her keyboard.

Not now, Yakoub answered. *I will think about your request and possibly contact you later. Good-bye.*

For five minutes Cara tried to get another response but nothing appeared. She slumped back in her chair and stared at the screen. "He's gone," she said to herself and then suddenly realized what she needed to do.

Cara saved and printed the message. Across the top of the page were his e-mail address and full name.

"Yakoub *Natshe!*" Cara exclaimed. "Now I know who you are!" She looked again at the piece of paper. "I'm sure there's enough here for Dad to eventually run you down." Cara picked up the telephone and punched in the number for the police department.

———

The sun had already begun to set by the time Sam returned home. Vera had arrived thirty minutes earlier. Sam walked into the kitchen and said, "Vera, let's both talk to Cara about this information she's come up with. I think we may be onto some significant data."

Vera laid her dish towel down. "Okay, let's see what our bright girl has found out this afternoon." She followed Sam into the bedroom.

"Hi, dear." Sam gave Cara a hug. "Your mother and I wanted to talk with you about the information that you called me about at the office today. You've got a sheet of paper?"

Cara picked up the printout from the top of her desk. "Take a look, Dad. I think this is an important breakthrough."

Sam held the page so that both he and Vera could read it. They quickly scanned the contents.

"No question about it, Cara. You've identified how we can run down the person who invented this descrambling device. Why in the world would someone with such a controversial invention make himself so vulnerable?"

Cara looked out the window. "Let me think for a second." She pondered the situation. "My hunch is that maybe this is a kid—somebody not far from my own age. Just a young guy and he's not devious. Most of these computer hackers are brainy nerd-types, you know." She glanced suspiciously at her mother and father.

"Hey, we never called you a nerd," Vera answered.

"Not saying that," Cara said, "*not quite*." She cleared her throat. "My guess is that he's a young guy who started out playing with a computer problem, and now the invention has blown up in his face. I bet he turned to the Internet seeking help, and out of desperation he contacted me."

Sam nodded. "Yes, I can see that picture. You're probably close to the truth. We do know that right now he's terribly upset. What do you think, Vera?"

"I think Cara needs to be careful. We're getting into deep water."

"Your mother's right. We don't want you getting caught up in what could become an explosive situation."

Cara looked exasperated. "You get me involved and then you're going to tell me to leave the problem alone? What kind of deal is that?"

"One that could protect you," Sam said sternly. "We have no idea what's happening in this scenario."

"Sam, obviously your next step is to make the police department aware of what's occurred," Vera reasoned. "Probably this young man's message has been picked up by others, but then again, you may be in the lead on this situation."

Sloan nodded slowly. "Yeah, we may have slipped into some strange variety of crime without even knowing what's happened."

"Look," Cara said, "we've got a family crime-solving team sitting here in my bedroom. Why can't we all work on this problem like we're one big operation?"

"Remember the last time we tried one of these efforts?" Vera said. "I wound up in the hospital in New York City."

"Yes, because you didn't include me fully in everything you were doing," Cara countered.

Sam smiled. "Sounds like the detective team's already broken down on the playing field. Okay, Cara, we won't close you out of the ballpark, but I want you to be very careful. We don't need any surprises sliding in under our noses. Agreed?"

Cara grinned broadly. "I promise to be careful."

Vera looked at Sam with doubt in her eyes. "I'm not sure I agree. Cara's got more than her big toe already in the water on this one."

"Mom," Cara countered, "after all, I'm seventeen! I'll even be leaving home shortly. Let's not try to put me back in the crib."

"I don't think we're worried about a baby bed," Sam answered. "But we don't want to be putting you on a hospital gurney either."

"Don't worry," Cara insisted. "You've got a great case to work on with *what I've found.*"

Vera raised an eyebrow and glanced at her husband. "That's what I'm afraid of."

7

In the spring and summertime, Nevada Street filled with travelers visiting Acacia Park and the tourist haunts that sold everything from expensive paintings to junk made in China. Sam Sloan parked in his usual space next to the Nevada Street police building and entered through the back door to avoid the tourists.

"Morning, Sam," the large lady seated at the metal detector gate said. "You've got that determined look on your face today."

Sam smiled for the first time since leaving the house. "Caught me in my sour face, didn't you, Hilda?"

"You look like your mind's certainly occupied," Hilda said. "That's all."

"Suppose it is." Sam smiled once more and kept walking.

A flood of thoughts had completely absorbed him. No other conclusion seemed feasible and Sam didn't like the possibilities, but he saw no other way to proceed. Whatever plans he might have had were now pushed aside, and more dramatic action was required.

"Hey, Sam!" Abbas waylaid Sloan when he turned down the hall leading to the administrative offices. "Have I ever got news for you. You know those names that you came up with for me on your computer—"

"Follow me," Sam snapped. "We're going down to Harrison's office."

"Harrison?" Abbas stopped and blinked several times. "But I want to tell you about what has—"

"I think we need to act quickly." Sam kept walking, gesturing for Basil to follow him.

"But—" Basil had already fallen ten feet behind and had to hustle to catch up as Sam entered Dorothy Waltz's office.

"Good morning, Dorothy. It's imperative that Abbas and I speak with the chief. Okay?"

Dorothy looked surprised. "Well, I guess so. Let me see if he's free." She picked up the phone. "Sam Sloan's out here with Basil Abbas to see you. Okay?"

"What's happened?" Basil half whispered to Sam.

"Sure," Dorothy said and hung up. "Go on in. Al can see you right now."

Again Sam beckoned for Basil to follow him. "Thank you, Dorothy."

Harrison was already standing up when they entered. "Morning, Sam. What's up today?"

"I think this computer descrambler problem is starting to move too fast, Chief." Sam and Basil sat down. "Let me bring you up-to-date." Sam detailed the theft in Amman and Cara's discovery of the inventor's identity. Basil listened as intently as Harrison did.

"Therefore, I think that Basil and I ought to fly to Amman immediately and see what we can uncover," Sam concluded.

"Go home?" Basil said with wonder in his voice.

"I don't want to fly into the Middle East," Sam said, "but I think that's the only way we'll get to the bottom of the matter. Basil can take me inside the Arab world of this Yakoub Natshe character, and that's where we need to go."

Harrison sat down and rubbed his chin. "I don't like your traveling halfway around the world either, Sam, but I believe you've summed up the matter accurately. Speed may prove important in this chase."

"I thought we could have Basil call the police and even the secret police in Jordan and have them identify who this Natshe is. They might run down his address while we're putting the details of the flight together. We could hit the ground running."

"Yes," Basil agreed, "the *Maukhabarat,* the secret police, would be an important part of this approach. I'm sure they could locate the man quickly."

The chief nodded. "No question about it. If we could get you there in twenty-four hours or less, we'd have as good a jump as we're going to get on this problem."

"Think the CIA might get us on an American military plane? Even if we got halfway there on a fast flight, that would be a significant distance."

Harrison's eyes flashed, the usual sign that his brain had gone into overdrive. "Basil, you get on the telephone and send this information out to the Jordan police establishment. I'll see what I can pull down through the CIA. Sam, you go home and pack. We'll try to get you boys on your way before noon."

"Excellent." Sam gave the chief a symbolic salute. "We're off."

"Be back with you as quick as I get something from Washington," Harrison said, reaching for the telephone.

———

Cara Sloan walked with steady determination down the hallway of Palmer High School. She'd been a student there for her entire high school career and could find her way around the halls with the lights out. The push and pull of other kids' changing classes failed to interrupt her thoughts.

"Cara, slow down!" someone called. "Where are you going so fast?"

Cara stopped and turned around, finding Jack Brown hurrying up the school hallway behind her. "Jack? Hey, what's coming down?"

"You went past me like a deer tearing down a forest trail. What's the rush?"

"Sorry, Jack." Cara smiled apologetically. "I guess I was completely lost in thought."

"Who's put the vise on your brain?" Jack reached out for her hand, then drew back.

"Yeah, the hall monitors will put the big pliers on you if you try to hold my hand." Cara grinned. "They catch everything happening in these corridors."

"Seriously. You looked like you were taking off for Mars."

"Jack, I'd like to tell you, but I've been helping my dad with a police assignment." She lowered her voice and whispered in Jack's ear, "And he warned me not to tell anyone. Sorry."

A frown crept across Jack's face. "I don't get it, Cara. I thought we had something special going on between us."

"We do, Jack, but my father's crime stuff is in an extra-special class. It's confidential."

Jack's eyes narrowed. "I can't believe that you're cutting me out of your life."

"Come on." Cara imitated a whine: "I can't tell you about only this *one thing*."

Jack took a step back. "Don't let me slow you down, Cara." He started walking backward. "I'll see you later when you've got more time for your common, everyday friends."

"Oh, Jack. Really."

Brown kept walking backward. "Yeah, sometime when you're all caught up on the stuff that counts, give insignificant me a ring." He disappeared into a crowd of kids.

Cara stood still with her mouth open. "I can't believe it." She turned uneasily and walked more slowly up the hall, feeling stunned. Why in the world would Jack have such a fit about her not sharing any of the details about the theft in Jordan? After all, her father would go off like a rocket if she talked about those issues.

Cara walked into the computer lab and sat down at her workstation. Surely this flap wouldn't amount to anything. Would it? She put her hands on the plastic keys but stopped as a funny feeling ran down her back. Maybe this problem with Jack was more serious than she thought.

8

SAM HURRIED INTO THE SLOANS' HOME ON TWENTY-THIRD Street and began packing his bag. He wasn't sure how quickly the police chief could put together a flight to Jordan, but if it were up to him, he wouldn't delay the start of the trip. Sam didn't think that he'd be gone too long, but who could tell? He still didn't want to carry a bag full of clothes across the desert. One pair of shoes. Maybe two suits. He'd wear one. Keep it simple.

Abruptly the back door opened. Sam stopped. Someone was breaking into their house? He reached into his shoulder holster and pulled out his pistol. Quietly Sam inched toward the bedroom door and slipped next to the doorjamb. He switched off the safety and held the gun in front of him. Then he leaped into the hallway with his pistol aimed at the kitchen door. "Don't move!"

"Ahhh!" Vera screamed and threw her hands up, hurling her purse across the room. "I live here!"

"Vera?" Sam instantly dropped the gun. "What are you doing home?"

Vera grabbed her chest and fell back against the doorjamb. "Great Scot. I thought you'd shoot me! I think I'm having a heart attack."

"Dear, I heard the back door open and thought that a burglar was breaking into our home. If I'd had any idea it was you . . ." Sam rolled his eyes and looked embarrassed. He quickly put the pistol back in his shoulder holster. "Oh, man. I'm sorry."

Vera fanned her face. "I wouldn't have expected to be held up in my own kitchen." She dropped down in a chair.

"What are you doing home, dear?"

"I called the police department to talk to you and got Basil Abbas. He said you were going to Jordan. I came home because he said you would leave soon."

"I was going to come by the All-City Detective Agency before we left. Honestly. I wouldn't leave the country without talking to you."

"Well, I hope so," Vera said indignantly. "I thought that you could use a little help in getting ready to go. After all, I am your wife."

"Sure, dear. Of course." Sam looked around nervously. "Actually I'm almost packed."

Vera reached out and took Sam's hand. "Oh, Sam, here you are about to take off again! We don't ever seem to slow down."

Sam pulled Vera up and toward the couch. He tugged Vera

down on his lap. "And I think you love every minute of the chase." He laughed. "Right?"

Vera blushed slightly. "I guess so, but I'd like for some of this madness to disappear." She hugged him. "I pray that God will keep His protective hand on you, Sam. You're going across the world, literally to the other side of the globe."

Sam bit his lip and nodded. "Yeah. A continent away."

"I don't want you getting into any dangerous situations."

Sam shook his head defensively. "Nah. I'm simply going to look in on a couple of matters. No big deal."

Vera abruptly squeezed his cheeks. "No big deal, my foot! Every time you go off on one of these trips, you end up in some wild chase or shoot-out. Don't you kid me. I know very well what can happen."

"I promise, Vera. I'll be very careful."

Vera leaned back and looked him straight in the eye. "You do that. Understand? We have old age to spend together. Don't you dare shortchange me." She hugged him tightly.

———

When Sam reached the police station, Basil and the police chief were waiting for him in the lobby. "Sam," Chief Harrison said, "we're going out to Peterson Air Force Base where they have an airplane waiting. I've worked out an arrangement with the government to get you flown straight to Frankfurt, Germany. They'll put you on a military cargo plane. The CIA believes there's no way faster to get you to Amman today."

Sam nodded appreciatively. "Al, you must have pulled every string you had in Washington."

"Like I told you the other day—the boys at the top are

quite upset about this invention. They want this device stopped before the entire DVD industry is affected and Hollywood starts losing money. They see you as a likely possibility to do the job for them."

Sam shook the chief's hand. "We'll do our very best, sir."

Harrison slapped Sam on the back. "You and Basil try to keep out of trouble and let me know what happens."

"I will, Chief. We'll be back in touch as soon as we land." Sloan quickly hopped into the police car and a sergeant drove the detectives away.

"We don't have much time," Basil told Sam as they zoomed down the street. "I think when we hit the airport, the jet will be ready to leave."

Sam nodded. "You get your call through to Amman?"

"I contacted the police at several different levels," Basil explained, "and I put Yakoub Natshe's name out on the table. I believe we'll get our best response from the secret police. The *Maukhabarat* shouldn't have much trouble running this man down."

"Really?"

"Sam, our secret police have extraordinary ties throughout the country. No one talks about it much, but the *Maukhabarat* is into almost everything happening in Jordan. Probably half the students at the University of Amman have worked for the *Maukhabarat* at some time or the other."

"Half the students?" Sam turned and looked at Basil with an amazed look on his face. "You're kidding!"

Basil shook his head. "Sorry. We have our own way of doing things in that part of the world. The monarchy keeps close tabs on everything that develops in Jordan. They make sure that any loose cannons are identified and properly labeled. I'll bet the *Maukhabarat* already has its eye on this Natshe. You'd be surprised how effective our local grapevine is."

"Whatever you say, Basil. I know absolutely nothing about that part of the world except that most of it is a desert."

Basil snickered. "Sam, you haven't seen anything yet. You're going to be hotter than you've ever been in your life!"

The police car turned off Highway 24 and down Peterson Road at the edge of Colorado Springs. "I bet that's our airplane over there." Basil pointed toward a military transport sitting on the runway. "Looks like the Air Force is ready to roll."

9

Sloan and Abbas were quickly hustled into the 737 jet and strapped into seats. Sam could see the ribs of the plane sticking out of the wall. *This jet is a long way from a commercial airliner,* Sam mused. *No first class on this thing; this is pure military style.*

The rear of the airplane had already been stacked with cargo. A few Air Force men moved the remaining equipment into place. "We'll be off the ground in a few minutes," an airman with a sergeant insignia told Sam and Basil. "Please stay buckled up until we give you further instructions. We're an easygoing bunch, but we must follow guidelines. Keeps the brass happy. Our flight path will take us straight out over the North to Germany. We'll be under way in a few seconds," the sergeant said. "Hang on."

"Don't see any flight attendant," Sam quipped.

The airman laughed. "Really? I'm as close as you get." He

pointed toward the back. "I ain't much to look at, but the mess hall threw in some sandwiches and a couple of thermoses of hot coffee. That's our version of airline food."

"I bet it will be better than what the commercials put out." Sam grinned at the sergeant. "We'll survive."

The airman stood up. "Yeah, we always do. Come up and knock on the cabin door if you want something. We'll be in there working on the flight."

"Thanks." Sam watched the man walk away. "Pretty basic operation, huh, Basil?"

The Arab looked around the cabin. "Actually there's plenty of space to spread out on the floor. If we could get a good seven hours or so of sleep, we'd feel better on the other end of the trip."

Sam glanced at his watch. "I got up about five hours ago. I don't know if I can get back to sleep. I feel more like running around a gymnasium."

Basil nodded. "Sure. But I can tell you that by the time nightfall comes in Colorado, a new day will be starting in Jordan. You're going to be stretched before this flight is over. Like the ancient church father Saint John Chrysostom once said—"

"Yeah, I get the picture," Sam cut him off. "I'll try to sleep."

The airplane lurched forward and lumbered down the tarmac. The roaring engines made talking difficult. Sam turned his attention to the window. As the huge jet sped down the runway and soared into the air, Sam peered down at Colorado Springs, watching the city become smaller and smaller until it finally disappeared beneath the clouds.

He prayed softly, "Lord, please be with Vera and Cara. Keep them safe and protect them from any trouble. I'd certainly appreciate a good helping of that same blessing myself. Please keep me from walking through doors I shouldn't enter." He took a deep breath. "I know You'll be with me. Thank You very much. Amen."

Sam watched the clouds billow up like giant balls of cotton, forming a soft bed of filmy white beneath the airplane. The serenity of the vast sky filled him with a quiet sense of peace. He needed to allow the hand of God to lead him through whatever lay ahead on this journey into a strange land. Though the thought of being immersed in a completely foreign society unsettled him a bit, it was time to let go and trust God. Sam decided to try to take a nap. He reached in his pocket for a couple of Sleep-Ease tablets.

———

Sam seemed to be running through a hazy world filled with strange colors and sounds when suddenly he felt a hard thump, sending him several inches into the air before he smacked back down in his seat. He blinked several times and abruptly realized the airplane must have landed and was now taxiing down the runway. Sam blinked and looked around.

"You missed everything," Basil Abbas yelled. "Should have seen the landing."

"Where are we?" Sam sounded disconcerted.

"We just arrived in Frankfurt. You slept better than you thought you would."

"Germany?"

"Yup." Basil nodded. "We'll be changing airplanes at this airport."

Sam unbuckled his seat belt and stretched. "I can't believe

that I actually slept through the entire flight." He shook his head. "I feel groggy."

"I think those Sleep-Ease tablets did the trick."

Sam shook his head. "Must have." He looked out the window. "Certainly is dark out there."

"It's the middle of the night over here in Europe. We're about eight hours ahead of Colorado Springs time now." Basil pointed down the runway. "Not much is happening besides several commercial jets taking off. I think they'll put us on a Jordanian Royal Airline flight that ought to get us there about breakfasttime."

The American military jet rumbled up to a hangar and the crew started preparing to open the doors. Several airmen hustled up and down the aisle. As soon as the door opened, two men in business suits hurried onto the airplane.

"Sloan and Abbas?" the first man asked.

"Yes." Sam extended his hand. "You're going to help us get on to Jordan?"

"I'm with the U.S. government," the heavyset man answered briskly. "We've got an airplane that will leave as soon as you board. The Jordanians are holding it for us. We've been instructed to get you men out of Frankfurt as fast as we can."

"Thank you," Sam answered. "We will get our bags and follow you."

"As quickly as possible," the second man said.

Minutes later Sam and Basil sat in the back of an electric cart buzzing down the long corridors. "Don't worry about your passports in Frankfurt," the heavier man instructed. "Just get on the airplane. They'll check you out when you land in Jordan."

Sam leaned forward. "Anything we should know?"

The man shrugged. "Not to our knowledge. All we were assigned to do was get you on that airplane."

Sam looked at Basil and shrugged. "Guess everything is going like it should."

Basil nodded. "Seems so."

Ten minutes later the cart pulled up to a gate at the opposite end of the airport. "Here you are," the heavyset man said. "Just walk down that corridor and you're on your way to Jordan. Good luck."

Sam thanked the men and grabbed his bag. Basil had already started down the entryway. "Appreciate the lift." The men only nodded and sped away.

"They didn't say much," Sam said to Basil.

"Probably American security people working in and out of the airport."

When they reached the hatch of the airplane, a Jordanian flight attendant greeted the men: "Mr. Sloan and Mr. Abbas?"

"Yes, ma'am," Sam answered.

The flight attendant smiled. "Good. We're ready to leave as soon as you are seated."

"Certainly." Basil headed toward his seat.

Sam quickly stowed his luggage in the overhead bin. By the time he was seated and had his seat belt secured, the door was closed and the airplane's engines revved up. The airplane immediately started backing out of the stall.

"We're on our way again," Sam told Abbas.

"Indeed! I can hardly wait to step off this airplane. I've been away from home for five years. I'm sure that my family will be there to greet us."

"Your family?"

"Of course. My mother, father, aunts, uncles, nephews! Everyone will be there to say, '*Ah-lan*'!"

"How many people are you talking, Basil?"

Abbas shrugged. "I don't know. Twenty . . . thirty . . . maybe fifty."

"Fifty!" Sam's eyes widened.

"I'm a returning hero, Sloan. A member of the American police establishment. They will be delighted to speak with me. Maybe a hundred will be there. Everyone will come out to shake the hand of Basil Abbas."

Sam looked out the window. "Fifty people!" he grumbled under his breath. "A hundred! I bet Chief Harrison would fall on his face if he had any idea this army was coming. I didn't expect half the city to show up."

10

THE ROYAL JORDANIAN COMMERCIAL AIRLINER DESCENDED over the city of Amman and quickly landed at the international airport. The burning sun had begun to rise over the hills, sending shimmering rays of heat across the arid land. Within minutes the doors of the airplane opened and the passengers began filing into the long corridors that would take them through passport control. The dry heat of the desert immediately settled over the travelers as they hurried into the air-conditioned airport.

"We must pay ten JDs to enter Jordan," Abbas explained as he walked. "That's ten Jordanian dinars. I already have the money in my pocket for both of us so you will not have to worry about changing your money."

"Excellent," Sam answered. "I'm sure that will expedite getting us through the passport line and into the airport. I have no idea where I'd get the local currency until we've passed the passport booths. Time is of the essence."

"Then I will see my family!" Basil exclaimed. "Yes, the hour is at hand."

"Wait a minute." Sam took his arm and stopped. "Listen to me. We've got a tight time schedule. I know you're excited to be home, but we can't be running around shaking hands with everybody who's possibly related to you and your family. Understand?"

Basil smiled and started walking again. "Of course. Of course. We will experience no delays. You will see."

Sam shook his head and hurried to catch up. "I mean it, Basil. We need to find this Natshe guy as quickly as possible. You got the picture?"

"I am sure that my friends at the *Maukhabarat* have already located the man. We will get there at once."

Sam frowned and stuck his hands in his pockets. Basil sounded like he was putting him off. Sam wanted more.

The two men quickly cleared the diplomatic passport entrance and within minutes were officially in the country. With bags in hand, they walked out of the holding area into the airport proper.

"Amm Basil!" a young woman shouted and charged Abbas. *"Ah-lan. Ah-lan."* Instantly a mob of people surged forward. The woman hugged Abbas while people of all sizes and shapes rushed toward him. Most of the women wore long, flowing black or white robes, and a few had veils across their faces. Men wearing white caps, some with long robes, joined the throng. Basil Abbas looked like the returning king greeting his loyal followers. People hugged him, shook his hand, and chattered like a sputtering car engine.

Sam stared. He'd never seen anything like the crowd greeting Abbas. Children pulled on Basil's coat and hugged his legs.

Finally Basil held up his hand. *"Heh-dee,"* he demanded. "Quiet!" He looked toward Sam, standing completely alone. "Please meet my friend, the great and world-renowned Sam Sloan!"

The crowd instantly broke into applause. People walking through the airport stopped and looked in their direction. Sam could feel his face turning red and wanted to hide behind a concrete pillar. He nodded modestly and waved feebly.

"Salute Detective Sloan," Abbas ordered.

The mob abruptly scurried in Sam's direction, pinning him against a concrete retaining wall, shaking his hand, and jabbering a thousand comments he couldn't understand.

"Minfadlak! Minfadlak!" Basil demanded. "I think they are overwhelming you, Sam. Don't worry. No problems here."

"Il-afsh-feyn?" one of the older men asked Basil.

"No problem," Basil answered for Sam. "We have our bags." Abbas motioned for Sam to follow him as Basil walked toward the front of the terminal.

Children grabbed Sam's hands. A small man took his bag, saying, *"Ish-shan-Ta dee."* Sam felt as though the flow of people whisked him along on a carpet of air. He kept smiling but wanted to run in the opposite direction.

Near the front door Basil Abbas began kissing people and speaking Arabic in a fast clip. The delirium of excitement continued as he talked. The Arabs smiled, nodded to each other, and clapped. Basil finally turned to Sam. "We will have a great feast tonight and all are invited. I will talk with them further at that time. Now we must depart with the police. Follow me, please."

Abbas abruptly turned and hurried through the front door, leaving the multitude of relatives waving after him. Sam tagged along behind without any idea of where they were going. Once outside the door, the rising heat of the day hit him. It would obviously be extremely warm by the time the sun reached the midpoint of the sky overhead.

"Let me remind you of the way things are." Basil talked as they walked. "The local police are called the *Shortah*. If you run into the police that regulate the University of Jordan, call them the *Al Amn Al-Jammee*."

Sam shook his head. "I'm sure I'll remember all those names."

"But the group we will work with most of all are the *Maukhabarat*, the secret police."

"Yeah, I've got that one nailed down."

"Good. That's probably all you will really need." Basil saluted a man waiting at the curb. Dressed in a plain, dark-blue business suit, the Arab immediately opened the door to a Mercedes and Abbas jumped in. Sam obediently followed. The door slammed shut and the car pulled away from the curb.

"Please meet my good friend Mohammed Farid," Basil said. "This is the great American detective Sam Sloan."

The man in the blue business suit turned around from the front seat. "My pleasure," he said without any hint of an accent. "Welcome to Jordan."

Sam said, "Thank you for picking us up at the airport. We've been concerned about using our time to the maximum advantage."

"Everything is under control?" Basil asked Farid.

"We have made a complete investigation of the matters you requested," the Arab policeman said. "I think our people have located everything that you might possibly need. Yes, the situation is now under our control."

"Where are we going?" Sam asked.

Mohammed glanced at his watch. "In precisely thirty minutes we will be in a neighborhood close to the University of Jordan. We will find our way to a white house on Al Abdullah Street. You will begin your interrogation of Yakoub Natshe."

11

SAM SAT QUIETLY LOOKING OUT THE WINDOW WHILE BASIL and Mohammed Farid talked furiously in Arabic with seemingly no end to the flash and fury of their words. The first part of the trip from the airport cut through flat, lifeless desert with only an occasional tree. A few stucco huts stood sprinkled across the sandy wasteland. After ten miles the road turned into the outskirts of Amman. Junk littered the ground around most of the flat-roofed houses. People walked down the streets wearing simple attire, some in brown robes, others in jeans, all looking poor. Periodically Sam saw a donkey or a pack of dogs yapping at everything that passed down the street.

Farid's Mercedes turned onto a street named El-Gumhuriya and soon passed by the entrance to Jordan's Hashemite king's presidential palace. In front of the regal gateway guards stood at military attention with carbines on their shoulders. The car turned onto Sheik Rihan Street. More automobiles sped up alongside them and the street filled with traffic. Sam noticed an increasing number of taxis. The buildings grew larger and many of the edifices on the street were impressive. Jordan began to look like a city on the move.

Basil spoke to Sam. "Mohammed's men have already taken the house, and the place is under police supervision. Secret policemen everywhere. Apparently everyone in the Natshe family is terrified of what we might do."

"Hmm." Sam rubbed his chin. "Anybody been smacked around?"

Basil looked surprised. "They've been bounced around a bit."

Sam studied Basil's eyes for a second. "Okay. Let's see what we find when we get there."

The Mercedes slowed and turned a corner. Farid's automobile inched up the street. "That's the house." Mohammed pointed to a flat, two-story, white-stucco house ahead. Similar houses stood on both sides of the street. Several black cars were parked outside along the curb. "Our men have secured the entire area."

Sam glanced up and down the street. The block looked like a typical residential neighborhood except that frightened faces peered out the windows as they passed. Everyone in the area knew exactly what was going on. The blue Mercedes pulled up to the curb and stopped.

"Here we are," Basil said. "Let's hope we can find out something."

"You will," Farid said in a flat tone.

Sloan walked through the dry dirt to the simple step up to the front door. An eerie silence had settled over the street. No one moved; everyone listened. As soon as he reached the entry, the large brown door opened in front of him. A big man in old jeans and a green T-shirt stared at him.

"H-hello," Sam said.

"It-shar-raf-na," the man answered.

"He understands you but doesn't speak English," Farid said. "The policeman said he's glad to see you."

Sam forced a smile. The man didn't.

"We have your suspect holed up back in the family's office," Mohammed explained. "Our people are all over the house. The rest of the family is huddled in the living room. Go on back and ask what you wish. You've got help if it's needed."

Basil nodded. "Thank you, my friend." He motioned for Sam to follow him down the long hall and opened the smudged white door.

Sam glanced around the small office. Three large, tough-looking men stood around the perimeter. They wore earpieces attached to black wires that ran down to receivers in their pockets. A frightened-looking young man in his early twenties sat shaking before a desk with a computer on it.

"Yakoub Natshe?" Sam asked.

The small, black-haired youth nodded. *"Ay-wa."*

"Speak English?" Sam pursued.

"Ay-wa." Yakoub nodded again. "Yes, sir."

"You can understand everything that I ask?" Sam pulled a chair over in front of Natshe.

"Yes. I study computer in English." He spoke with a heavy accent.

"You're the person who discovered the sixty-kilobyte

content scrambler decoding device?" Sam looked Yakoub square in the eye.

The young man glanced nervously around the room at the hostile faces surrounding him. "Yes, sir."

Sam pursed his lips. "You did this by yourself?"

Yakoub nodded.

"And what happened after you made this discovery? I want to know what's occurred in the last couple of days."

Natshe looked down at the floor and wrung his hands. "I should put no information on the Internet," he said. "Someone bad come see it. Come here."

"Who?" Basil pushed.

"American. Say he is businessman and want to buy my invention. He offer me fifty thousand American dollars."

Sam moved closer and glanced around the plain office. "That's quite a hefty sum for Jordan. You work out a deal with this man?"

The young man shook his head. "No. Price is low."

One of the guards immediately pulled a Makarov 9-millimeter automatic out of his pants and stuck it next to Yakoub's head. *"Ma-a s-sa-leh-ma!"*

Yakoub grabbed his head, doubling up and falling with his face to the floor. *"La! La!"* he shouted.

Basil held up a finger and gently waved it at the guard while he shook his head *no*.

Sam looked at the guard angrily. Then he bent down close to the boy's head. "What was the man's name?"

"He says only A.M." Yakoub kept his arms wrapped around his head. "At least he have an A.M. printed on briefcase."

Sam pulled the boy back into the chair. "Sit up here," he

said and motioned for the guard to back off. "I don't think that you believe A.M. was the man's name."

Natshe shook his head.

Sloan looked at Basil and around the room again. No one had moved and the guards still appeared threatening. "This happened two days ago?"

Yakoub nodded and peered up at Sam. For the first time Sam noticed a large red welt on the side of the young Arab's face. The guards must have slapped him before they arrived. Sam didn't appreciate that approach.

"Don't lie to us," Basil growled. "We won't be easy on you!"

Sam shook his head at Basil. "Please tell us what happened, Yakoub. No one will hurt you." He looked into the young man's eyes. "I promise you, no more injuries."

Yakoub glanced nervously at the guard still holding his pistol in front of him. "Please don't hurt." He straightened up slightly. "Man come here with briefcase filled with money. Offer money. I do not take it. He get mad. Angry."

Sam studied Yakoub's eyes. The thin man looked frightened, too afraid to lie. Sam felt the young man was telling the truth. "Listen to me," the detective said softly. "No one will hurt you anymore. We just want to know what happened. I understand the man came back and stole a copy of the device. Right?"

Yakoub reached out and grabbed Sam's hand. "No," he said. "He steal copy *and* the original disk. I not know it until last night. This bad man steal everything."

Sam stiffened. "Everything?"

"Yes. He take all my work." Yakoub suddenly stopped talking and started crying. "You see my error," he sobbed. "Everything that I invent is now gone."

Sloan looked at Basil. The Arab's mouth dropped and he looked startled. "Stole it all," he mumbled.

"Where was this man staying?" Sam pushed. "What hotel?"

"I first met him at Hilton downtown, then he come to this house."

"What'd he look like?" Sam probed.

Yakoub ran his hands nervously through his hair. "Average height. I think he had on a wig . . . but it was brown . . . I think he also wear a false mustache. His clothes looked like they had been purchased in Jordan and not fit him so good. Very plain look."

"This man knew what he was doing," Sam said.

"Definitely an American," Yakoub added.

"I know he gave you a name in addition to the initials A.M." Sam looked straight into the Arab's eyes. "I want that name."

Yakoub looked anxiously at the guard holding the pistol and then at Sam. "The man call me back and says that if I tell another the name he gave, then he kill my family." Yakoub glanced again at the guard. "You can kill me if you intend, but I don't put Father and Mother out to die. I'm too afraid to say anything more right now."

"Okay." Sam stood up. "I want you to get a coat, your things, whatever you wear, and come with us. Understand me?"

Yakoub nodded.

"We're going to talk to your parents, then you will go down with us to the police station." Sam looked at the guards. "Anyone got any problems with that plan?"

The three men shook their heads.

"Okay, Basil." Sam opened the office door. "I want you to come down with me to—"

At that moment a roar erupted underneath Sam's feet, and he felt himself suddenly flying down the hall toward the living room. Pieces of wood hurled past his body, and the hall turned black with smoke. Abruptly all sound stopped and he felt himself crumbling into the front door, which seemed to give with the weight of his body. The feeling that wood was splitting was the last thing he remembered.

12

SAM OPENED HIS EYES SLOWLY BUT HEARD NOTHING. HE seemed to have dropped into a world of total silence. He blinked several times before realizing that he was lying facedown in sand and gravel. Turning his head, the detective could see feet running past him. He closed his eyes again and was back in the world of total silence. No running. No cars. No noise. Nothing. Total quietness. Only then did he realize how much his shoulder ached.

Wherever Sloan looked, Arabs were racing in all directions. He could see white-robed men dashing in and out of the house, carrying people, things, objects, appearing to be yelling at each other; but he heard nothing. Sloan's body slowly told him how much he hurt from his head to his feet, but none of the rescuers rushing past Sam even noticed him. He seemed strangely isolated in the sand and the silence.

Rolling sideways, Sam pushed himself up on one elbow and the sharp pain increased. His entire upper chest hurt. He looked at the building in front of him and discovered that the side of the white house was burning. Bellows of smoke drifted upward from the fiery roof. He sniffed and for the first time recognized that his clothes smelled like smoke. The stale odor turned his stomach.

Sam suddenly began to wonder if an explosion had occurred with a roaring boom that had left him deaf. He felt his forehead and discovered blood running down the side of his face. His coat looked tattered and torn. Gently flexing his back muscles, Sam was sure that the back of his jacket was gone. His movement only added to the pain.

Sam rolled over on his side but didn't think he could get up. His hip hurt and his knee was a bloody mess. For the moment, he could do no more than watch the frantic surge of people running in and out of the house.

Nothing made any sense. Why was he sitting in front of a smoldering, white-stucco house with the sun burning down on him? Sam couldn't remember why he was there. He rubbed his head but only stillness surrounded him. What in the crazy world had happened?

Suddenly a man dropped down on his hands and knees in front of him. Sam stared but couldn't quite put this scene together. He could see the man's mouth moving but didn't hear a syllable. For some reason *Mohammed Farid* came to mind. The man abruptly leaped up and ran back into the house, disappearing as fast as he had appeared.

Sam suddenly felt overwhelmed. Overhead the brilliant blue sky covered him like a hot blanket, and the sun's heat felt like it would roast him alive. He closed his eyes and slipped back into the darkness. Silence joined hands with blackness, and Sam no longer felt the gravel gouging his face.

———

When Sam awoke, he felt something soft and comforting underneath him. The sharp rocks had disappeared. The side of his face didn't hurt so much; the ground had turned into a bed with white sheets. Somewhere off in the distance he could hear faint noises. He raised his head and looked around. He was in a small white room. Sam closed his eyes again and immediately fell back into the realm of unconsciousness.

———

A voice above Sloan chattered in unintelligible syllables and phrases. All sense of time had vanished. Had he been there hours, days? Sam felt like it had been longer than a day. He took a deep breath but couldn't remember. Before he opened his eyes, Sam realized he seemed to be hearing now, obviously not clearly or correctly, but he was picking up sounds. The noises were faint but felt more reassuring than the total silence.

"Where am I?" Sloan mumbled.

"You are in the hospital in Amman, Jordan," a man's voice said in heavily accented tones.

"Amman?" Sam tried to remember why he would be in a place that he'd never been before in his entire life. "Amman?" he asked again and opened his eyes.

A dark-complexioned man in a long white coat stood next to his bed. "I'm a doctor," the man said. "You've been recovering from a concussion. You've been here two days."

Slowly a memory returned. "I was in an explosion." Sam tried to recall. "Yes, I think an explosion."

The doctor nodded. "You're lucky to be alive. The force blew you through the front door of the Natshe house. You've been unconscious for quite a while."

"Natshe?" Sam said, trying to remember where he'd heard the name. Another name popped in his mind. "Basil? Basil Abbas! My friend." Sam looked at the doctor. "What happened to Basil?"

"The blast blew him through the side window into the backyard. He was hurt, but less than you were."

Sam nodded slowly. "He's here? In this hospital?"

"Your friend was treated and released." The doctor raised an eyebrow. "Yesterday."

"Yesterday?" Sam's mouth dropped slightly. "I've been here all night?"

"You went into shock, Mr. Sloan. As I said, you've been here two days. Getting you completely conscious again hasn't been easy."

"There were others!" Sam abruptly remembered the three policemen and Yakoub Natshe. "What about the other people in that room?"

"You're the only person that I've worked with." The doctor sounded defensive. "I knew about your friend because he's been around here most of the day." The doctor looked toward the door. "In fact, I think he's coming in right now."

Sam tried to hear but no sound came to him. *The impact of the explosion must still be affecting my hearing.*

The door swung open and Basil Abbas walked in. "Sam! Sam Sloan! Praise the living God, you're awake!"

"Basil!" Sam held out his hand. "You look like you've been through a war." Sam stared at the large bandanna around the top of Abbas's head and the cuts on his face and hands. "You've had stitches!"

"A few." Basil pulled a chair up close to the bed. "Actually I look worse than I am. By God's grace, I went through the window and out into a pile of soft dirt. Yakoub's family, who were in the front of the house, survived. But the rest of the people who stayed in the office really took the full force of the explosion."

"What happened to them?" Sam asked.

Basil shook his head. "The blast had been well planned. Set up with a timer to catch Yakoub at his desk." He pursed his lips and shook his head again. "They didn't make it."

"Didn't make it?"

Abbas inhaled deeply. "Apparently the bomb had been placed under the house and ripped through the floor. Falling debris inside the room was part of what killed the other four people. Of course, they took the full impact of the explosion and the fire. I think the fact that you crashed into the front door was what did you the most damage—but also saved your life."

Sam looked at the doctor. "How bad am I?"

"You have had some injury to your hearing," the Arab answered, "but we think it won't be permanent. You wrenched your arm and severely bruised your knee. Shouldn't take too long to heal. The rest of the aches and pains are relatively minor." He pointed to Sam's forehead. "You have a nasty cut up there on the top of your forehead."

Sam felt his brow. "Must have taken a few stitches."

"About fifteen," the doctor confirmed. "Not a small problem.

We worried because you have stayed asleep for a while, but you don't seem to have had any severe head damage beyond the deep cut."

"I guess I can sit up?"

"Sure," the doctor said, "but you're going to be sore. That was quite an explosion."

Sam looked at Basil. "Where do we go from here?"

"I've been talking with Mohammed Farid about that very issue. I think you've asked the jackpot question. No one seems to know."

Sam stared at the ceiling. *Four dead?* He winced. *Tragic.*

13

ON THURSDAY EVENING THE HOSPITAL RELEASED SAM. With his arm strapped to his chest, he was wheeled out to a car that Basil Abbas was driving. The hospital personnel were friendly enough but it was obvious that Sam Sloan had been more like a visitor from another planet. He didn't look like the locals or have any idea of what they said. Sam waved appreciatively to the nurses and attendants as he was rolled down the hall.

Sam's knee hurt but he thought he could probably walk slowly. The problem would be getting around with his arm strapped to his chest. Balancing on crutches wouldn't prove easy. The entire scene wasn't anything like what he had on his agenda for this visit to far-off Jordan.

Sam's memory had returned, and he now remembered why he'd gone to the Natshe house to talk with Yakoub. His body hurling through the front door was the point where his memories blurred until he woke up in the hospital.

"Here I am!" Basil Abbas waved and shouted from beside an old red Ford parked on a distant curb. "Bring Sam over here."

The nurse reversed her direction and pushed Sam toward the car. "In one minute we be there," she explained apologetically.

"No problem," Sam answered. He really wanted to stand up.

"I think we can get him in the front seat," Basil told the nurse. "You help him stand up and I'll slide him in."

The nurse locked the wheels so the chair wouldn't slip away. "Yes," she affirmed.

"Actually, I can take care of myself," Sam said defensively. "No kidding. I can get up out of this wheelchair without any problems."

Instantly the nurse put her arm around his back. "I help you into the car," she insisted, pushing with all her might.

Once Sam was in and seat-belted, Abbas shifted into low and they drove away from the hospital. "We're staying at my parents' home," he explained. "I think we will be safe there. Plenty of room for you to stretch out, Sam."

Sloan nodded. "I wonder if the news about this bombing has gotten back to Colorado Springs."

"I doubt it," Abbas said. "Our people play their cards close to the vest. I don't think anyone has released information on what's happened."

"I need to get a message back to my family. Your parents have a computer? Internet access?"

"Of course!" Basil sounded almost indignant. "We have all the modern conveniences in this country."

Sam raised an eyebrow critically. "Really?"

"Okay, okay," Abbas admitted. "Some things aren't here, but I can guarantee you that everybody has a television and a computer."

———

Cara Sloan's computer lab class occupied the first hour of the morning. Normally she expected Jack Brown to meet her before class and walk into the room with her. It was no big deal, but she appreciated the friendly gesture.

But Cara hadn't seen much of Jack for the past several days. Since their argument over her not divulging what she had been researching on her computer, Jack had kept a significant distance, acting as if Cara had betrayed him. That made her angry. Disagreements were part of any relationship, but she felt Jack was just being a jerk. She wasn't about to buckle under his silent treatment and in turn gave him nothing back but an indifferent look. Their standoff continued.

When Cara walked into the computer lab, Jack was at the front of the room talking to the teacher. He didn't look at her and Cara was sure his unusual early appearance in the class was only a ruse, a next step in their running war. Jack wasn't leaving her any alternatives. She had to act as if he weren't in the room.

Cara sat down at her computer and started firing it up as if she had something important to do.

Maybe I'll access the Internet and see if I've got any e-mail that came in overnight, she thought. Cara quickly typed in the information to access her account. *Might as well get it here as at home.*

To Cara's surprise, she had a message waiting. She quickly discovered that it was from her father. "All right!" she said more loudly than intended.

Sam Sloan hadn't contacted his family since leaving home, and the delay hadn't sat well with either Vera or Cara. After all, he'd promised to keep them up on every detail of the trip and hadn't even called once yet. Cara knew her mother worried when they didn't hear from him.

Special Message, the e-mail said. *From Sam Sloan to Sloan family.*

Cara smiled. "Let's hope he's got a good explanation for this long wait," she mumbled under her breath and scrolled to the message.

Please don't panic, regardless of what is reported, as I am okay, Sam's message began. Cara leaned forward, frowning at the strange beginning. *I am now out of the hospital and staying with the Abbas family in Amman.*

"Hospital!" Cara blurted out.

I was in an explosion and was in the hospital for several days, Sam wrote.

"Explosion!" Cara nearly shouted.

I strained an arm and injured my knee, and I had to have a few stitches, Sam explained, *but I am recovering well. Don't worry. I'll be back on my feet shortly. Just wanted you to know why you haven't heard from me.*

"Oh, no! No! He's been hurt!" Tears started running down Cara's face. "Oh, Daddy!"

"Cara?" the lab teacher called out from the front of the room. "What's happened?" Students turned toward her, and Jack looked at her with surprise.

Cara could only shake her head.

The teacher hurried toward her with Jack behind him. "What have you found on the computer?" the teacher asked urgently.

"My d-dad," Cara stammered. "He's been in an explosion."

"What?" Jack Brown dropped down on one knee beside her workstation. "What do you mean?"

Cara pointed at the message on the screen. "It sounds terrible."

Jack quickly read the lines. "Oh, no," he uttered softly. "Mr. Sloan is in Jordan," he told the instructor. "Sounds like he's been hurt."

Cara felt herself starting to shake. "I've got to tell my mother. I don't know what she'll say. She'll be very upset."

"Yes, of course," the instructor said. "Let's print this message so you'll have all the data in hand." He immediately began punching in instructions to the computer. "Jack, can you help Cara get to a phone?"

"Absolutely." Jack reached out to put his arm around Cara's shoulder. "I'll take her down to the principal's office. Let me help you," he said to Cara.

Cara brushed the tears out of her eyes. "I'm sorry," she muttered. "I didn't mean to get this upset. It's just that my father has gone to . . ." Her words trailed off.

"I'll take her down to the office," Jack insisted. "I probably ought to take the printout with us." He reached out to take the sheet of paper from the teacher.

"Certainly." The instructor gave him the information. "Let us know what happens."

"We'll be back as quickly as possible," Jack called over his shoulder. "I know where to find Mrs. Sloan."

14

BY THE NEXT MORNING, SLOAN WAS WALKING SLOWLY AND cautiously around his bedroom in the Abbas house. Each day Sam felt more flexible than he had the day before. The aching knee appeared to be healing well. After a few small "laps," he plopped down in a straight-backed chair and stuck his feet out in front of him, wishing he were back in Colorado Springs.

No one in the simple home spoke English except Basil, so Sam had plenty of time alone. The only phrase Basil's family could say in English, which they did over and over again, was, "Welcome, welcome, we bid you welcome." By now Sam felt quite welcome in Amman.

Around ten o'clock Mohammed Farid drove up in the big Mercedes with three other men. From his bedroom window Sam observed one of the *Maukhabarat* officers staying by the car while the other two stood by the front door. Their visit looked official. Farid came inside and Sam could hear him talking in Arabic with Abbas.

"Sam," Basil called from the living room, "can you come in? Mohammed Farid has arrived."

Sloan pulled himself out of the chair and started hobbling down the hall. His chest hurt and every movement made his arm ache more. Nevertheless, he kept pushing himself forward one step at a time, jockeying with crutches.

"Good morning, sir," Sam said.

"Mr. Sloan." Farid bowed at the waist in a formal manner, as if greeting a dignified head of state. "I trust you are improving. The leg is better?"

"Thank you, Mr. Farid. I am getting around somewhat more easily, but walking is slow yet." Sam sat down.

"I understand." Farid bowed again. "Perhaps we might have a discussion this morning. I am sure that you are eager to return to the United States, so I thought we should discuss our next steps in the investigative process." His English pronunciation remained excellent but each utterance had a subtle twist, as if the man were implying more than he was saying.

Sam sensed a hidden undercurrent as the Jordanian police agent kept talking. The words were fine—too fine. No one had mentioned their leaving the country, but Farid was hinting that they should be on their way as soon as possible. Something wasn't sitting right with the Jordanian government. Maybe the explosion and the subsequent deaths proved to be an embarrassment to the government. Maybe the quicker he and Basil left, the better for Farid and company. Maybe . . . who knew?

"These matters have proven difficult for all of us," Farid said.

"No one anticipated bombing or violence of this order. Of course, we have kept this news confined to our organization for the time being." He cleared his throat. "We did allow your e-mail to go through because it offered reassurance to your family."

Sam stiffened. No one knew he had any intention of contacting the family back in Colorado Springs except Basil, and he wouldn't have conveyed Sam's plans to anyone.

"I felt we should review the facts about what we have gathered to date." Farid looked at Sam, waiting for his comments.

Sam nodded. "Good idea. Let's talk. Yakoub Natshe described a man wearing a disguise—a wig and local clothing—which didn't give much of an appearance that Yakoub could identify later. Natshe was sure the man's initials were A.M., but he didn't give us any more of a name to go on." Sam straightened his aching knee out in front of him and shifted his weight uncomfortably in the chair. "The man stayed in the local Hilton. At best I'd say we're looking for an A.M. who is quite clever at making bombs. Not much to go on. All we have to do is find someone of American or English ancestry running around your country with those qualifications and we've got our man." Sam smiled. "If he's still in the country."

Farid looked pained. "We also know this man has stolen all the copies of the descrambling device. In fact, he's probably carrying them with him."

"Have your people checked the airports?" Sam asked.

"We've had the *Shortah*, the city police, run down every flight passenger list for an A.M., but they have found nothing so far," Farid answered. "We've also put out restraint and hold orders to all of our passport-control officers around the country, but nothing has come up."

Basil pursed his lips. "Let me be perfectly honest with you, Sam. If someone was trying to flee the country and stay undetected, there are many ways to escape. Jordan is a desert country. It wouldn't take a great deal of skill to find one's way across the sand, going somewhere like Damascus."

Farid stiffened slightly. "We must be candid with each other," he agreed. "What Basil has said is absolutely true. This man wouldn't have nearly as difficult a time escaping Jordan as he would leaving the more sophisticated European countries."

"Hmm." Sam rubbed his chin. "Sounds like our bomber is a man of more capacity than first appeared. He must have come to Amman with the sole purpose of obtaining the software. Sounds like he thought Yakoub would sell the device, but the thief didn't offer Natshe enough money and had to change his plans—blowing Yakoub's house up."

"This is the exact picture that we've picked up from the family," Farid explained. "Apparently, Yakoub talked with his father about selling the device, but his father pushed him to hold out for more money. In the end, Yakoub decided that he didn't trust this American—I'm assuming he's an American—and wouldn't talk with the man anymore."

"That's what created the theft and finally the bombing," Abbas added. "Our thief certainly knew how to make a bomb."

"Not only that," Farid continued, "he knew how to make what seemed to be a simple device while actually creating a sophisticated-enough bomb to cause a major explosion. I think A.M. is far more skilled in explosives than he'd like us to think."

"How so?" Sam asked. "What kind of a bomb did he make?"

"We think he used an improvised radio-detonation device put together with materials that could have been purchased at many small stores around Amman." Farid raised an eye-brow. "Remember your Radio Shack stores? That's what I am describing."

"The sort of places that sell radio paging systems, wireless intercoms, toy walkie-talkies?" Sam asked. "But dynamite? Plastic explosives?"

"Correct," the *Maukhabarat* officer answered. "We think the actual detonation material came into the country with him. Our hunch is that this man was watching the house when you arrived and thought time was running out on him. He caused a Servo device to release a depressed microswitch that completed the circuit and resulted in the explosion."

"I suppose this man could still be in the country," Sam observed.

Farid nodded. "Yes. He might be floating around, waiting for the heat to cool down."

"And he could be holding several passports," Abbas added. "If the man is a U.S. citizen, he could carry a passport from a foreign country without jeopardizing his American citizenship. You know, it's not that hard to obtain a fraudulent passport in America. If an applicant has a birth certificate with another name, or a naturalization certificate from another person, he could attempt this exchange through the mail and probably would be able to perpetrate such fraud."

Mohammed agreed. "Beyond the initials A.M., we don't have much to go on, but we will maintain constant vigilance here, at the airport, and at all border crossings. We are already trying to find out what room he used at the Hilton. I can assure you of this fact."

Sloan studied the man's face. The Arab looked sincere

enough, but Sam knew he was getting nothing more than a whitewashed version of events. The bottom line was that Farid had no idea where A.M. might be, and the bomber could be roaming down the street this very minute, planning to plant another bomb along the way in some innocuous little house like the Abasses' residence.

"Therefore," Farid continued, "if you need to return to America fairly soon, we will continue pursuing these leads with our officers. I am certain that you would feel more comfortable back in your native land where the medical care is more familiar."

Sam watched his eyes. Farid's words sounded friendly, but his eyes looked nervous and edgy. Whatever was going on with the man, Sam saw no point in pushing him.

"You might even want to leave as quickly as tomorrow," Farid continued. "Please let us know your intentions, and we'll be ready to assist you."

"Thank you," Sam answered in the same diplomatic tone. "Please allow Basil and me time to discuss our options, and we'll be back in touch as quickly as possible."

"Certainly." The *Maukhabarat* agent stood up. "Basil knows how to call me. I'll be waiting to hear from you."

Sam smiled pleasantly. "We'll be contacting you shortly."

Farid nodded stiffly to each man and quickly left.

Sam turned to Basil and started to speak, but Basil put his index finger to his lips. "Shhh." He shook his head and whispered, "Not now."

15

BASIL WATCHED MOHAMMED FARID'S MERCEDES DRIVE off with his crew, and only then did he beckon to Sam. "Let's step outside and get some fresh air. I think a walk around the yard will be good for us."

A ripple of pain slipped across Sam's face. "Walk?" he groaned. "You're kidding!"

"Slowly," Basil said and pointed toward the back of the house. "Yes, slowly. We can exercise with care."

Sam hobbled behind Abbas at a grudging pace, lifting his sore knee carefully. "Whatever you say," he moaned.

Once Abbas stepped out in the backyard, he became much more serious. "Over here," he said, pointing toward the fence, "where we can talk without observation."

"Why couldn't we talk in the house?" Sam asked.

"Because every area is bugged. My guess is that miniature

transmitters have been placed somewhere in every room."

"Transmitters? Are you sure? We're on their side. Remember?"

Abbas shook his head. "We came here on a relatively simple journey to find out what was going on with a computer invention. Instead, we became the center of an explosion that's killed four people. I'm sure the *Maukhabarat* is still trying to decide if we're not possibly part of some terrorist organization invading the country or something of that order. They know me, but they don't know you, Sam."

"Come on!" Sam shook his head and frowned. "We came here from Colorado Springs and our passports show that—"

"In this part of the world people make new passports every day of the week. Don't forget that not very many years ago, the Jordanians threw the Palestine Liberation Organization out of the country because they had secret information that the PLO planned to overthrow King Hussein. This government has learned to live on the edge of its seat."

Sam rubbed his jaw and shook his head again. "I'll take what you say at face value, but you sure this is possible?"

"Listen." Basil spoke intensely under his breath. "I didn't get to the United States because I won a local lottery for a free trip. My English has always been excellent and my family's reputation impeccable, but I also worked with the *Maukhabarat*. My employment with the secret police proved to be the lever that pried me loose from this country. Get it?"

Sam looked over his shoulder and around the area. "We could be bugged in your own parents' home?"

"No question about it. The *Maukhabarat* report directly to

the monarch. They are not about to leave any stone unturned. I'm sure the house was wired the instant Farid discovered we would stay here. My parents will eventually find some of these transmitters. You must remember that fact every time you use the phone or make computer contact with someone."

"So they want us out of the country until they're sure about what's actually occurred with this Natshe guy's death?"

Abbas nodded. "Cooperation is the key word. We must do everything that will put us in the best possible light. Farid wasn't kidding when he said they'll keep running A.M. down, because they want to know where he is worse than we do."

"Then you're saying that we need to go back to the USA as quickly as possible?"

"I think so," Basil concluded. "I believe that Mohammed Farid will contact me quickly if something turns up over here. That's my honest conclusion."

"Has our trip across the world actually been worth anything, Basil?"

Basil patted Sam's shoulder. "Sure, the trip has been important. We've got a lead on this A.M. person, and the entire police force of Jordan is working the case. Don't worry. They have significant data to go with. We'll see the benefits eventually."

Sam rubbed his chin again and scratched his head nervously. "Strange turn of events." He looked around the yard quickly and over the fence. "I have nothing to go on but what you think we should do, Basil."

"Jordan is a good country, Sam. You have to put everything in historical perspective. There's been a war going on over here forever. Today it's between Israel and the Palestinians. The

Iranians and the army of Iraq are always dangerous. No one can take any chances without getting hurt. The Jordanian government has to keep itself covered with careful investigative efforts. They can't assume that our interests were only a computer problem."

Sam sighed and started back to the house. "Let's see what we can put together to get a flight out of this country. I'm certainly ready to get back home to my own bed."

———

At seven o'clock in the morning, the phone rang beside Vera Sloan's bed. She had been awake for ten minutes but was still thinking about getting up. She picked up the receiver.

"Sam! Thank God! It's so, so good to hear your voice."

"Been a difficult trip, dear, but I'm all right."

"All right, nothing! It sounds like you've gotten hurt pretty bad."

"I'll tell you all about it later, but I'm getting around slowly. Think I'm improving every day."

"Oh, Sam. Cara and I have been praying for you like crazy. She picked up your e-mail message at school and was quite shaken. We've been hoping you would call."

"I can't say too much, Vera," Sam said cautiously. "I wanted you to know that Basil and I will be on our way back to the States shortly. We are still working on some of the details, but I believe we'll be on a Jordanian airplane to Paris first thing in the morning."

"Sam, tell me what's happened."

"Many of the details are police secrets," he said softly. "You understand how this works."

Vera paused for a moment, considering carefully what he'd said. "You can't tell me *right now* exactly what's going on?"

"Yes," Sam said. "That is correct."

"I see," Vera said slowly. "Yes, I think I understand. I will wait for you to call me from Paris tomorrow. Will you be able to do that?"

"I think so. I hope so, but I'm not sure what our timeframe will be. We could be rushed through the airport without time to grab a phone. I don't want you to panic if you don't hear from me."

"Don't worry, dear. I will understand."

"Good." Sam sounded relieved. "Just don't worry about me. I'm doing fine."

Vera pushed the telephone closer to her ear. "You're sure?"

"Of course. I'm fine." He forced a laugh.

"Let us know when we can pick you up at the airport, Sam. We'll be there with bells on."

"I love you, dear. Hope to see you as soon as possible."

"We love you, Sam. I love you with all of my heart."

Vera hung the phone up and stared at the ceiling. *Something isn't right,* she thought. *I know he's been hurt, but Sam sounds like he's caught in some kind of bind. Oh, I pray he's okay.*

With one swoop, Vera threw the covers back. "Cara!" she yelled across the house. "Cara! Come here as quickly as you can. We've got to pray for your father!"

16

CARA KNEW HER FATHER SHOULD BE HOME IN A COUPLE OF days, and hopefully he was okay. But until he walked off the airplane, no one could be certain. The thought of her dad being hurt in an explosion rattled Cara again and made tears come to her eyes. She wanted to help, but what could she do?

Cara got up off her bed and took a shower, brushed her teeth, and started fixing her hair, but she kept thinking about her father. With each stroke of the brush through her long hair, Cara thought about the problem from a different angle. Different ideas bounced around in her head, but most of them were not practical.

After all, I'm the person who came up with the discovery of this software theft in Jordan, she thought. *I'm the one who found the information on the Internet because I knew about the Reverse Engineering Web site. I ought to have something to contribute.*

Cara put the hairbrush down and slipped on her shoes, still feeling troubled. Suddenly she stopped and stared at the wall. "Of course!" she cried. "I'll try working on my computer again." Sitting down at her desk, she immediately turned the machine on. Maybe some twist had occurred. Possibly a new message her father didn't know about.

She quickly found her way to the Internet and onto the MoRE Web site. "Come on, boys." Cara started scrolling through the chat room. "Talk to me. You've got to have come up with a new idea or two in the last couple of days. Something important must be out there."

The comments were typical. Nothing novel, unique, or helpful. She kept running through the network of material, chats, promotions, stuff, hoping to see anything that might help her quest, but nothing useful appeared. After several bounces through the listings, she hit the memory-retrieve button and came back to the original message received from Jordan.

Warning! Warning! rolled up on her screen. Cara studied the words for a moment. *Yakoub calling for help. A copy of the sixty-kilobyte device I invented for copying DVDs has been stolen from me.* Cara reached over and printed it again. Leaning back in her chair, she waited for the printout.

"Let's take a second look," she said to herself. "I can take this material to school and think about it." Cara started reading the message out loud. "*Only a few hours ago I discovered he had stolen one of my disks. I am angry. He uses the initials A.M. and the name Alvin Marshal.*"

Cara stopped and read the last line again. "My gosh! My screen didn't pick up that last line earlier. The data had been there all the time and didn't come up. I missed it!"

For a full minute Cara stared at the printout. For some inexplicable electronic reason, that sentence had been hidden all the time. She certainly hadn't seen it when she quickly typed in her response, *Can you tell me more?*

"My father doesn't know any of this!" Cara exclaimed. "Now I've got my own lead." She looked more carefully at the monitor. "A.M., Alvin Marshal! Names I can chase. Who is this guy? I can pursue this person."

Cara switched the computer off and slipped the piece of paper in her purse. She would have to hurry to keep from being late, but she was back in the big game her parents were playing. If she could only come up with some sort of a lead on this A.M. guy, this Alvin Marshal, would her father's eyes ever roll! She actually had information that would startle him.

Cara slammed the door behind her and ran to her car in the driveway. She whipped out backward and sped off in the direction of the high school, driving faster than she should. "I don't know how this information will help, but I'll run this lead to the ground. Until I get some additional insight, it will be my secret."

On Saturday night, an American Airlines commercial airplane landed at the Colorado Springs Municipal Airport. Inside Vera and Cara stood anxiously waiting for Sam to step through the door. A seemingly endless line of passengers filed out. Sam and Basil were the last people to deplane.

"Sam!" Vera called out and waved. "Sam. Here we are!"

Leaning heavily on the crutches, Sam walked slowly through the gate, trying not to put weight on his damaged leg. His arm was in a canvas sling attached to his chest. Dark circles hung under his eyes and his clothes looked badly wrinkled. Basil Abbas walked at his side, helping to stabilize him.

Vera rushed through the crowd and started to hug him but stopped. "Oh, Sam. Can I touch you?"

"Sure." Sam grinned and held out his good arm.

Vera raised up on her tiptoes and hugged his neck. "Dear, dear, Sam. You look like you've been in a wreck."

"Sorta have." Sam winked at Cara. "But I came out alive."

Cara stared at the large bandage across her father's fore-head. She turned slowly and glanced at Basil's face. Tears filled her eyes. "Daddy, they really hurt you." She started to cry.

"No, no." Sam reached out to his daughter. "We just got banged up a bit. I'm fine."

"Sam, sit down here in this chair." Vera gently pulled him toward one of the airport seats. "Please sit down and rest for a moment."

Sam gently slipped into the chair. "The long ride in that airplane almost did me in. I do feel a bit weak."

Cara dropped down on one knee next to Sam. "Daddy, what kind of an explosion was it? You didn't ever say."

Sam looked at Basil and raised an eyebrow. "Shouldn't be any miniature transmitters out here in the foyer. I think we ought to level with them."

Abbas nodded. "Why not? They will know soon enough anyway."

Sam quickly told the story of the bomb that ripped the office off the Natshe house and how he and Basil had been hurt. He told them that the explosion killed several men.

Vera kept taking deep breaths and Cara's mouth dropped when he said Yakoub Natshe had been murdered.

"In a word," Sam concluded, "we're dealing with a danger-ous man. We need to stay aware of that important fact. To put it in computer lingo, someone was serious about deleting us."

Vera nodded. "You bet. We won't forget that part of the puzzle. Now I understand why you couldn't tell me on the phone."

The color drained from Cara's face and she looked light-headed. "This bomber character is much worse than we ever expected," she said.

"I think we need to go home," Vera concluded. "Basil, we'll drop you by your apartment." Vera looked a second time at her daughter. "Cara, you all right? You seem a little on the peaked side."

Cara only nodded and followed them out to the car.

17

THE SUN ROSE IN A BRILLIANT BLUE SKY ON MONDAY morning. The fresh, invigorating smell of spring hung in the air. With his arm in a sling but without his crutches, Sam trudged slowly into the Nevada Street police station, moving like winter had returned. No one needed to tell Sam that he resembled a refugee more than a first-class detective. Even the lady at the metal detector station looked concerned when Sloan limped past.

"Sam," Basil Abbas said when Sloan stood in his office door, "the chief wants a verbal report on our trip. You ready to talk to the big man?"

Sloan nodded. "I haven't felt up to writing much on paper yet. Most of the weekend I lay around the house and slept. Talking will certainly be the easiest way to go this morning."

"Okay, let's go." Basil started toward the chief's office with Sam following him down the hall.

When the two detectives walked up to Dorothy Waltz's desk, consternation flashed across her face. "Oh, my!" she gasped, staring at Sam. "I had no idea your injuries were that severe. You okay?"

"I look worse than I am," Sam explained. "Can't keep a tough detective off the beat."

Dorothy shook her head. "Maybe not, but the crooks made a good effort at trying to. The chief is expecting you. Go on in."

Al Harrison sat behind his desk, reading police reports. He looked up and immediately jumped to his feet. "Sam! You don't look well."

"Thanks for the cheerful thoughts, Chief." Sam slipped into a chair in front of the desk. "Actually, *I must* feel better than I look."

Harrison pursed his lips and rubbed his chin. "Tired, aren't you?"

Sam took a deep breath. "Let's say that jet lag has proved to be a problem. I feel like going to bed right now."

"And you're in pain?" Harrison added.

Sam nodded. "Really, I'm fine. Why don't we let Basil give you his version of what occurred in Jordan."

Harrison nodded. "Sure."

Abbas immediately launched into a detailed description of what they'd found and how the explosion had blown Yakoub Natshe into oblivion.

"We still don't have any idea where the DeCSS software is?" Harrison asked.

"And we know only the thief's initials," Sloan added. "The Jordanian police are working the case, but the leads are slim."

"This guy could be producing those disks right now, getting

ready to sell them like hotcakes, for all we know," Harrison concluded.

Sam shook his head. "He's killed several men now. He can't go public after committing murder. He may have something else in mind. Obviously killing is no longer a limitation."

"What's this man after?" Harrison pushed.

"I don't know." Sam looked thoughtfully out the second-story window. "The use of this device may yet prove to be an important ingredient in the entire case. I believe there's more to this than we thought."

Harrison leaned back in his chair. "I'll prepare a preliminary report for the CIA and have both of you review it before I fax it in. I'd suggest you push finding out this A.M. character's complete name. Obviously that's one of our next steps."

Sam nodded. "Seems so to me."

"And I believe that we are still trying to run down Charlie Boyles?" Basil asked. "Dick Simmons didn't get him yet?"

"No, Boyles is still out there. If Simmons gets a lead, I'll want you to join the chase."

Sloan pushed himself up out of the chair. "At least I can drive the car."

"I'd think you'd do better to spend time in physical therapy," Harrison said. "You know that I'd let you go home if you needed rest."

"Thanks," Sloan said, turning toward the door. "I'm fine. Just need to get myself adjusted to the Colorado clock."

"I'll check with you boys as soon as my report is done," Harrison said. "Shouldn't take too long."

The two detectives returned to Sam's office. The room

looked exactly as it had before they rushed out to board the military airplane. For a moment Sam walked around the place, touching knickknacks, papers, the desk, looking at the local map on the wall. Finally he settled into his chair behind the desk.

"You love this old haunt?" Basil asked.

Sam smiled. "It's kinda beat up and could use a good coat of paint, but I've spent many fine hours in this office. Sorta my second home."

Basil looked around thoughtfully. "Who was it that said home is where the heart is?"

"I don't think it was one of the ancient church fathers you love to quote constantly."

Basil grinned. "It wasn't until we walked off the airplane in Amman, that I realized how much I've missed the world I came from. I'm sorry that explosion sent us out of the country so quickly. I could have spent much more time with my family and friends."

"You'd like to go back?"

Basil stared at the floor. "Compared to this country, Jordan has many problems . . . certainly economic problems, but . . . they are my people, my kin." He scratched his head. "After you live in America for a period of time, you realize how great the opportunities are here. That makes returning difficult, but I am sure that someday I will go back for good."

"I understand," Sam said. He reached for the phone. "Let's get Dick Simmons in here and have him update us on the situation with our old friend Charlie Boyles. I'm sure Pretty Boy has been chasing Boyles like he was number one on the FBI's most-wanted list."

"Sure."

"Dick!" Sam barked in the phone receiver. "I'm back and wanted to—" Sam stopped. "Right now? This minute?"

"What's happening?" Basil asked.

"We're ready!" Sam snapped. "Meet you downstairs immediately."

Basil frowned. "Sam, what's—"

"Simmons has found Boyles's location." Sam felt under his arm to make sure his shoulder holster was in place. "Make sure you've got your gun and let's get downstairs immediately." Sam pushed away from his desk slowly. "Rushing is going to be somewhat difficult." He caught his breath. "But I've got no choice. Let's go."

The two men hurried out of the office as fast as they could. Dick Simmons was already standing beside an unmarked brown Taurus. He started to open the car door and then stopped. "Sam? What's happened to you?"

"I'll tell you on the way," Sam answered. "Sounds like we need to hurry."

Simmons slid in behind the wheel. "We don't have time to fool around, but you look like you've barely survived the last attack of Lawrence of Arabia."

"Nah, I'm fine." Sam slipped carefully into the backseat. "Let's go."

Simmons pulled out of the parking space, and Abbas gave him a quick, sketchy account of the bomb explosion in Jordan. Within five minutes, they were on the highway headed out of Colorado Springs.

"We're going to Woodland Park," Dick explained. "We have information that Boyles may be holed up there in one of the RV areas that tourists fill up in the summertime. We have a good chance of cornering him this morning, but it'll probably involve a gunfight."

"What did you uncover while we were gone?" Sloan asked.

"We turned Ralph Oliver's Sierra Madre Street office upside down and inside out," Dick explained. "I tried to discover how deeply the link between Oliver and Boyles ran. Turned out Oliver was also starting to work the computer angle." Dick looked at Basil and raised an eyebrow. "He had been dabbling in the world of using people's credit cards. Sound familiar?"

Basil blinked several times. "I was running that crime down before all of these other computer problems popped up. Sure. I know about those capers."

"Remember that movie I told you about several weeks ago? *Six Degrees of Separation*? Well, these crooks appear to be linked far more closely than by six people. We're onto an important web of criminals working out of this area."

"Catching Boyles is part of a larger picture?" Basil asked.

"I think so but don't know for certain," Simmons answered. "I'm betting on the fact that this man can lead us to a number of other hoods before the chase is over."

"He won't be easy to bring in," Sloan said more to himself than to the other two. "I suspect that Charlie Boyles will prove to be one tough act to shut down."

18

CARA WALKED OUT OF HER ENGLISH CLASS WITHOUT speaking to her friends. She didn't want to be distracted from thinking about the name she'd discovered on her computer.

Alvin Marshal. Alvin Marshal. Alvin Marshal.

Cara walked down the hall, wondering how the name Alvin Marshal and the initials A.M. fit the whole scenario. Why hadn't her father discovered the link in Jordan?

Kids filled the hallway as always, moving from one classroom to another, but Cara didn't look at them. The entire weekend Cara had wanted to tell her father about her computer discovery, but Sam had been so tired, it didn't seem right to bother him. Cara also worried that he'd think she was foolish for not having caught the computer glitch earlier.

"Hey, Cara!" a friend called out. "Doing okay?"

Cara smiled at the girl but kept walking. "Yeah," she answered weakly.

The entire A.M. name problem needed a quick fix. Her father wouldn't be happy that she'd missed something so obvious on her computer. On the other hand, maybe she was misreading the entire situation. Sam usually proved to be more gentle and understanding than Cara expected. Maybe he'd take the whole thing in stride and just be glad she'd found out the name. She just didn't want to have done something wrong.

"Cara!" a boy's voice called from behind her. "Wait up. It's me."

She turned around and recognized Jack Brown walking behind her. "Jack! Sorry, I didn't see you."

"You look like you're back on one of those mental clouds where you occasionally float away." Jack fell into step with her. "Your father's okay?"

"Dad went to work today, but I don't think he should have. He's still really sore, and he still sleeps a lot of the time."

"Hmm." Jack grimaced. "Doesn't sound like he's in the best shape."

"You know my dad. Nothing stops him. He'll be down there at that police station if it's the last thing he does."

Jack smiled. "Yeah, your father's a hardworking man."

The bell in the hall rang a warning buzz.

"Got to run." Jack squeezed her hand. "See you later." He hurried away in the opposite direction.

Cara walked into her biology class and sat down. Students flocked in and took their desks around her. She remained stuck on one thought: *Alvin Marshal. Alvin Marshal. Alvin Marshal.*

Simmons slowed his car. "About a half mile ahead is the RV park where Boyles is supposed to be hiding. I think our best bet would be to go into the manager's office and let the man know what's about to happen. Then we'll hit Boyles's hideout."

"Sure," Sam agreed. "Give the local citizens time to duck. Sounds right to me."

The manager's office turned out to be an old house identified by a small, marker-scribbled sign as that of Pedro Gomez. The one-story white house needed a paint job and more than a little repair. A quick glance around the area picked up litter and no small amount of junk. Seven RV units sat parked in the rental area.

Simmons walked up on the porch, shaking his head. "Bad scene." He knocked on the screen-door frame.

"Yeah?" a woman with a Spanish accent called from a back room.

Simmons knocked again.

"Okay, okay," the same voice protested but grew louder as the woman came to the door. The battered door opened slightly, and a heavyset, dark-skinned woman peered out of the door. "Whatcha need?"

"*You* are Pedro Gomez?" Dick asked with seeming innocence.

"Pedro!" the woman shouted over her shoulder. "Come here!"

Half a minute later a short, overweight man came to the door. "Can I help you?" he asked in similarly accented English.

Simmons held up his badge. "We're with the Colorado Springs Police Department," he explained briskly. "I need to talk with you. We're coming in." He reached for the knob on the screen door.

Pedro Gomez looked nervous but didn't move.

"Thank you." Simmons opened the door and walked in. Sloan and Abbas followed. Gomez backed up reluctantly, but the woman started for another room.

"Hold it," Simmons demanded. "I want both of you to look at a picture." He pulled Boyles's photo out of his pocket. "Do you know this man?" Dick held the photograph in front of their faces. "Take a good look."

Gomez and the woman exchanged glances but didn't say anything.

"Look," Dick spoke sharply, "we can talk here, or I can run you down to the police station for a more aggressive discussion of the matter. I know you've seen this man."

The woman looked down at the floor, but Gomez nodded. "Sure. We know him."

"Where is he?" Simmons pressed.

"I don't know." The man shrugged. "Don't watch the rentals."

"Look!" Basil pointed out the side window. "There's Boyles. He is going for that car parked beside one of those old trailers in the back. He's seen us!"

"We've got to stop him." Sloan pulled a gun from his shoulder holster.

Basil and Simmons instantly ran through the front door, but Boyles had already started the car and was driving toward the manager's house. When he reached the entrance to the area where the RVs were parked, Boyles hit the gas pedal and the car leaped forward. Leaning out the car window, he started shooting at Basil and Simmons, hitting only the manager's house. One shot caught the rear tire on Simmons's car.

Dick jumped off the side of the small porch and Basil fell to one knee, trying to aim. Simmons landed in a small flower bed with a thud and dropped his gun. Basil got off three shots that hit the car, but Boyles's bullets flew past him when the car sped by. Sloan leaned against the window, taking careful aim at Charlie, but Gomez's woman suddenly hit his hand with an old kitchen plate. The ceramic shattered, showering Sam with clay slivers and causing his shot to miss even the car. Boyles's bullets scattered the glass in the window above Sam.

Seconds later, Charlie Boyles disappeared down the highway. Basil dashed to their brown Ford and then remembered it didn't have a transmitter radio. "Dick! We've got to call backup to get someone chasing Boyles."

Simmons stood up. The knee of his classy suit pants had been torn open and the coat was smudged with dirt. He looked at his pants in disgust, then noticed that his car's tire had been ruined. "Yeah," he said. "I know. I know." He cursed and pulled out a cell phone, starting to tap in the number.

"Help us!" Sloan called from inside the house. "The woman got hit!"

Abbas and Simmons rushed back into the house. The heavyset woman lay sprawled on the floor with a small hole on the left side of her thick chest. Blood had already begun to form a pool under her. She wasn't moving or making a sound.

Pedro Gomez stood frozen in place, looking terrified.

"Get an ambulance out here!" Sam demanded. "She got hit by a stray bullet." He reached over and grabbed her wrist.

For a moment he struggled to find her pulse. "I don't think we're in as big a hurry as I thought. There's no pulse."

Simmons dropped down on his knees, trying to get some response from the woman. "Afraid so," he concluded. "She's gone. Hit through the heart."

Sloan looked up at Gomez. "Why did she strike me with that plate?"

Gomez didn't move but looked panicked. His eyes darted back and forth. He didn't speak.

"You're friends with Boyles, aren't you?" Sam demanded.

Gomez started breathing harder but still didn't speak.

"We know Boyles hid out here," Simmons said. "He obviously had friends who covered for him." He pulled out a pair of handcuffs. "We'll take you in, Gomez. Aiding and abetting a fugitive of the law can get you time over there in that big pokey in Canon City."

Gomez stared at the floor but didn't move.

Sam stood up. "These thugs are trying hard to put me completely out of business." Putting his pistol back in the holster, he clenched and unclenched his hand. "All I need is to get my gun hand broken. That woman certainly gave it her best shot."

19

"BOYLES SHOT YOUR TIRE OUT?" CHIEF HARRISON YELLED at Dick Simmons. "Before you even got in the car?"

Simmons shrugged and looked embarrassed. Sloan and Abbas stood behind Simmons in the police chief's office, trying to appear as innocent as possible. Sam bit his lip and glanced out the window.

"This is ridiculous!" Harrison pounded his desk. "This is the second time this Boyles thug has escaped from you people. I expect better work than this."

"Honestly, Chief," Simmons tried to explain, "this creep and his woman covered for Boyles. Maybe they even signaled him as soon as we drove up. At the least, somebody alerted Boyles we were coming."

"'Honestly'?" Harrison's voice became more shrill. "I think the better word is *stupidly*. You shouldn't have roared into that place like you were starting a Fourth of July parade." The police chief pointed toward the door. "Okay, you people get back out there. Simmons, you keep the investigation running on nailing Boyles down." Harrison shook his finger in Dick's face. "I want that man found!"

"Yes, sir," Simmons answered apologetically. "We'll stay right after him."

"You do that!" Harrison started looking down at letters on his desk.

The three men walked back to their offices. "Don't take his tough demeanor so hard," Sloan told Simmons. "Harrison always explodes when things go wrong."

"He certainly sounded mad to me," Dick answered.

"Next time you see him, the chief will be in a much better mood. It all goes with the day's job."

"I'm back to square one in trying to find Charlie Boyles," Simmons complained. "If the guy was smart, he'd leave the state."

"Usually crooks aren't that bright," Sam said. "He's probably out there hiding in the mountains someplace. Don't worry. The man will turn up."

Simmons shook his head. "Man, I hope so—and soon."

———

An hour and a half later, Cara left school with her mind glued to her problem. During the last hour of her final class, she kept thinking about telling her father about the Alvin Marshal name. She'd come to the conclusion he should have been told, regardless of how bad he felt. Cara knew she'd made a big mistake. The issue was too serious, and her father needed to have the man's name, regardless of how he reacted. Rather than disturb him on his first day back at the office, though, she decided she would tell him as soon as he returned home that evening.

At home Cara threw her books on her bed and sat down in front of her computer. The copyright description and a basic explanation of the capacities of the system flew past. She watched the icons appear on the screen until the many programs stood in front of her.

At that moment an idea flashed across Cara's mind. Her mother had told her that all of the complicated word processing and computer data had basically originated as a gift from God. The Bible said that God desired truth and that in the hidden place, He would cause His people to know wisdom.

Cara flipped open her Bible and thumbed through a portion she'd read several nights earlier. In the first chapter of James she silently read: "If any of you lacks wisdom, let him ask of God, who gives to all liberally and without reproach, and it will be given to him." She had a right to petition for divine help.

"Oh, Lord," Cara prayed. "I truly need You to help me deal with these issues in the right way. I could certainly use some wisdom." She paused for a moment and thought about what else she should ask. "Please lead me to answers that will make things right. Amen."

Cara took a deep breath and started typing. From the memory banks she brought up the conversation that she'd seen earlier. As she read through the old messages, a new idea began to take shape in her mind. Had A.M. or Alvin Marshal been involved in any of the chat rooms when the announcement of Natshe's discovery first came up? Could this mystery man have first picked up information about the discovery of the sixty-kilobyte program from the same place that she learned about the invention?

Cara scrolled to the conversations about the DVD descrambler, which appeared with details of how the device would permit recording of movies from original DVDs. Cara began following the discussion of how the invention of an unidentified man in Jordan made the breakthrough possible. Putting her finger on the monitor screen, Cara followed the excited discussion bouncing back and forth from all over America with interjections from around the world.

"Here it is!" Cara shouted. She abruptly stopped. "I've found the A.M. initials on the conversation list."

She read the line out loud: "Please describe this device more explicitly to me. A.M."

"Got ya!" Cara shook a clenched fist at the ceiling. "Here you are—bigger than life!"

She followed the unfolding discussion down her monitor. Experts from California offered thoughts about how the software must be constructed. Contributors from England added comments and asides about the financial possibilities of such a device.

Cara did a double take. An *Alvin Marshal* had abruptly joined the conversation, asking questions about how such a device might be used for other possibilities, like editing movies. She carefully followed his questions, comparing them to comments from A.M. After a number of lines, Cara observed that A.M. and Alvin Marshal both periodically used "therefore" and "dubiously" in extremely similar ways.

"Tricked yourself!" Cara exclaimed. "Old buddy, you're

talking in the chat room *twice*, trying to appear to be two different people, but you are only one guy: A.M.!" Cara leaned back and crossed her arms over her chest. The young woman thought about what she had observed. Clearly this one man, using the names A.M. and Alvin Marshal, was sending his messages from the same location. What she needed now was to figure out how to hack her way back into the Columbia On-Line system and find out where this one guy with two voices had been coming from. This would exceed anything Cara had done in the past. If she could manipulate and maneuver through the system extensively, she'd be able to give her father an incredible bit of information on who the man was.

"Thank You, Lord!" Cara beat on the desk with her fist.

20

When Sam arrived home, Vera met him at the kitchen door. "You look exhausted," she told him. "How did work go today, dear?"

"Tough!" Sam walked into the living room and plopped down in a big easy chair. "The police chief was light-years away from happy when the crook we were chasing escaped."

"I was afraid returning to work today would turn into problems of this order." Vera shook her head. "How's your arm feel?"

Sam flexed his hand several times. "I think my arm is working much, much better. That's one of the reasons I need to stay on the job. Exercise helps." He raised an eyebrow. "The other reason is that I don't want to go crazy moping around the house by myself. I've got to keep moving."

"I understand, but I still feel that—"

"Vera," Sam interrupted, "I have to stay on my feet."

"Dad!" Cara hurried out of her bedroom. "I have some really big-time news for you!"

"Thank you, Cara, but I'm truly bushed tonight." Sam kicked off his shoes. "Been a highly demanding day. Couldn't we talk about your schoolwork later?"

"This isn't school. I think I've found the name of the man you were chasing in Jordan."

Sam straightened up in his chair. "What?"

"I think I've found out who this A.M. is—or at least one name that he's been using."

"What?" Sam's mouth dropped slightly. "Where in the world did you pick up those particular initials? You didn't get them from me."

"How does Alvin Marshal sound?" Cara smiled.

Sam leaned forward. His voice was low and intense. "Where'd you find that name?"

"I went back over all of my computer data and found some material that had slipped through the cracks." Cara shrugged and paused. "I even rechecked all of the conversations that I had accessed and saved earlier. The initials and name originally came from Yakoub Natshe in Jordan. That's how I linked them together. In rerunning the e-mail messages, I found the initials A.M. and the name Alvin Marshal everywhere."

Sam leaped straight out of the chair, pulling his arm out of the sling. "Show me!" He started hobbling toward Cara's bedroom. "I've got to see this name with my own eyes."

Cara slipped in front of him, Vera behind him. "I've got the facts up on the screen right now," Cara said. She walked into the bedroom and slid onto the chair in front of her computer. She started with Natshe's message and then began running down the conversations, pointing out the A.M. and Alvin Marshal entries. "See? The same man appeared in this conversation twice. Now, all I have to do is run down where his responses originated on both the A.M. and Marshal responses, and I'll have an exact location for you." Cara beamed.

Sam pulled up one of Cara's chairs. "I want you to listen to me carefully. This information is of the highest importance and has to be considered confidential." He reached over and held her hand firmly. "You must not share this data with anyone. You understand? *No one.*"

"Yes, sir."

"When did you find this information?" Sam stared intently into her eyes.

Cara blinked several times and then looked down at the floor. "I didn't want to bother you this past weekend. Dad, you looked so tired and were struggling with pain."

"When?" Sam pushed.

"Last Friday," Cara admitted reluctantly.

"Friday!" Sam yelled so loud the room seemed to vibrate. "You've known this all weekend?"

Cara bit her lip and nodded slowly.

"Good heavens, child!" Sam kept shouting. "Don't *ever* allow such information to sit here without telling me immediately."

Tears began to well up in Cara's eyes.

"Sam." Vera patted him on the back. "Don't make Cara cry."

"Dad, I was afraid you were too sick to talk about this stuff.

I thought about telling you but decided to wait until tonight."
Cara sniffed.

Sam shook his head and took a deep breath. After a long
pause, he said, "I appreciate your concern for me, but let's not
let this occur again."

"Of course," Cara mumbled. "I won't."

Vera patted her daughter on the shoulder. "It's all right,
dear. We both appreciate the fact you've come up with highly
significant information."

"Yes," Sam agreed. "You've done an important job in iden-
tifying this man, Cara."

"Would you like for me to keep trying to find out where he
is, or at least what address he used?" Cara sounded reluctant.

"Absolutely!" Sam patted her on the shoulder. "No question about it. Certainly. Most certainly!" He started rubbing
his hands together.

Suddenly a smile broke across Cara's face. "Good! I think
I'm going to have to do some hacking that could get complicated. This probably takes more skill than I've acquired." She
looked out of the corner of her eye at her father. "Could I
expect any help?"

Sam broke into a grin. "You bet!" He hugged Cara. "I'm
always here at a moment's notice."

"Excellent!" Cara beamed. "Want to see what I can find
right now?"

Sam pulled his chair up even closer. "Let's see what we can
dig up together."

Vera smiled. "I'll let you nerds go to work while I fix supper." She walked back toward the kitchen.

Sam scooted closer until he was nearly in front of the computer screen. "I think your first step is to do a little shell programming." He put his hands on the keys.

"Shell programming?"

"Cara, a shell program is essentially creating a file that you can operate by typing in only one line. It's a good way to protect yourself. Sorta like a DOS batch file. You write a series of DOS commands and save them in a file ending with *bat*. Got me?"

"I think so." Cara sounded hesitant.

"We've got to make sure that you have a personal defense in place. We want to make it as hard as possible for somebody to come back on you. Particularly someone using the initials A.M."

"Got ya, Dad."

Sam began typing in commands. "Of course, a real pro might make an end run and still find you. Watch what I'm doing. You'll get the drift of it after a while."

"Sure." Cara watched intently. The screen filled with strange messages: *helo Cara@commandcentral.org 250 callistro. uoffoo.edu Hello Cara@commandcentral.org250<Cara@commandcentral.org . . . Recipient Okay data.* "You're using my name?"

"Yes," Sam said. "You're going to need to patrol your Web site frequently, as we don't want any surprises."

"Yes, sir."

Sam studied the screen for a moment. "Hmm. Getting into the world of Columbia On-Line isn't so easy, because Columbia is not an Internet service provider but an on-line service. We may need to use an old Columbia installation disc to allow us to work our way in with the tools we've got."

"I think I've got one around here somewhere." Cara started opening drawers on her desk. "Let me see now . . ."

"Hang on." Sam hesitated a moment. "Let's try another approach. We have three domain servers for Columbia. I think we can go a different route right now."

———

An hour later Sam closed his bedroom door. Vera lay on the bed reading a book. She marked the page and closed the cover. "Cara's done an amazing job."

"Yes. Yes, she has."

Vera looked thoughtful. "Sam, are you concerned that she might get into trouble? After all, wandering through the Internet can get scary. When I see what she's doing, it concerns me."

Sam sat down on the bed. "I've had those thoughts. The truth is that young kids today use computers like we did when I finished college. Cara's learned a thousand secrets from me, and she's capable of surfing the Web like a California beach boy hitting the waves on a summer day."

"Do you think she could stumble onto some data that would backfire or get her in legal trouble?"

Sam rubbed his neck. "I don't think so. And of course, I'll cover her as working for me if any legal problems arise."

"She's putting in a great deal of time working for you."

"That's less time she's spending with Jack Brown," Sam said. "Can't be all bad."

21

LATE MONDAY EVENING VERA STOOD IN THE DOORWAY TO Cara's room and watched her daughter for a few silent moments. A dozen teddy bears on a wall shelf, a thimble and a Mickey Mouse watch, one wall filled with pictures of her teenage friends, another with photos of rock stars—all of these marked the room as singularly belonging to Cara. The young woman sat at her desk staring so intently at whatever she was doing on her computer that she didn't hear Vera enter.

"How's it going?" Vera asked.

Cara jumped. "Mom! You scared me to death."

"Forgive me. I didn't mean to startle you. Everything's been so quiet in here that I stopped by to make sure you were all right."

Cara wiggled her fingers. "I've been so involved with Dad's hacking project that I'm nearly getting muscle cramps." She leaned back and folded her arms across her chest. "I can't get through the tangled maze out there on the Internet, but I know it can be done. Just haven't fit the pieces together yet."

"Don't worry, dear. You'll eventually get through that electronic labyrinth. It's essentially a matter of practice."

For a moment Cara stared again at the screen, now filled with a maze of words, dots, @'s, bars, > signs, and strange configurations. "I asked you earlier about how the maze of information, this strange computer alphabet, and the rest of the stuff that computers produce fits into the plan of God. I still think about that at disorienting moments like tonight."

"Cara, as I remember our earlier talk, I told you that the closer we come to the truth, the closer we come to God. Right?"

"Yes. I guess that I'm still not really sure about how God and the truth fit together with each other. I have been reading my Bible about it, though."

"As I remember from my college philosophy classes, the ancient world struggled to discover what truth was and how you find veracity. Stoics tried to suspend their emotions while the Epicureans took a different tack. One group moved into monasteries to escape the world, while others became hedonists and lived without restraint. Behind all this bizarre behavior was a genuine desire to get in touch with what was real and everlasting."

Cara nodded her head. "I've studied some of these people in high school, but the subject didn't fit together for me. At least, I didn't get my questions answered."

"Dear, the ancient world struggled to know the source of insight and intelligence. Light? Fire? Water? The sun, the stars, the elements? No one was sure."

"I think we're as confused today," Cara said.

"Today?" Vera laughed. "Absolutely! We bump into people every day who aren't any more aware of the truth than people were two thousand years ago. You think that killer you're chasing has any sense of what truth is? I doubt it. Your target, A.M., isn't particularly different from the gladiators who fought to the death in their struggle to survive the Romans and their cruelty. I imagine this character has trouble even thinking about what's right and wrong. Criminals often have problems with moral issues."

"Okay. You had said that the Christian philosopher Augustine changed the search."

"Yes, Saint Augustine stopped the frantic quest. He helped people to see that God is our final source. The answer isn't a *what* but a *who*. All truth comes from God, who created the world and authenticity. If we follow the truth persistently, eventually we will be led to Him. That's why we know that computers and all forms of complicated knowledge will, in the end, be finally good. Of course, we don't worship the truth or get caught up in believing that knowledge is our final hope, but we do know that the closer we come to consistency, cohesion, balance, and the right use of what is in our world, the closer we come to God and His work."

"Not only do I want to do what is right, but what God wants me to do," Cara said. "I guess it helps to know that I'm on the right track."

"You are, Cara. Stopping someone who is out to rob and kill people is more than right. Every day when your father leaves for work, I know he's going to face danger and difficulties, but I have no doubt that he's doing something extremely important for the kingdom of God. He's one part of the way truth is at work correcting error. By catching criminals, he's part of God's purpose in our world. Your father is fighting evil."

"And that's what I'm trying to do!" Cara scratched her head and looked doubtful. "It's proving to be so difficult that

I'd certainly be happy if God would come down here right now and give me a hand."

Vera laughed. "But that's how our heavenly Father uses truth. God doesn't want us to be His little puppets, floundering around on the end of long strings like mindless dolls with sawdust-filled heads. Everything the heavenly Father does is an attempt to make us stronger and sufficient. He gave us free will and the ability to decide right and wrong. Without that capacity, we wouldn't be able to choose to love Him. That choice makes us persons. We're free entities who can love God or not. Our struggle is to become increasingly competent while advancing our ability to love."

Cara grinned. "I've struggled for hours, but I haven't accomplished one crying thing."

"No." Vera shook her head. "You've achieved more than you have yet recognized, because you have already ruled out approaches that won't work. You're asking important questions, and the more you choose right solutions, the closer you come to understanding how important the truth is."

"I guess you're right." Cara nodded. "I wasn't looking at issues that way before. Tomorrow I'll start in again and see where it takes me."

Vera hugged her daughter. "When the sun comes up again, you'll go much farther than you imagine. Just wait and see."

Cara began shutting down her computer. Vera watched, keenly aware that her seventeen-year-old daughter was a bright girl with a considerable capacity to ask the important questions. In this room filled with childhood mementos, Cara was finding her way to adulthood.

Vera smiled. A little girl turning into a loving woman? Maybe she and Sam were doing better than she thought.

22

BY TUESDAY MORNING SAM FELT SIGNIFICANTLY BETTER. His arm seemed to be working well enough that he didn't need to wear the sling all the time, but Vera urged him to wear it for at least one more day. Sam's knee still ached but he was getting around better and better.

He walked into the kitchen and sat down at the breakfast table. "I think another day ought to put me back in running condition."

"Easy, Lone Ranger." Vera set a cup of coffee in front of Sam. "I still think you're pushing your luck too far. Take it slow for a couple more days."

"I can't. Now that I *finally* have the name that Cara gave me, I've got to pursue this individual."

"Go easy on the girl, Sam. She worked until way past bedtime last night, trying to come up with the location of this character. Cara wants to please you very much."

Sam nodded. "I know she does and I appreciate her efforts. But I certainly hope she doesn't tell that boyfriend of hers about this name business."

"You made that clear. Jack Brown is a nice boy and I'm sure that—"

"He's a boy," Sam charged. "I don't trust any of them."

Vera chuckled. "You sound worse than my father. Honestly, Sam! You've got to lighten up."

Sam grumbled while he drank his coffee.

A minute later Cara bounced into the room. "Sorry, Dad. I couldn't get the address located last night, but I'll be on it as soon as I come home from school. I promise."

Sam reached an arm around Cara's waist and hugged her. "Thanks for all you're doing for me. You are saving me an enormous amount of time, and that allows me to investigate other things. In fact, you're helping the entire police force. Remember we said that this business will stay completely confidential." He glanced at Vera. "We won't be telling *anybody*. Right?"

"Of course, Dad."

"No one like, let's say, Jack Brown?"

Cara kissed Sam on the cheek. "You're funny. Of course, 'no one' includes Jack. See you this evening." She walked out the back door.

"I've got to finish getting ready for work," Vera said. "I know you want to leave for the office. Call me during the day if you get a chance."

Sam stood and set his coffee cup in the sink. "I will," he said, doubting it. The pace of the police department usually pushed all private business aside. "I'll try."

Ten minutes after Sam got to his desk on Nevada Street, Dorothy Waltz called him to the chief's conference room for a special meeting. When Sam walked in, Basil Abbas was already seated at the large, oblong table.

"How are you feeling today, old man?" Basil asked.

"Better," Sam responded. "Looks like I'll live."

"Like you'll live?" Basil rubbed his chin and the predictable strand of long, black hair dropped down over his eyes. "Hmm. I believe that Saint Origen once said about living that—"

"Thank you, Basil," Sam said, cutting him off. "It's too early in the morning for me to think about Saint Origen. I'm sure he would have wished me well."

Chief Al Harrison stormed into the room. "Good morning, gentlemen. We'll start immediately." Dick Simmons came in behind him with a cowed look in his eye. "Simmons and I have already had a . . . little conversation."

Sloan straightened up and Abbas snapped to attention.

"Sam, you feeling better?" the police chief asked.

"Yes, sir. Much better." Sam answered with considerably more enthusiasm than he'd given Basil. "Probably don't need the sling, but I'm wearing it one more day in case."

"Hmm." Harrison nodded. "Good." He walked around to the head of the table. "As I told you yesterday, I was far from happy about Charlie Boyles's escaping one more time." Harrison crossed his arms over his large chest and glowered at the men. Since their meeting was the first one of the day, he still looked fairly well dressed, but Harrison had already started a downhill slide in the wrinkled clothing department. "I assume everyone knows about my unhappiness. We can't have any more of these erratic escape flights. Do we all understand?"

Sam glanced at Simmons, who was staring at the floor with a hangdog look on his face. "Absolutely," Sam answered for the other two.

"Good!" Harrison started to pace. "We need to make careful plans about what we'll do next."

"Sir," Sam said, "I have new information that should prove vital to our efforts on the Jordan case."

The chief stopped walking and stared at Sam. "What do you mean?"

"I believe I have one name that the initials A.M. stand for. I now know that the man who killed Natshe and bombed us has used the name Alvin Marshal."

Harrison blinked several times. "Really?"

"My daughter was able to ferret the name out on her computer. There is no question that the killer used this particular name in Jordan. I believe Natshe would have eventually told us if the bomb hadn't gone off."

Harrison dropped down in the chair at the end of the table. "Now that's important," he said quietly. "Real important. You've got something to work on."

"I think so," Sam answered. "At the least, the CIA is going to be delighted to run this information down."

"Good. Good." Harrison rubbed his chin. "Now we're moving!" He clenched his fist. "All right, men! This is exactly the sort of information we're looking for." Harrison turned abruptly to Simmons. "What lead have you picked up on this Boyles guy?"

Simmons looked uncomfortable. "We've sent his picture to all the state airports to prevent any immediate flights out of the area." He wiped his lips awkwardly. "We've also put Boyles's pictures to all law enforcement personnel. My hunch is that he's up there in the mountains somewhere. He might have easily taken Highway 24 going toward Buena Vista or dropped back on Highway 9 down toward Cripple Creek. Those are all good possibilities."

"Got anybody down there looking for him?" Harrison growled.

"We've notified the local police," Simmons answered.

"Humph!" Harrison slumped back in his chair. "You personally been over there yet?"

"No, sir. The escape only happened yesterday."

"Maybe you should get out of your desk chair and take a good look, Simmons." Harrison turned back to the rest of the group. "We've got two problems here, but both involve computers in one way or the other. Simmons, I expect results in this Boyles business. You read me?" The police chief leaned over the table and glared.

"I understand." Simmons looked apprehensive.

Harrison straightened up and turned to Sam and Basil. "I want you two to stay available to assist Simmons on this chase. In the meantime, Sam, you get in touch with Washington, D.C., and find out what they can do with this Alvin Marshal name." Harrison ran his hands nervously through his thinning hair. "The CIA has the top authority in this matter, and you need to do what they tell you. Any questions?"

The three detectives shook their heads.

"Okay, then!" Harrison stood up. "You boys get out there and catch these bad gorillas."

23

SAM SAT AT HIS DESK WITH BASIL ON THE OTHER SIDE. Their conference with Chief Harrison had finished a few minutes before. As always, Sam's office had a worn look from years of use. The floors maintained a consistently dull appearance. A pile of files sat on the corner of Sam's desk. Faded green file cabinets lined the wall under a large map of the city.

"The chief certainly was on Simmons's case this morning," Abbas commented.

"Yeah, but Dick was in charge of a raid that failed, and then he fell in the flower bed with the agility of a schoolboy kissing his first girlfriend. He came back here with the knees of those expensive pants covered with mud. You can't do much worse."

Basil grinned. "Old Pretty Boy didn't look like a winner today."

"Harrison goes overboard on escapes, and the officer in

charge always gets chewed on. I think Harrison is afraid the mayor will come down here to eat his lunch." Sam waved his hand as if dismissing the subject. "He'll forget it by noon . . . unless Simmons makes another gigantic *faux pas*."

"I'm sure you're right." Abbas stood up. "I'll go down and console Dick. He'll need me to help him run Boyles down."

"I'll start working the Alvin Marshal name. Let me know what happens, Basil."

"Certainly." Abbas walked out and went down the hall.

Sam turned back to his computer and brought up the e-mail address of Mohammed Farid in Jordan. He envisioned the *Maukhabarat* agent driving up in the large blue Mercedes. Farid had been friendly enough but also left no doubt about what he wanted done. This man needed to be treated with caution. And Basil Abbas should be protected in any communication Sam had with Farid and the secret police.

Sloan quickly typed out a warm, personal greeting, also extending Basil's affection. He typed in the name of Alvin Marshal and suggested that the police run down this clue as quickly as possible, sending any response directly back to Sam. He signed off with his best wishes for King Abdullah and the people of Jordan.

At least the *Maukhabarat* would chase this name through the hotels and places they had already identified as possible links in this chain of mystery. Maybe they'd find something; maybe not.

Having finished the e-mail, Sam picked up the phone and called the CIA agent in Washington assigned to cover the entire DeCss affair.

"Yeats here," the agent answered succinctly.

"Sam Sloan in Colorado Springs."

"Ah, Mr. Sloan. How are you feeling?"

"I'm back on the job."

"Surprised to hear it," George Yeats said. "From the data we garnered from the Jordan hospital, you got hit rather hard."

Sam paused for a moment, realizing the CIA missed nothing. The mere fact that Yeats had picked up the hospital's records was indicative of the comprehensiveness of the agent's operation.

"I do better if I stay on my feet," Sam answered. "In fact, I've already picked up an important piece of evidence."

"Really?" Yeats sounded surprised.

"I have at least one name that the bomber in Jordan used for the initials A.M., and it may be the same name he used all the time in Amman."

"A name?" Yeats seemed taken aback. "How'd you find that?"

"On the Internet. The man called himself Alvin Marshal."

"Alvin Marshal!"

"You'll need to run that through your computers as quickly as possible. I am available to follow up immediately. Forget about my physical condition. I'm down here as on any normal workday."

"I see," Yeats said slowly. "Yes, I see. We'll be back in touch with you hopefully sometime today."

"Thank you." Sam hung up. *That ought to get their merry-go-round spinning.*

———

Throughout Tuesday, no matter what class Cara was in, she thought about breaking into the Columbia On-Line system. Idea after idea bounced around in her mind. She even tried to avoid Jack Brown. If the computer search issue came up, he'd press her for information on what she was doing at home, and that would only lead to another fight. At four o'clock, Cara slipped away to get back home without anyone picking up on the singular issue that absorbed her every thought.

The quietness of the Sloan household helped Cara concentrate and made her feel more confident about trying to ferret out this Alvin Marshal's location. She quickly got her computer up and running. In a few minutes Cara started working on breaking into the Columbia company's records. She quickly ran into the same brick walls she'd encountered the night before.

After a few minutes, she stopped and sat back in the chair. Everything seemed fuzzy and disorganized. It occurred to her that A.M. must have been using the Columbia On-Line system because it had international connections. He could tap in from anyplace in the world. There was no telling where this man had been. Cara took a deep breath and started her search again.

Remembering what her father had said the night before, Cara pulled out an old version of a setup disk to reinstall the program. As Sam had instructed, Cara began by unchecking the box at the top of the screen marked "Dialing" and "Connect to the Internet as needed." She worked quickly, punching in instructions.

After twenty minutes of intense work, Cara stood up and walked around the room for a moment. She could feel the tension rising and didn't want to become nervous. Another deep breath and she was back at the job. Within thirty minutes, she was struggling to get around the fire wall that surrounded the Columbia On-Line address system. She was finally getting farther than she had the night before . . .

Suddenly the telephone rang. The noise startled her.

"Hello," Cara said harshly.

"Hey, it's me. It's Jack."

"How you doing?" Cara sounded distant.

"You okay? I mean at school you seemed to be floating on another planet."

Cara realized that Jack Brown knew her too well to be easily fooled. She had tried hard to avoid him and he'd picked up on what she was doing. "Sure, Jack. I've just been under pressure to get some things accomplished."

"I bet you're back working on one of those projects for your father."

"I've let some assignments stack up." Cara avoided a direct answer. "I think by next week I'll be back on top of things."

"I wanted to make sure you weren't mad at me or something like that." Jack sounded earnest.

"No, no." Cara laughed. "Nothing of that sort. I'm here trying to get this work done. I'll call you back later this evening."

"Okay." Jack hesitated and added, "I'll be waiting."

"Great. Talk to you then." Cara hung up quickly.

Jack meant well but the intrusion irritated her. She needed to concentrate as intently as possible. Cara loved to talk on the phone but this wasn't the time. She leaned back and stared at the screen.

The problem was finding the right code word to get inside the Columbia system. No matter what she did, the search couldn't go any farther until she cleared this one hurdle that seemed a mile high. And if someone in the Internet network caught her at this moment, she would be in serious trouble. At that moment, a new thought popped up. What if she tried a different site from the one she was trying to access—what if she tried to work her way through by going around?

Cara started typing feverish instructions. Suddenly the system opened up in front of her. She was on the other side of the fire wall!

Catching her breath again, Cara slowly, carefully, typed in Alvin Marshal's name. She waited, watching the computer shift through screens of numbers and instructions. For a moment, the screen went blank and then suddenly the name came up again.

This time a list of cities from which A.M. had accessed the Columbia On-Line system was attached!

24

FOR SEVERAL MINUTES CARA STUDIED THE COMPUTER printout listing both the name Alvin Marshal and the initials A.M. with the locations from which he had made calls into the Internet, as well as the dates of the computer contacts. The distance between points seemed strange and unconnected. Alvin Marshal had made calls from Amman, Jordan; Cairo, Egypt; Washington, D.C.; Alexandria, Virginia; and Paris, France. He hit one place after another like a traveling salesman blowing through the planet. Cara reached for the telephone.

"Please give me Sam Sloan," she told the operator at the police department. "I'm his daughter."

After about a minute Sam picked up the phone.

"Dad, I've located the origins of the Alvin Marshal calls."

"Cara! That's excellent!"

"I know you'll be home soon, but you said to let you know

at once." Cara read Sam the list of locations and dates. "I can't make any sense out of this. Can you?"

"That's okay. I'll work on it and have some other specialists take a look. Calling me immediately was exactly the right thing to do."

"I told you that I'd find his location," Cara boasted. "See, you can depend on me!"

"Absolutely. No question about it. Now I've got one more problem for you to work on."

"Shoot."

"I believe this will prove more difficult than what you've done to date," Sam said. "Do you think you could locate the billing address for this man?"

"I don't know," Cara answered carefully, remembering how the entire venture so far had taken hours of labor. Her father was asking her to go back through the arduous process again and probably knock on an even larger and tougher door. "I imagine addresses are the most difficult area to crack."

"I know that we're dancing on the edge of the sword," Sam added. "And you probably shouldn't be nosing around that area. It's just that this is such important information, and you are saving me an enormous amount of time. That's the only reason in the world I'd even hint at this idea. I'd even buy you a new—" Sam stopped.

"Don't stop now. You'd buy me a what?"

"You name it and I'll do my best."

"Let me think about it for a second." Cara took a deep breath. "I'll try, but I certainly can't promise anything. I'm not sure I can break through the fire wall around the directory of subscribers. All I can do is try. It will take time."

"That's fine. If you run into any problems with someone catching onto you, tell them you're my secretary and refer them directly to me. I can cover the problem."

"All right, Dad. Let's see where the search takes me." Cara hung up. An icy dread ran down her back. Trying to get the address of A.M. would probably prove *completely* impossible— and this was even more dangerous than what she'd done before.

———

Sloan stared at the list of locations Cara had given him. From the dates next to the calls, he could tell this man did a significant amount of hopping from one country to the next. No question that he'd been in Amman in the early stages of Natshe's discovery of the decoding device. His first questions about the invention had to come from within driving distance of Yakoub Natshe's neighborhood. Then A.M. had abruptly flown to Egypt, made a few other stops, and then traveled to the United States before going back to Jordan and leaving again. *The man must work for a company with significant funds to fly him around the world like a king,* Sam thought. *No question but that A.M. was in Amman when the bomb exploded.*

Sam picked up the phone and dialed the CIA agent George Yeats again. The phone kept ringing but no one answered. Sloan hung up and went back to his address book, looking for a cell phone number that would locate Yeats anywhere at any time. He found the number and dialed it.

"Yeats here," the agent answered in his usual crisp tone.

"Sam Sloan in Colorado Springs."

"Uh . . . yes." Yeats lowered his voice. "I am not at a good place to talk right now. I'm in a restaurant."

"Let me do the talking," Sam said. "Have you found anything on the name yet?"

"Initial inquiries are still being run."

"I understand. Listen carefully. I now have the cities from which this man called the Internet."

"Excellent."

"I'm going to read them to you. Got a pencil handy?"

"I'm prepared."

Sam quickly read the list, including the dates. "I think this will help your computer people check the records. We're still trying to get an exact address."

"You're amazing, Sloan. Unless something unusual happens, I will call you in the morning."

After Yeats hung up, Sam looked at the piece of paper one more time. Cara had no idea how important this information was.

25

ON WEDNESDAY MORNING SAM RETURNED TO HIS OFFICE to wait for Yeats's call from Washington, D.C., knowing that the two-hour time difference could cause the response to come earlier than people on mountain time generally expected. He thought about how matters had gone at home the previous evening. The search project had proved to be good for the family as well as the detective's guest.

For a moment Sam's mind wandered, and he briefly remembered Dick Simmons's comments about the movie *Six Degrees of Separation*, which was constructed around the idea that all the people in the world are separated from each other by a maximum of six people. If the right people are identified, the film contended, anyone can eventually find and meet anyone else. While it may take less than six, that's the most needed to reach anyone from the pope to the president of the United States.

"Six people," Sam mumbled to himself. "I'd love to know who could connect me with Alvin Marshal."

He thought about the wide range of acquaintances that he had around the world. In his travels he had met everyone from sneaky snitches to mild-mannered little old ladies, and all had played a role in running down deranged or diabolical murderers. If he could only put together the right combination to fit the final pieces in this puzzle.

Sam glanced at his watch. It was already well past ten o'clock in Washington. Yeats should be calling.

"Sam?" Dick Simmons appeared in the doorway. "Can you come down to the conference room? I've got some important information that you and Basil need to consider."

"Sure. Let me call the office operator and tell her where I'll be." He quickly made the receptionist aware of where to find him and put his cellular phone in his coat pocket in case Yeats tried that number.

Sam found Basil in the conference room sitting at the table, wearing the same clothes he'd worn the day before. With the usual strand of black hair hanging in his eyes and his half glasses at the tip of his large nose, Abbas again looked more like an absentminded college professor than a policeman. At least he was consistent.

Simmons walked to the head of the table. Sam noticed Dick was wearing a tie that he had never seen before. The startling dark blue and bright gold colors had to be what the glitterati were wearing in New York City today. Even though he labored to be stylish and competent, Dick still looked nervous and edgy.

"I've got some important information for us," Dick began in an unusually blustery mode. "Regardless of what Harrison thinks, I've been working hard on this case. Several dimensions of the chase are coming together." He handed sheets of paper to Basil and Sam.

"The matters have turned out to be global," Sam noted.

"That's the CIA's problem," Simmons snapped, "but I do have data that ties this together locally. You'll find it all on this sheet of paper. Basil, you started out working on a local angle of Internet manipulation where local folks were stealing credit-card numbers to the tune of twenty, thirty thousand dollars. Right?"

Abbas nodded. "I've been working with several computer experts to get inside this problem."

"Sam, you went flying off to the Middle East to run down the inventor of the descrambling device. Correct?"

"Afraid so."

"I've been calling people all over the United States," Simmons continued in an arrogant tone. "I even talked to some man named Paul Miller in California with the Motion Picture Association of America. We've got a world of people struggling with this problem."

"Yup!" Sam leaned over the table as if Simmons's assessment of the details had begun to border on the boring side. "What's your point, Dick?"

"Last night we made a big discovery. Remember this Alfred Harris that got shot in Ralph Oliver's office? Turns out that he and Charlie Boyles are the people running the scam that Basil's been working to uncover."

"You're kidding!" Basil pushed the hair out of his eyes.

"That's what was behind the attack on Oliver. They were fighting over control of an extortion scheme that was far larger than the amount we've known about. We're looking at an operation that probably would have run into several hundred thousand dollars."

"How'd you find this out?" Sam asked.

"All yesterday I worked on a computer angle and had several pros help me. Things started coming together. Then, around nine o'clock last night, who should show up using the Internet but our old friend Charlie Boyles."

"*You* found this?" Sam pushed.

A slight look of embarrassment flashed across Simmons's face. "No, one of my experts picked it up. But I was on top of the problem immediately."

Sam smiled. "My, aren't you an industrious little man."

Dick ignored the comment and kept talking. "At least I'm the one who put this operation together. We found out Boyles was working out of Denver, and—"

"Denver?" Sam interrupted. "Whatever happened to that Cripple Creek or Buena Vista route you thought he'd taken yesterday?"

"Looks like he took Highway 67 up to Sedalia or possibly Pine Junction. At least, Boyles appears to be in Denver." Simmons stopped. His eyes looked desperate. "Come on, guys. I had to tell Harrison something yesterday. Good heavens, the man was all over me. Everything I said made the chief angry. I threw out the names of those towns to stop the personal attack."

"We understand." Sam slipped into a professional mode. "Look, Dick, we're completely on your side. Are the Denver police aware of and looking for Boyles?"

"I alerted them this morning. I am sure that they are onto the problem now." Simmons sat down, looking less nervous.

"I've got to give the chief a report, and I wanted to be able to tell him that you men were on board."

Sam smiled. "Tell Harrison we're backing you 100 percent. You're made an important breakthrough. You can quote me."

Simmons took a deep breath and exhaled slowly. "Good. A positive report will help."

"Hey, man!" Sam reached over and patted him on the shoulder. "Tell us what you want us to do."

"I think we ought to hit Denver and see if we can find Boyles's tracks up there somewhere."

"Good." Sam stood up. "Lay your report on Harrison and let's get on the way. After all, it will take an hour to get there."

Simmons started gathering up the sheets of paper. Color started returning to his face.

"Don't let that old barking dog scare you," Sam told Simmons. "His teeth aren't that sharp and he's been vaccinated. Meet you at the car."

26

SAM HAD ALREADY FOUND SIMMONS'S CAR IN THE PARKING lot and was waiting when Basil and Dick came out of the police station. Before he left the office, he told the receptionist to refer Yeats to his cell phone number if he called. Everything about the day felt positive and good. Maybe the trip to Denver would take them to a new level in the investigation; maybe Yeats would be able to fill in some of the blanks.

"How'd your report to the chief go?" Sam asked.

"Like yesterday never happened," Simmons said. "You'd think that last night I had discovered where Jimmy Hoffa was buried."

"What did I tell you?" Sam asked.

Dick took his coat off. "No matter what happens in Denver, I feel great. Went from a minus six to a plus ten in the chief's book."

"You know," Basil said, rubbing his chin thoughtfully, "I am reminded of what the church father Tertullian once said about the inevitable reversals that happen to all of us."

"No!" Simmons said firmly. "If you want to ride in the car, you cut out those endless quotations. Otherwise, you can ride on the fender."

Sloan's cell phone rang and he immediately pulled it out. "Sam Sloan."

"George Yeats. We have made progress."

"Excellent."

"But we need you to come to Washington, D.C., immediately."

Sam blinked several times. "You mean *today*?"

"As soon as possible. We have some matters that can only be covered from here. If it takes another day, the CIA will understand, but we actually need you to get here this evening."

"What about my partner, Basil Abbas?"

"Yes, we want both of you. If he can't get here, you're the man we need most."

"Just a moment." Sam lowered the telephone. "Basil, can you go to Washington, D.C., *right now*?"

Basil's mouth dropped and the long strand of black hair slipped farther across his eyes. "You're serious, I presume?"

"I mean in the next few hours," Sam said.

"I guess." Basil sounded surprised. "Other than making this raid on Denver, I'm not doing much else. Why not?"

"We're both coming," Sam spoke back into the telephone. "Please have two tickets for us at the airport for the earliest afternoon flight."

"They'll be there."

Sam slowly clicked off the telephone. Simmons stood by the car looking at him in dismay. "Looks like you'll be going to

Denver by yourself, Dick. The CIA seems to have an urgent wish for us to go east." Sam rubbed his cheek. "Apparently about as quick as we can run."

"You're kidding," Dick said.

"I hope your stock holdings went through the roof this morning, because you're on your own for a while."

Simmons rubbed the back of his neck and frowned. "I think we just had a stock market crash. I needed your assistance."

"You've always got the Denver Police Department to back you up."

"I guess so." Simmons shook his head. "Well, here goes nothing." He reached for the car door.

———

By early afternoon Sloan and Abbas were on an American Airlines plane flying due east. Sam had called Vera at the All-City Detective Agency and let her know where they were going. He promised to call Cara that evening if possible. By the time they hit the airport, the two detectives were hustled onto a Boeing 727-200 with the door slamming behind them.

Sam glanced at his watch. "Why do these exits always occur with the speed of Michael Jordan making a layup shot? We came close to missing this plane."

"Hard to thoughtfully throw everything into a bag so quickly," Basil said. "I'm not even married and I thought I wouldn't make it. Your CIA buddies don't fool around."

"I guess not." Sam settled back into the padded seat. "We're back on the roller coaster again. I hope this ride is smoother than the last one."

"I notice you left the sling behind," Basil said. "Your arm must be nearly well."

"And I'm walking better. Hurts a little every now and then, but pushing myself seems to work. All this exercise is like special therapy sessions."

Basil pushed back in the airplane seat and closed his eyes. "I think I'll take a little nap." He yawned.

Sam stared out the window, watching the clouds gather underneath the ascending airplane. He hoped Cara could make some progress on finding an address, but he knew such a task would be formidable, even for a technician.

The clouds congealed into billowy masses that seemed to bear the airplane through the skies like a foamy cushion. Sam marveled at the mystical ways of the world, the scientific laws of physics and aeronautics that could send a hunk of metal flying through the air like a giant eagle. He thought about the astonishing application of knowledge that had produced a craft that would land on the eastern coast in three to four hours when it had originally taken weeks and weeks to cross the vast prairies. The hand of God had blessed the human race with an extraordinary ability to use their minds in profound ways. He could only pray that the heavenly Father would touch him with the same magnificence of imagination and vision.

Sam rethought every detail of the case. He knew nothing about Yeats except that the man seemed to be a shadowy character with the CIA. Yeats must have been selected for his job because he was a man of considerable stature. Since the financial giants of the industry had scrambled with such fury over the discovery of the decoder device, the entire electronic world was obviously worried about what might come next. Hopefully George Yeats had some of the answers.

27

THE FLIGHT ATTENDANT OPENED THE SIDE DOOR OF THE airliner, and passengers began filing down the steps and into the van that would take them across the tarmac to the terminal. Sloan and Abbas pushed their way to the end of the shuttle so they would be ready to get off quickly when the transportation bus pulled into the main terminal.

"What's this guy look like?" Basil asked, pushing his hair back out of his eyes.

"I have no idea. His follow-up message said he'd meet us. Probably Yeats will have a sign with our names on it or something of that order."

"A sign?" Abbas shrugged. "Sounds a little amateurish."

"Keep your eyes open." Sam held his attaché case firmly. "We'll see something." He felt his coat pocket to make sure the cellular phone was there.

The large vehicle pulled into the station and people hurried out. Sam and Basil stood at the door for a moment but didn't see anyone.

"Nobody's out there with a sign," Abbas observed.

Sam looked carefully at the people standing around the gate. "Well, he could be downstairs. Probably down in the baggage area." Sam started walking. "I can always call Yeats on my cell phone."

"Whatever you say." Basil fell in beside him.

The two detectives had walked about twenty feet when a man spoke from behind them. "Good evening, gentlemen."

Sam whirled around. A short, heavyset, plain-looking man wearing a sport coat and a sweater-vest had come from nowhere.

"Just keep walking," the man said, "and don't look so startled. I have both your passport pictures with me."

"You're George Yeats?" Sam asked quietly.

"Correct. We will walk downstairs and pick up your luggage." His appearance was totally bland. In contrast to his obscure appearance, Yeats spoke with a direct and authoritative voice. "I will stand to one side, but when you've collected your things, a car will be available."

The escalator descended to the luggage area. Sloan and Abbas looked straight ahead while Yeats stayed behind them. Just as they reached the bottom, he spoke again. "I will wait for you over there by the exit marked seventeen. See you in a moment." Yeats turned toward the door.

"My gosh!" Basil groaned. "I'm supposed to be trained to see people, and I missed him when he was right there, bigger than life."

Sam said nothing but stood by the conveyor belt, waiting for the luggage to come out of the shoot. The bags started tumbling out, and within a few minutes each man had a suitcase in hand. Sam looked toward the door. Another man was now standing next to Yeats.

"Let's go," Sam said. "The welcome committee is certainly here."

The four men walked silently out to a plain blue Chevrolet in the parking garage. Only after the doors were closed did Yeats speak again.

"I want you to meet Jefferson Meacham," George Yeats said. "He's one of our agents who covers a multitude of details. He'll be available to take you anywhere you need to go. You may simply call him Jeff."

"Glad to meet you." Meacham shook hands with Sloan and Abbas and then turned back to driving them out of the parking garage.

"We're going to our headquarters outside of Washington," Yeats explained. "We'll talk out there in my office. Lots to discuss."

Sam settled into the backseat but kept watching Jeff Meacham. The man was no chauffeur, he thought; Meacham was there to be a source of constant information back to Yeats. Looked like Mr. Plain Face didn't miss a beat.

Little was said as the car sped down the Dulles Airport access road toward Washington, D.C. They traveled through thick groves of trees and wooded forests that lined the highway. When they reached the city, Meacham skillfully wove his way through the heavy traffic and drove toward the Central Intelligence Agency's headquarters. Meacham slowed as they approached the entry gate but halted only for a moment. The car and the front-seat passengers were obviously well known to the guards.

Meacham parked the car to one side of the building. "Follow me," Yeats said. "I will take you to my personal office."

Sloan and Abbas followed closely behind him. At the entrance they received passes admitting them to the building. Five minutes later they found themselves in a moderate-sized office.

George Yeats kept a picture of his wife on the bureau behind his desk, upon which also sat a large computer. His office appeared neat and probably highly sanitized—a definite contrast to Sam's cubbyhole on Nevada Street.

"Please make yourselves comfortable." Yeats hung his sport coat on a rack behind the door. "We need to go over several items of business as we start our work." He paced in front of them with his hands behind his back, like a general preparing for an attack.

"Obviously the task of our agency is to disappear into the woodwork. Being invisible is our preoccupation. During your time with us, we trust you will do the same."

"Certainly," Sam answered. "I am already aware of this responsibility."

"If possible, don't acknowledge any connection with the CIA in any form or fashion," Yeats continued. "You can disclose that you are from the Colorado Springs Police Department, visiting here on business. Beyond that I suggest you say little."

"We understand," Sam said.

"The CIA generally delves into the foreign concerns of the United States government." Yeats stopped and lit his pipe. "By the way, in my office I set the rules and smoking is one of them." He raised one eyebrow knowingly and blew a cloud of smoke in front of him. "But you don't have to."

Basil laughed. "Always good to be with the man in charge."

"You are," Yeats answered dryly. "I guarantee you are." He walked behind his desk and sat down. "Ready to proceed?"

"Definitely." Sloan forced a smile. "We are here to follow you down any path you select."

Yeats nodded. "Good. We have run the name Alvin Marshal through our system and had it fully processed by the *Maukhabarat* in Amman." He paused and looked directly at Sam. "By the way, you won't be hearing personally from Farid and company. They communicate through us."

Yeats stood and started pacing again. "Turns out a man using the name was registered at the Hilton Hotel. The clerk remembered him with a brown mustache and wearing local clothing. Suits made in the Middle East never fit well and always look on the blocky side. In contrast with Western-made clothes, the colors were flat and dull. He stood around five feet, ten inches tall and seemed to be working hard to maintain an average appearance. But his expensive shoes made him stand out. The hotel people recognized him as an American and the plain appearance didn't fit with how most Westerners dressed."

"So we've found the man?" Sam pushed.

"No." Yeats shook his head. "The problem is that there is no record of an Alvin Marshal coming in or going out of the country. The name proved to be fictitious."

"Dead-end street!" Basil concluded.

"Not necessarily," Yeats retorted. "For some reason, this man used this name with some consistency. Our hunch is that he was trying to establish a reputation of some sort in case Yakoub Natshe started trying to check on him or who he was. I believe he told you that he met the man at the Hilton."

"I remember that Natshe made such a statement," Sam said.

"Before you arrived at the Natshe household, Farid had already put the poor man through an intense two-hour examination." Yeats put his pipe into a large ashtray on his desk. "Our good friend Farid neglected to tell you about the hot seat Natshe had already sat in. A slight 'oversight' made with every intention. He wanted to see if you'd drag something new out of our young inventor."

"Did I?" Sam asked.

"We don't know. If you'll remember, Farid stayed in another part of the house, appearing innocuous, thinking that the guards, or possibly a hidden tape recorder, would tell him what was said. Unfortunately, the bomb brought the entire matter to an abrupt end."

Sam ran his hands through his hair. "You seem to know every detail there is to know about this matter."

"We stay informed." Yeats broke a slight smile. "As you know, that's our business."

"Then why are we here?" Sam shrugged. "You don't need us for anything."

"Ah, the time has come for us to take you through a detailed debriefing session to make sure we've not missed anything. Then we want you to help us by making some inquiries in this city. Because you've been in Jordan, you may be able to recognize something or someone our local agents might miss."

"I thought you said Alvin Marshal was a fictitious name. This issue is dead—gone," Sam argued.

"Not necessarily." George Yeats smiled and winked. "In fact, not at all."

28

DURING THE ENTIRE MORNING FOLLOWING SLOAN'S AND Abbas's arrival in Washington, CIA agents grilled them in separate rooms, asking every conceivable question about their investigation. After an hour with one set of agents, another group came in and went over exactly the same issues. Question after question, the process ground on through the morning and into the early afternoon. The examiners weren't hostile but neither were they friendly. The interrogation proved to be firm and relentless.

At three o'clock in the afternoon, Sam talked with Basil for the first time that day. The usual strand of black hair hanging down in Basil's eyes had become thicker. He looked fatigued, even a bit frazzled. Abbas still wore the same shirt, tie, and coat that he'd worn flying the day before.

As the detectives stood alone in George Yeats's office, Sam asked, "Having fun yet?"

"These people want to know everything, down to and including the size of my underwear." Basil rubbed his mouth nervously. "I've never been through a more intense questioning."

Sloan nodded. "You know how this works. They look for an inconsistency, an error, a misstatement and then go to work on the issue. No big deal. You tell them the truth and let it stand."

"I'm not worried so much about errors. Right now I feel talked out."

Sam laughed. "Yeah, but that's their game."

George Yeats opened the door and walked briskly into his office, carrying a file in his hand. "Relax, gentlemen." He sat down behind his desk. "I have everything necessary in here."

"Did we pass?" Sam asked caustically.

"Of course," Yeats said indifferently and opened the file. "I believe we now have a comprehensive picture of what our investigation has uncovered to date. Today's interrogation proved helpful."

"What did you learn?" Sam asked.

"That our previous data were correct." Yeats picked up his pipe from the ashtray and lit it. He took a big puff and blew smoke in front of his face. "I think we are beginning to get our culprit in perspective, with some sense of how this man acts." He winked. "And we know *you* much better."

"Good," Sam answered. "I hope we can nail this mystery man down."

"Interesting that you should say that." Yeats smiled as if Sam had just walked into his preconceived trap. "That's exactly what we want you to help us with next. Even though

you weren't in Jordan long, we think you might be able to recognize some aspects of the man and the case from your time
abroad." Yeats looked intently at Basil. "It appears you have
more than a small relationship with the *Maukhabarat.*"

Basil blushed. "Of course, I am a Jordanian and they are my
friends."

"Friends?" Yeats frowned. "Come now. Wouldn't *colleagues*
be more appropriate?"

Abbas's eyes narrowed with a hardness Sam hadn't seen
before. He didn't say anything.

"I am getting a different picture from my conversation with
Mohammed Farid." Yeats puffed on his pipe. "I think you
work for the *Maukhabarat.*"

A crimson cast began working up Basil's neck, and the tip
of his large nose turned red. His usually jovial, casual appearance shifted into a straightforward stare. "You must be more
specific."

"Specific?" Yeats growled. "I'm asking you a simple question. Do you work for the secret police in Jordan?"

"You have my vitae sheet. You know the description of my
personal history."

"Basil, I must assume that your failure to respond directly
is in fact an affirmative answer to my question."

"You can assume whatever you wish." Basil's posture became
rigid. "I will say no more on this subject."

George Yeats settled back in his chair and kept puffing on
his pipe. After a few moments, he said, "I'm not trying to
unmask you, Abbas. My point is to clarify that you might be
our best point of contact to talk with the secret police. Am I
correct?"

Basil pushed his hair out of his eyes. "You are continuing to interrogate me by clever innuendo. I will answer no more questions on this subject. You can refer to my credentials."

Yeats smiled. "As you wish." He turned to Sloan. "We want you to pursue the name along with the initials that you've pulled off the Internet, as we believe the decoder thief may have been too clever for his own good," he said.

"Oh?" Sam said. "How's that?"

"We have an FBI agent who has been doing some intelligence work in the Middle East. He's been going in and out of several Arabic countries and knows names and faces. The man has handled sensitive data and could give you an edge if he's able to hook you up to the right sources."

"Okay." Sam glanced at Abbas out of the corner of his eye. His face was still red and he looked irritated. The sudden change in the man's composure amazed Sam. He'd never seen Basil quite so upset. "What's the man's name?"

"Angelo Martinez. He obviously has a Hispanic background but everyone calls him Freddy. I have no idea where he picked up that American moniker."

"Strange name," Sam said. "Maybe you ought to bring him over for a little interrogation. I'd bet your agents could run the source of the name Freddy down."

Yeats ignored Sam's jab. "His dark skin and black hair make him fit in well with the Arab world. He gets by okay, but he's definitely an American."

"I see." Sam pulled at his chin. "Where do we find friend Freddy?"

Yeats pointed over his shoulder. "You don't have to worry about an address. Jeff Meacham has that information and will give you a copy. Jeff will drive you to the FBI headquarters. The office is some distance from here."

Sam had been silently drumming on the arm of the chair with his fingertips. He stopped. "Jeff has the information?" He forced a smile but his voice was cold. "Why don't we all quit kidding each other, George. During the last few minutes you've tried to rattle Basil with this Jordanian secret-service business, and now you want to send us out with one of your best boys, keeping an eye on everything we do. Jeff is nothing more than a spy's spy. Right?"

Yeats's eyes narrowed and he took one more long drag of his pipe. "I'm not playing games with you, Sam. We have our ways of doing business. Yes, Jeff will be paying attention, but not because we don't trust you. You and Basil wouldn't be sitting in my office if I had any question about your veracity."

"Really?" Sam chuckled. "I'll bet! My point is that I play straight up, and I like people who operate in the same way. I'm basically a cop from Colorado who doesn't work well with nonsense floating over his head."

"Good." Yeats sounded unmoved. "We'll do well together." He stood up. "You're ready for Jeff to drive you now?"

Sam looked at Abbas. "I suppose so. We still have time this afternoon?"

"The clock is not our friend, but I'll let Freddy know you're coming. He'll wait for you."

"Whatever you say," Sam answered.

"Excellent." Yeats picked up his phone. "Please send Jeff Meacham in," he told the receptionist.

Almost instantly the door opened and Meacham walked in. The day before, Sam had not paid much attention to the man's appearance. He had been dressed in a T-shirt and a pair of jeans, looking more like one of the luggage handlers at the airport. Today Meacham wore a well-tailored, three-button suit with a maroon tie. His ruffled brown hair was combed back in place, giving his muscular and angular face a handsome look.

"Ready to go?" Meacham asked as he pointed toward the parking lot.

"Sure." Sam smiled at Yeats. "We'll be back." He beckoned to Abbas to follow and walked out of the room with a determined stride.

29

BEFORE THEY REACHED THE PARKING AREA BESIDE THE CIA headquarters building, Sam caught Basil Abbas's arm and pulled him to a halt. Jeff Meacham kept walking toward the blue Chevrolet.

"You okay?" Sam asked.

"Sure," Basil answered without looking at him.

"Yeats was trying to shake you. Looks like he did."

"The man had some objective in mind that I don't completely recognize. He found my hot button. Obviously he enjoys being the fry cook for people like us."

Sam put his arm around Basil's shoulders. "Hey, it's fine. Don't worry about the big squeeze. The guy is giving both of us the total treatment."

Abbas seemed to relax. "I don't like being fried on a hot plate by some American fat boy. I don't trust the guy, that's all."

"Nobody likes to be embarrassed." Sam patted him gently on the back. "But what about his question? Do you work for the Jordanian secret-service police?"

Basil looked at the sidewalk. "What difference would it make if I did?"

"Wouldn't change anything with me whatsoever."

Basil looked at Sam. "I appreciate you, Sam. Thank you for standing with me."

"Now don't launch off into what Saint Tertullian might have said about the CIA, FBI, or the *Maukhabarat*, because they didn't exist back in those days. I just want to know where you're coming from."

"I can't say any more than I've already told everybody. My record is the only statement I can make. We all have secrets we can't tell, Sam."

Sloan shrugged. "You know me: I love to chase a mystery, and your complete identity is turning out to be one of the unexpected twists in this case."

"You men coming with me?" Jeff Meacham called from the car. "The clock's running."

"Sounds like ol' Jeff's afraid he is missing what we're talking about, so he won't be able to give Yeats a hot, firsthand report," Sam said. "Let's go allow him to be our chauffeur and walking tape recorder."

As soon as Sam and Basil got in the car, Meacham drove out of the parking lot. Within a few minutes they were back on the highway, driving toward downtown Washington. Meacham said nothing and just drove quietly. As they approached the outskirts of Washington, Sam broke the silence.

"We're going to an FBI office, right?"

"Yes," Jeff said. "The location is their main office for the national area here in Washington. The J. Edgar Hoover Building is on Pennsylvania and Ninth Street. It's a big building. Lots of offices."

"You know Freddy Martinez?"

Meacham shook his head. "Never met the man, but then again, there are many FBI people floating around the city I've never met."

"How long have you been with the CIA?" Sam asked.

"Ten years."

"Hmm," Sam mused. "You've probably been many places around the world."

Jeff smiled. "A few."

Sam reached up from the backseat and patted him on the back. "Tight-lipped, aren't you?"

Meacham smiled but said nothing.

Sam grinned at Basil. "Should turn out to be an interesting afternoon."

Meacham wound his way through heavy traffic and then sped down Constitution Avenue. Sam sensed that Basil was still digesting what had happened back in Yeats's office and was bothered by the entire scenario.

Basil never talked about his private life, and in the past Sam had only fleeting thoughts that Abbas could actually be a Jordanian secret-service agent. After all, Farid obviously knew who Basil was before they even got off the airplane. The man had a knack for appearing innocent and naive, but when it came to responding, Basil could be as accurate, fast, and deadly as anybody on the police force. He probably was among the best in Jordan.

"Here we are," Meacham said, pulling into a large parking area under a large granite building with *Federal Bureau of Investigation* written in metal letters across the front. "Freddy Martinez will be expecting us." He turned off the car and got out.

"Lead the way," Sam said, falling in beside Meacham. "We have no idea where you're going."

Jeff maintained an easy stride. "Shouldn't be that far." He trotted up the front stairs. "We'll check in with the receptionist, and she'll show us the way to his office."

Ten minutes later, the three men walked into an office on the second floor. The man sitting at the desk stood up immediately. Although he was of Hispanic descent, Martinez could have passed for any of several nationalities. His skin had a rich, dark tone, and he had black hair and brown eyes.

"Ah, you must be Sloan and company," he said.

"Glad to meet you, Mr. Martinez." Sam extended his hand.

"Welcome to the FBI." Martinez shook hands with all three men. "Please sit down. George Yeats told me that you'd be coming."

"We understand you recently returned from Jordan," Sam began.

"I spend a considerable amount of time running all over the world," Freddy began. Martinez wore a charcoal suit with a white shirt and a dark black tie. He looked suave, professional. His clean-shaved face had a youthful quality that probably concealed an older age. "I was in Jordan this spring as well as in several other Arab countries."

"You are aware of the case we are pursuing?" Sam asked.

"More or less." Freddy shook his hand. "As we'd say *en español, mas o menos.* Please fill me in."

"We are looking for a man involved in a bombing in Amman named Alvin Marshal."

Freddy blinked several times. "I see," he said slowly. He looked startled.

"Yeats believes you might help us. We already have the Jordanian police following the man's footsteps in Amman," Sam explained. "I'm not sure why, but he wants you to process this name through your offices."

Martinez rubbed his chin. "Yes." He scratched his head and looked perplexed for a moment. "We can run a location search through our computers," Freddy said slowly. "It shouldn't take too long, as we have a comprehensive system that moves quickly." He picked up the phone. "Let me see what I can put into action."

For a few moments, Freddy told someone on the other end what he wanted and asked how long it would take. They chatted for a moment and then he hung up.

"Looks like it will take a little over an hour to get the detailed information I requested." Martinez looked at his wrist-watch. "Maybe we could eat a bite and get better acquainted. By the time we're finished, the report ought to be on my desk."

"Sounds fine with me," Sam said. "How about you, Basil? Jeff?"

Both men nodded.

"Sure," Sam agreed. "Lead us to the nearest restaurant, Freddy. Lunch was a little on the sparse side today, as the CIA people were chewing mainly on us. You'll find Basil and me to be quite agreeable to anything tonight."

"You'll like the restaurant." Freddy stood and reached for his coat. "They have great Chinese cuisine." He opened the door. "After you, men."

30

CONVERSATION AROUND THE LARGE CIRCULAR TABLE IN the Red Dragon Restaurant was casual. Sloan kept the talk on the light side and Martinez followed suit. No one pushed in any particular direction. Sam and Basil proved to be as hungry as Sam had hinted. Near the end of dinner, Sloan leaned over the table and asked the FBI agent a question.

"How'd you get the name Freddy?"

Instantly Martinez's eyes hardened, but he forced a smile. "Ever hear of Freddy the Freeloader? Red Skelton once did a scenario on a bum by that name. Came from there."

Martinez's grin seemed to say, "No problem. It's all fun," but the man's eyes signaled a hard, cold dislike of the name.

"You prefer us to use a different name?" Sam asked.

"No." Martinez kept the grin in place. "The name's fine. Everybody uses it."

Sam nodded but said nothing more. As Yeats had done with Basil, he'd hit a hidden button.

By the time the four men returned to Angelo Martinez's office, darkness had settled over the streets. Freddy went out to the secretary's office and brought in a report. Martinez gave it a quick look and handed the pages to Sloan and Abbas. Meacham read over their shoulders.

"We have a few people with the name Alvin Marshal on the East Coast," Martinez said. "You'll notice that the page has people listed by their street addresses. You say this man set off a bomb?"

"Yes," Sam said. "Killed several people."

"I'd stay downwind if I was you," Freddy quipped. "He might hit you on the next go-round."

"We'll be paying better attention this time," Sam answered. "You can count on it."

Martinez smiled pleasantly. "The experience should prove interesting."

"Can you get pictures of these people?" Jeff Meacham asked.

"Only if they have a criminal record. Apparently none do."

"Okay." Sam folded the paper and stuck it in his inside coat pocket. "We'll go to work on this tomorrow and be back in touch in the late afternoon. You can always reach us through George Yeats's office."

"If anything additional comes up, I'll call." Martinez shook hands with the men and they left.

As they walked out of the building, Sam said to Basil, "Looks like we could have a long day tomorrow. Running these people down is going to take some time. You reading me?"

"Of course."

"I'll drive you," Jeff said. "I know the area."

"You know," Sam said, "I'll bet you do."

———

For the second night in a row, Cara sat in her bedroom hunched over her computer, trying to work the complex Internet system from every possible angle—but little moved forward. Her stomach growled and made her feel even more uneasy.

Cara got up, walked into the kitchen, and poured popcorn into a large black kettle with oil already on the bottom. She kept thinking about her problem and where to go next. Having gotten back inside the Columbia On-Line system, she found that nothing took her to the information she needed.

The popcorn started to sizzle. Quickly the buzzing turned into full-scale popping. Cara listened as the exploding kernels bounced off the sides of the metal container. She poured the steaming popcorn into a large ceramic bowl. As she walked back to the bedroom, Cara felt her thoughts bouncing just like popcorn: in every direction. She began to think about approaching the problem from a totally different angle.

Abruptly, a totally new aspect of the search crossed her mind. Pushing the bowl to one side, Cara started typing furiously. Taking an entirely circuitous turn, she began to reaccess the Columbia file system and started searching for the bank transit system for customer billing. After a few minutes, she found herself in the section where accounts were held for all subscribers. She quickly tried A.M. Nothing came up, but when she typed in the Alvin Marshal name, Cara found a long list of accounts. Instantly, she started running off the list on her printer.

"Hmm." Cara made a quick scan of the names. "There must be a couple hundred of these guys." She ran down the list with her finger. "Scattered around everywhere in America."

For a few moments, Cara silently studied the list, checking the names, the initials, the addresses. If she knocked out the names with an initial in the middle, the long list dropped dramatically. Several hundred names turned into a list of only forty. Cara carefully looked at each one of these individuals.

Some Alvin Marshals lived on the West Coast, in the Los Angeles and San Francisco areas, but that seemed like the wrong side of the United States. Several men apparently lived in the broad midsection of America. She kept studying the list. Only five men were billed from the East Coast . . . and only one in the Washington, D.C., area.

Only one!

Cara looked more closely. The Marshal address sounded like it was in the northwestern part of Washington, D.C. She hurried into her father's office and found his thick atlas of the United States. Back in her bedroom, Cara opened the atlas to the District of Columbia and started searching the streets.

Sure enough! Cara said to herself. *There is a Corcoran Street!* With her index finger she ran up Fourteenth Street until the two streets crossed. *Got to be the right place. Not far from something called Logan Circle.*

She grabbed a pencil and began writing down the address and the map's description of the location. This Marshal address could be in the area where her father was staying tonight. If nothing else, he wouldn't have any trouble running the address down.

"Mom!" Cara yelled. "Please come in here as quickly as possible."

Vera appeared in the door. "You want me to get you a Coke this time?" she asked. "Or a sandwich?"

"I've actually got an Alvin Marshal address for Dad to run down in Washington. I mean, this is a real person with an actual street address!"

Vera looked at the address for a moment. "This might prove to be significant, Cara. We need to get the information to your father immediately."

"You have his telephone number?"

"You bet." Vera hurried out of the room and returned quickly. "Here's the phone number. I keep it in my daily planner."

31

THE CIA HAD RESERVED ROOMS FOR SAM AND BASIL AT the Phoenix Park Hotel, not far from Union Station. Sloan had already turned out the light and was in bed when the telephone rang in his hotel room. He flipped on the light and discovered it was past midnight.

"This better be good," he mumbled, reaching for the phone. "Very good."

"Dad! It's me. Cara!"

"Well!" Sam pushed himself up in the bed. "How nice to hear your voice, even if *it's after midnight.*"

"I'm sorry it's so late, Dad. I know there's a two-hour time difference, but I had to get this information to you before tomorrow morning. I finally have an address for Alvin Marshal."

"What?" Sam pushed the phone more tightly against his ear. "You're kidding."

"I had a terribly difficult time hacking into the Columbia On-Line system, but I kept remembering that you promised me legal coverage if I got caught doing something wrong. I hope what I found is acceptable."

"Sure. Sure, Cara. What did you find out?"

"It took me two whole evenings, but I finally discovered the billing lists for all the Alvin Marshals in the Columbia system. Turned out to be a long list."

"Hmm—about what I expected. Lots of subscribers in the Columbia system. But you said you had a specific address for me."

"Dad, I've got a street address right under your nose in Washington, D.C. Got a pencil?"

Sam grabbed for the ballpoint on the nightstand. "Don't stop now. I also have a notepad with me."

"Write down 1305 Corcoran Street," Cara said. "Ever hear of a place called Logan Circle?"

"I think that's a subway station. Several similar stops, like Dupoint Circle, are scattered around the city. My hunch is that's a major stop on the underground line."

"My map says Logan Circle is about four blocks from this place on Corcoran Street. It might prove to be something of a walk. You can check it out. Of course, if you've got a car, you can drive straight to the house."

"Cara, I can't tell you how pleased I am with this information. I'll make it my number one stop tomorrow. You know that what we do is police business and confidential, but I'll let you know if anybody significant is in the building."

"Thanks, Dad. I'm really excited."

"Cara, you've made a big breakthrough. Is your mom around?"

"She's right here."

When Vera came on the line, Sam explained, "Dear, I didn't call because I got here so late and was exhausted. Cara's truly done an amazing job."

"She certainly has. Are you all right?"

"It's been a hard day and I'm worn out, but we're making progress."

"Call me tomorrow," Vera said. "I love you."

"Me too. Take care." Sam hung up. He put the telephone back on the stand and looked at what he'd scrawled across the notepad: 1305 Corcoran Street. He got out of bed and walked to a small closet, opened the door, and reached inside the inner pocket of his coat.

Sam quickly ran down the list of names and addresses he had received from Martinez. The only name in Washington, D.C., proper was on Garfield Street above Georgetown, not far from the National Cathedral.

"How strange," Sam said to himself, thinking that surely the FBI had a comprehensive computerized listing of all the people living in the city. "How could they have missed this?"

Sloan sat on a hotel chair and stared at the piece of paper. Something didn't fit.

———

The next morning, Sam met Basil for breakfast in the hotel's restaurant. Meacham wouldn't show up for another forty-five minutes, and they could talk without the walking tape recorder sending a message back to George Yeats. Hunched over the table with his glasses down on the tip of his nose, Abbas was already devouring the morning newspaper. He was still in the same clothes, except he'd changed shirts. Progress was possible.

"I've come up with some unexpected information," Sam said, slipping into the booth. "I've got to run it down today without anyone following me."

Basil pushed the black strand of hair out of his eyes and peered over the top of his half glasses. "Won't be easy. I don't think Meacham will let you out of his sight."

"Sometime during the day I want you to help me lose him. You'll go one way and I'll disappear in the crowd. Something of that order. When Slick Jeff figures out that I'm gone, you tell him I was checking out another location to save us time. He won't like it, but by then I'll have vanished like the breeze. I'll call you later in the day on your cell phone and let you know where to pick me up."

Abbas grinned. "I can't think of anything more that I'd love to do than give Yeats the slip. It'll be my payback."

Thirty minutes later Jeff Meacham came into the restaurant. He was ten minutes early; Sloan and Abbas exchanged a knowing glance but said nothing. By nine o'clock the three men were back in the plain blue Chevrolet and on their way across town.

Meacham drove them toward Mt. Vernon Square. He would probably take this boulevard, Sam surmised, all the way up to the address on Garfield Street they had received from Martinez.

As things now stood, Sam thought, Cara's information might be a mistake, but it seemed to hold more promise than anything else he had. The more he thought about the Corcoran address, the more important it seemed to be.

Sam saw they were approaching the Washington Plaza Hotel. In the center of the circular exchange was Thomas Circle—the perfect place to catch the subway and check things out on his own. He wouldn't have much time to make up his mind. It was a now-or-never situation.

Meacham slowed for the stoplight.

"I'll catch up with you guys later," Sam said. "Be careful in this traffic."

"What?" Meacham whirled around. "What'd you say?"

Sam leaped out of the car and slammed the door. The light changed and the cars surged forward. He had to jump quickly to the curb to avoid getting run over. For a moment the blue Chevrolet sat there, and then cars started blaring their horns.

"See ya around." Sam waved good-bye.

Meacham had no choice but to pull away.

Sloan hurried into the subway tunnel. Just to be on the safe side, he waited in the shadows until he was convinced no one was following him. Once satisfied, he quickly grabbed the next metro coach that would take him directly to Logan Circle. He sank into the seat and caught his breath. If nothing else, he enjoyed the solitude of bumping down the tracks alone.

32

SLOAN STEPPED OFF THE COACH AND WALKED INTO LOGAN Circle. The hour was early enough that passengers were still leaving for work, so the station was crowded. He edged his way through the mob of passengers and walked out into the neighborhood. In contrast to the metro station at Thomas Circle, the area around Logan Circle appeared to be largely residential.

He started walking north on Thirteenth Street and in a couple of blocks found Corcoran Street. Lined with trees, houses, and apartment buildings, Corcoran looked like a pleasant neighborhood. Sam checked the address in his pocket again—1305 shouldn't be more than a couple of blocks away. Turning to his left, he strolled past Kingman Place Street and kept walking toward Fourteenth.

The morning air smelled good. Walking along by himself, Sam felt almost as if he were taking a stroll down Twenty-third

Street in Colorado Springs. The exercise stretched his muscles and felt invigorating. Sam picked up the pace.

The fact that Freddy Martinez and his people didn't know about this address bothered Sam. He didn't like the long nose of George Yeats and his bird dog named Jeff, but the intrusions were understandable. The CIA didn't take chances—but neither should the FBI. The obvious oversight made him feel uncomfortable.

Shortly after crossing Fourteenth Street, Sam slowed down. Checking the house numbers, he could see far enough down the street to recognize the location of the 1305 address. A two-story apartment building signaled problems. He would have to find a way in the front door and then figure out which unit belonged to Alvin Marshal.

Sam walked over to the building and stood on the front landing for several minutes, thinking about the best way to proceed. He finally concluded that the door lock shouldn't prove too difficult to pick, but it could set off an alarm. Not a good situation. Maybe he could use a credit card to slip inside the lock. Sam heard a noise. Moments later a woman came out. He grabbed the door.

"Morning," Sloan said pleasantly.

"Good morning," the black, middle-aged woman answered. She walked down the sidewalk.

Sam hurried inside. In the hallway, he found a row of mailboxes. He slowly walked down the length of the row, checking each box. In a small slot at the top, the residents had affixed their names. Halfway down the row, he found the right box: Alvin Marshal. Apartment 25.

Sam grinned. "Great!" he mumbled under his breath.

Across from the mailboxes he could see an elevator, and down at the end of the hall, a stairway. Using the stairs, Sam hurried up to the second floor, walking as quietly as possible. He quickly slipped up to the door with a small metal number 25 nailed on the front. He knocked quietly. No one answered. Sam knocked again more forcefully, but no sounds came from the other side.

After a minute, Sloan pulled out a set of keys and lock picks from his coat pocket and started working. The door lock was old and simple. He quickly worked it open and gently pushed. Sam didn't hear anybody inside, but he found he could open the door only a couple of inches. A chain safety lock had been slipped into place at the top. Sam immediately shut the door and hurried back to the stairs.

Something was wrong. No one could bolt the safety lock unless he were inside, but no one had answered the door. Alvin Marshal, his wife, girlfriend, whoever, could be in there . . . unless Alvin Marshal had gone out some other way. Like a back door—or a fire escape. If this was the man they were chasing, Sam thought, he might avoid the front door to keep from being observed.

Sloan looked back into the second-floor hallway. At both ends of the corridor stood two large windows. Sam noted where apartment twenty-five stood in the arrangement of the hallway, then went back down the exit steps. He quickly walked to the back door of the building and looked out.

"Ah, there it is," he murmured to himself. "A fire escape!" Someone had already placed a large garbage container with a lid under the stairwell. It appeared that Alvin Marshal used this setup with some frequency. Once on top of the bin, Sam grabbed the ladder hanging overhead and the steps came down silently. Marshal apparently kept the system well oiled.

Sam scampered up the steps and quickly counted down the housing units until he found the right back door. Through the window on the back door he could see the kitchen area.

Sam knocked on the back door but no one came. He could see through the kitchen to the front door. The chain safety lock still hung in place. The apartment appeared to be genuinely vacant.

"Here we go again," Sloan said to himself and pulled the lock picks and keys out of his pocket. The back door proved to be even easier to open than the front one. Sam quickly entered the kitchen.

To his surprise, the entire apartment had little furniture. The small living room proved to be completely bare, but in the back bedroom, Sam found a computer console and tables with electronic gear scattered around the carpet. In the center of the room, a small television sat on a little table. Wires ran to a DVD recorder. DVDs sat on top of the recorder and a few lay scattered on the floor. On one side of the room stood a pile of VHS movies and another recorder to play them. Other wires ran to the back of the computer. Behind the desk sat an office chair. Everything stood ready to be used.

"Well, well," Sam said to himself, "no one but a lonely computer lives here."

He carefully walked around the entire apartment several times but found nothing that gave any indication of who rented the place. The name Alvin Marshal or the initials A.M. had not been stamped on or attached to anything.

Sam sat down at the computer console desk and studied the

monitor. The 1.7 GHz Pentium model computer had the capacity to do about anything. Sam saw that it was hooked up to the
television set. He reached down and turned on the console,
watched the monitor screen pick up color and come to life.
Then he ejected the disc. Immediately a three-and-a-half-inch
Sony popped out. Some notation had been written in Arabic
across the front of the index label.

Sam stared in astonishment. Was this the sixty-kilobyte
decoding system that Natshe had invented?

33

FOR AN HOUR SAM SLOAN WORKED WITH THE COMPUTER and DVDs in the bedroom of the apartment on Corcoran Street. By eleven o'clock, the nature of the system was clear to him. Apparently the thief had used this apartment as a hiding place to do his deciphering business. Alvin Marshal seemed to be playing with DVDs of old movies, breaking through the protective shield with the decoding device, and copying each of the films. Perhaps he was copying rented movies, but that was hardly a task worth blowing up a house and killing people on the other side of the world. If this device were going to make big dollars, it would need to be mass-produced. The one-room operation at Corcoran Street hardly fit that scheme of things.

Sam pushed back from the computer and stared at the mess around the room. He had one of the DeCSS disks Alvin had stolen in Jordan; the thief probably carried the other disk with him. Maybe he'd made others by now. Sam searched the room but found no other copies of the device.

Sam quickly decided it was possible that the thief might show up during the noon hour to work with the machines. He had to make up his mind about what to do next.

Clearly the problem was more complex than could be handled by one man. Apartment twenty-five needed to be watched day and night. If Sam walked out with the DeCSS disk, Marshal would know the place had been discovered. On the other hand, leaving the decoder disk invited a disaster—it could disappear again. Sam felt the squeeze and knew he needed more information.

Slipping the computer disk into his coat pocket, he unlocked the front door and went downstairs to find the manager's office. Another rundown of the row of mailboxes revealed that apartment three belonged to a Ted Donavan, listed as manager.

Sam knocked on the door. A few seconds later, a tall, thin, older man opened the door. "Can I help you?"

"You're the manager? The person who rents apartments?"

"Sorry. We're completely full with no openings in sight."

Sam held up his police badge. "I am with the police and making a search. I need to ask you some questions."

Donavan raised his white eyebrows. "Oh! I see." He obviously didn't notice that the badge was from Colorado Springs. He coughed. "Please come in."

Sam walked into the simple but pleasantly decorated living room. From the accumulation of clutter around the room, Sam surmised that the man had lived there for some time.

"Who ya lookin' for?" Ted asked.

"I'm interested in the person who rents apartment twenty-five upstairs. I believe the name is Alvin Marshal."

Ted nodded. "That's what I understand, but I never seen the man nohow."

"Never seen him?"

Donavan shook his head. "Everything about that rental was done by mail. Strange. He signed the lease and sent the money all through them mailin' envelopes, don't ya see."

"You've not seen him once?" Sam pushed.

Ted scratched his head. "Well, about a year ago, one time, I seen him come in the front door. But I was a far bit away and couldn't see much."

"Did you see *anything* you can tell me about him?"

"Trouble was, this here Marshall was obviously wearing one of them thick brown wigs. Not all that good, as a matter of fact. Sorta covered his head in such a way that I didn't get a good look at the man's face. Kept lookin' at that awful wig. After that I didn't see him none."

"Nothing?"

"Not at all."

"Do you have a sample of his writing?"

"Let's see here." Ted Donavan turned around and walked slowly to a small, two-drawer file cabinet next to a desk. He opened the bottom drawer and pulled one out. "See. Here's where the stuff is."

"I'll look over your shoulder."

Ted fanned out the contents across his desk. "Looks like he's done typed everything on plain white paper." He held it up to the light. "Looks like common ol' paper you'd buy anywhere. All's I got is one signature, here on the lease."

"Thank you, Mr. Donavan," Sam said. "You have a copy machine here?"

"Sure do."

"I need to take these originals with me today," Sam explained. "How about you running off copies for your file?"

"Certainly. Just take a minute." Donavan took the pieces of paper and walked to a back bedroom. Sam stayed in the living room, carefully looking at everything in the apartment. In a couple of minutes, Ted came back.

"Here ya are, Mr. Sloan."

Sam took the originals. "I need to talk to the neighbors on the second floor, and I may need to come back later. Any problems with that?"

"No, siree! We completely support the police in every way in this place."

"Thank you." Sam opened the front door and stepped back into the hallway. "I'll go up there right now and see what I can find out."

"Sure thing. You call me now if there's anythin' you want." Ted shut the door.

Sam took the elevator to the second floor and quickly started down the hallway, knocking on doors. Because most of the people were gone, he covered the first ten apartments quickly. At the eleventh, a petite Hispanic woman opened the door.

"We don't want none," she began. "No salesmen welcome."

"I'm with the police," Sam said and held up the badge again. "Need to ask you a few questions."

The woman pulled her robe tighter and her dark brown eyes widened. "Oh!" She took a step back. "My goodness! We done nothing."

"You know the man who rents apartment twenty-five?"

"We don't know nobody."

"Ever see him?"

The woman clutched the throat of her robe and looked frightened. "Never."

"You've not seen him even from a distance?"

"Never," she repeated.

"You can't tell me one thing?"

She shook her head furiously and her black hair quivered. "I don't know nobody in this place. Okay?" She hung on to the door like she wanted to slam it.

"Thank you," Sam said.

"Good-bye." The boom followed immediately.

No one on the second floor had ever seen Alvin Marshal. Sloan tried the first floor with the same results. They obviously kept to themselves. The thief had selected the building because anonymity was the primary order of the day.

Having demonstrated what he suspected was true, Sloan went back to apartment twenty-five and fastened the safety latch in place on the doorjamb, locking himself in. Sitting on top of this apartment was too difficult a task for Basil and Sam to do alone. He had a tough decision about whom to trust next.

Sam pulled out his cellular phone and dialed. When Abbas answered he said, "Basil?"

"Well, it's my former partner, Sam Sloan."

"You found anything?"

"You kidding? We've been driving all over this city. Needless to say, my driver isn't a happy camper."

"Give Jeff my best regards. He's sitting next to you?"

"As a matter of fact, Meacham is right here. You want to speak to him?" Basil laughed.

"I don't think so, but I do want to talk with you. Where are you now?"

"We just finished checking one of the addresses in Arlington, Virginia, on the other side of the Potomac River. Actually we're not that far from Georgetown University."

"Okay. I'm going to give you the address of where I am. Tell Jeff to come by for me and then we'll go back and see your friend George Yeats. Sound acceptable?"

"Sure."

Sam gave him the address and general directions on how to get to the Corcoran apartment building. "I'll be waiting outside," he said and hung up.

Putting the cellular phone back in his pocket, Sam made his way out the back door and down the fire escape. His mind raced. He had a hard decision to make.

34

When Jeff Meacham pulled up in front of the Corcoran Street apartment, Sam Sloan had been standing in the shadows for thirty minutes. A few people had passed by but no one even vaguely resembling his flimsy description of Alvin Marshal had appeared. Possibly the thief wouldn't come back soon . . . or ever.

"Good to see you again, Jeff," Sam said into the window of the blue Chevrolet.

Meacham looked disgusted but only nodded.

"I hope you've had a profitable morning and afternoon," Sam added.

"Probably would have if you'd been with us," Jeff said cynically. "I could have let you out back there at Thomas Circle if you'd asked."

"Didn't want to bother you." Sam opened the car door and

got in the backseat. "I want to get back to the CIA headquarters now."

Jeff pulled away from the curb slowly. "I thought you were checking out possible locations for this missing man."

"Changed my mind." Sam settled back against the seat. "I ran into several other problems that demanded my attention. Let's go."

Jeff said nothing but pulled away. He drove straight back to the CIA offices without any conversation, obviously peeved at Sam's escapades. He passed security with the usual ease and parked in the predictable slot; then the three men walked into the building.

"I am going to talk with Yeats alone," Sam said. "You and Basil will wait outside."

"But I need to—"

"Not now," Sam said, cutting him off. "We'll call for you when Yeats is ready for your report on what you and Basil did today."

"I'm not sure that—"

"Thank you." Sam stopped Jeff again. "Wait for me, Basil." Without stopping, Sam nodded to Yeats's secretary and kept walking.

"Mr. Sloan!" the woman called after him.

Sam opened Yeats's door and closed it behind him without slowing his stride. "Yeats," he said, "we need to have a little talk."

George Yeats bolted slightly. "You always come in without knocking or telling my secretary?"

Sam sat down across the desk from him. "I understand that I'm supposed to be working with you—maybe even for you—

but we need to get some problems cleared up before we go any farther."

Yeats lowered his pencil and picked up his pipe. He eyed Sam suspiciously. "Oh?"

"I found Alvin Marshal's apartment," Sam said.

Yeats stopped and lowered his pipe. "You what?"

"I lost your man Jeff and went on my own. I'm not ready to talk about the details until we get some matters settled."

"Do I understand you right? You found this thief?"

"I'm not sure who I can trust," Sam began. "I've worked with you people before. You know my history and it's impeccable. Nevertheless, when I came up here this time you gave me the third degree. I want to know why."

Yeats put his pipe back in the ashtray. "I read your file before you arrived, Sam. Yes, I know your history, but I didn't have the same information on your friend Basil Abbas. From my conversations with Mohammed Farid, I had already deduced that Abbas probably worked for the *Maukhabarat*. I wanted to know what makes this man tick."

"So you gave both of us the treatment?"

"Exactly. You were interrogated because that covered what we needed to do with Basil Abbas."

Sloan folded his hands in front of him and stared across the desk. "I don't believe you sent Mr. Meacham with us because we needed a driver."

"Correct." Yeats looked back intently at Sam. "I imagine you consider him to be my personal spy."

"Yes."

"Wrong."

"Then what?"

Yeats thumped on his desk with his fingers for a moment. "Sam, I work in a most complex and procedurally organized institution. The CIA does everything with a mission and a purpose. We have the responsibility of thinking through every move quite carefully. This matter with the DeCSS device is no different."

"I don't understand." Sam twisted in his chair.

Yeats smiled. "Jeff was sent to protect you. He is an excellent marksman. I didn't want someone shooting you in the back."

Sam rocked back in his chair. "You're not serious?"

"Quite. I personally believe something more is afoot in this DVD decoding device theft than any of us have yet ferreted out. I don't think the ultimate objective is to steal movies."

Sam rubbed his mouth nervously. "Now you are playing straight with me. This morning I found an apartment with a computer, television set, DVDs, and this little device." He laid the disk with the Arabic notations on Yeats's desk. "I found one of the two sixty-kilobyte disks that our killer stole in Jordan."

Yeats picked up the disk and stared at it for a moment. "Amazing, Sloan. How'd you find it?"

Sloan didn't smile. "For the moment, that is my secret. What's important is that I didn't get any of this information from the FBI. Understand? Your buddy Freddy Martinez had no idea that anyone named Alvin Marshal lived at this address."

Yeats's eyes narrowed. "I see." His voice sounded flat and slightly suspicious.

"Isn't Freddy supposed to be the expert on Washington, D.C., or have I missed something here?"

Yeats looked at his desk.

Sam nodded his head. "I don't expect you to fill me in on

every secret that you've got stored around this office, but I do anticipate being treated like an insider. I want you to level with me on this assignment."

Yeats nodded. "I will do the best I can."

"Okay." Sam leaned over the desk. "I think you suspect something about Martinez that you haven't revealed to me. You wanted us to go over there and get a good look at the man, hoping we'd come up with something unexpected and important. Right?"

"I suspect everyone, Sam, including you. It's what makes me a successful and significant agent for the CIA. However, in the case of Freddy Martinez, I have my own special fears and suspicions. At this moment I can't yet speak about them, but I do need your help."

"Shoot straight with me, George, and you've got it."

35

SAM CLOSED THE DOOR AS HE LEFT GEORGE YEATS'S office, only nodding to the secretary as he spoke to Jeff Meacham. "I think Yeats will talk with you now. We'll be out here in the hall when you're ready to leave."

Jeff eyed Sam nervously but said nothing. The secretary looked confused and silently watched Meacham disappear into the inner office.

"Come out here." Sam motioned for Basil to follow him into the long hallway. "I got the air cleared," he began. "I think matters will unfold more smoothly now."

"Oh?" Basil raised an eyebrow. "You beat him with a stick? Hit the man with your gun?"

"I explained a few things," Sam said and launched into a lengthy description of what had happened throughout the morning. "I think Yeats will treat you better now," he concluded.

"Excellent." Basil pushed the long strand of black hair out of his eyes. "What an incredible discovery. I suspect that Cara had something to do with finding the right address."

Sam grinned. "Why, Basil. You sound devious."

"I have a devious partner. Where do we go next?"

"I believe Yeats is giving his bird dog Jeff some new instructions for our next field assignment. We'll be going back to the FBI offices as soon as he comes out."

Basil looked at his wristwatch. "He better not take long."

Sam heard the door open and close inside Yeats's office suite. "I think our man is on the way even as we speak."

Once Meacham joined them, they quickly walked out of the building.

"We'll have to hurry," Jeff said as they headed for the car. "The afternoon is slipping away from us."

Sam reached over and put his hand on Meacham's shoulder. "We appreciate you," he said. "Yeats explained your function more clearly. I always have a definite affection for a man whose job is to keep my back covered."

Jeff appeared to relax. "Thank you," he said. "I'm sure we will work together in an acceptable manner."

"Oh, far more than that," Sam answered. "I believe we are making definite progress on this case, and I promise not to lose you again." He chuckled.

The men got back in the blue Chevrolet and drove toward the center of Washington. Meacham maneuvered through the heavy traffic and soon found his way down Constitution Avenue. By the time they reached the FBI building, Sam's watch said four-thirty. Jeff turned into a special entrance under the building. Five minutes later, the three men walked into Freddy Martinez's office.

"Gentlemen," Martinez said, looking surprised and standing up. "Welcome back. I trust you had a good day."

"Most successful." Sam smiled thinly. "Yes, we found some unexpected clues that are proving helpful. The material is being analyzed right now."

Martinez looked puzzled. "Oh? Well, I'm sure that's positive."

"Yes," Sam answered, "our leads turned out to be more than productive."

Freddy Martinez blinked several times. "I see," he said slowly. "How can I be of assistance to you?"

"I'm going to need more information," Sam said. "We must access your computers for personnel data. I have been given a top security clearance by the CIA."

"Hmm." Martinez adjusted his tie nervously. "I am not authorized to give you such freedom on our computers. Those matters are in other hands."

Sam smiled broadly. "I understand. I simply wanted you to be aware of what we are doing. Please send me to your immediate supervisor."

The FBI agent took a deep breath. "As you wish." He picked up the telephone. "My supervisor?"

"Exactly," Sam said and looked at Basil and Jeff. Neither man changed his stoic expression.

"Dale?" Freddy asked. "This is Freddy Martinez. I need to send three men from the CIA up to speak with you."

Sam turned back toward Jeff and Basil, winking at them.

"Yes, they are here at this moment," Freddy said. "Thank you," he concluded and hung up.

"Dale Beck will see you immediately. I'll go with you."

"Thanks," Sam said, "but we'll find our way. We need to talk with him alone."

Martinez's eyes narrowed and for a moment he looked angry. "You'll find him in office 3207," he said.

"Thank you." Sam didn't smile. The three men walked out.

After they were on the elevator, Sam spoke again. "You think we rattled ol' Freddy's cage?"

Jeff nodded. "He didn't like what you said or what you are doing."

"Good." Sam smiled and walked through the door of the elevator. He pointed down the hall. "Beck's office should be right over there. At least, that's the direction that Yeats gave me."

"'Yeats gave you'?" Jeff echoed.

"Hang on," Sam said. "We're riding a roller coaster." He opened the office door, allowing Jeff and Basil to enter ahead of him. "Get ready for another sharp turn."

A secretary with black hair and flashing, dark brown eyes looked up from her computer. "Can I help you?"

"I'm Sam Sloan. We're here to talk with Dale Beck."

"Oh yes, he's expecting you." The woman picked up her office phone and relayed the information. "Mr. Beck will see you now." She stood up.

"Thanks," Sam said. "We'll find the way." The three men walked to Beck's office door.

Dale Beck proved to be a physically strong-looking man, probably in his fifties. A flat nose gave him the appearance of a boxer. His ruddy complexion added to the brawler look, but a white shirt, tie, and business pants balanced his appearance.

"Please sit down," Beck began. "I've been expecting you since George Yeats called earlier this afternoon."

"Thank you." Sam sat down and the other two men followed. "I think you know why we are here."

"I know what Yeats said." Beck broke into a big grin. "If anyone ever knows exactly what's going through George's mind, they are way ahead of me."

Sam smiled. "I understand. We need to check some personnel matters that we're working on for the CIA. I believe George said to give you this card, which indicates that I have a top-level security clearance." Sam handed the document across the desk.

Beck looked at it carefully. "You've obviously passed their big test. These men have similar clearance?"

"I do," Jeff Meacham said.

"I'm still in immigrant status," Basil said. "I'm afraid that keeps me from even being considered."

Beck nodded. "I understand. Sorry, but I'll have to ask you to sit out in the lobby with my secretary."

"Your secretary?" Abbas smiled. "Now there's a woman I could get to know."

"You probably would enjoy her husband too," Beck added in a low voice. "He's about six-foot-four and once played college football at Purdue."

Abbas pursed his lips and rubbed his forehead. "I believe Saint Simeon once said—"

"Thank you." Sam cut Basil off. "I'm the only one who needs to look at your personnel files. Jeff can stay with Basil."

"Sure." Jeff glanced at Abbas. "You and I can handle this assignment by ourselves."

36

DALE BECK WALKED SAM DOWN A LONG BACK CORRIDOR and then up two flights of stairs. At the end of the fifth floor, Beck took Sam into a large room filled with computers, electronic equipment, and many smaller computer stations. Stretching nearly to the ceiling, several massive machines clicked away, busily transacting the nation's secret business on spinning reels of magnetic plastic tape. Against the far wall, a single computer was not being used. Beck pointed toward a chair sitting in front of it.

Sam nodded to several of the agents tending the other machines but no one spoke. He sat down in the small padded chair and looked at the blue screen already prepared for service.

"Let me be frank with you," Beck said quietly. "I've worked with George Yeats for a number of years in a successful professional relationship. We generally level with each other."

"That's the way I like to work."

Beck nodded. "George didn't tell me a great deal about what's happening in this matter, but I take it that you're looking for something that involves my staff."

"I'm not completely sure," Sam said candidly. "I'm hunting right now."

Beck rubbed his chin and squinted thoughtfully. "Of course, all government agencies have their turf, and usually we don't share secrets. Sloan, I want you to know that if you need my help, I'm here to do what I can. If you find any of my people have crossed the line, you let me know. We'll deal with the problem."

"Thank you," Sam said. "Yeats indicated I could trust you completely." He studied Beck's eyes. The FBI agent's intensity signaled that he meant business.

Beck nodded. "I'll be in my office." He walked out of the computer room.

Sam watched Dale Beck disappear and then began typing in instructions. Data concerning FBI employees appeared on the screen. For several moments, Sam surveyed the screen. The instructions indicated he needed only to type in a name and that file would appear. His fingers glided across the plastic keys. He hit the enter button and instantly the file of Angelo Martinez came up.

Sloan slowly studied the information. Apparently Martinez had been born in McAllen, Texas, to parents who had immigrated from Matamoros, Mexico. An unusually bright young man, he had graduated from the University of Texas in Austin, working to keep himself in school and using government aid programs to pay tuition. His field of study had been languages.

His résumé indicated he could speak Spanish, English, Arabic, and Italian with fluency.

"My, my," Sam mumbled to himself. "Freddy has quite a history."

The employment record indicated that in 1999, Martinez had been given an assignment for the bureau outside of the United States in the Middle East. Trips on official business took him to countries including Turkey, Jordan, Israel, Saudi Arabia, and Egypt.

"Confirms what I've been told," Sam said quietly. "He's been where they said he went."

Sam typed in a different set of instructions. The employment page disappeared and another group of materials appeared. He quickly typed in more directions and the pages started moving fast. After five minutes, a set of names appeared with addresses affixed. Sam ran his finger slowly down the monitor screen.

"Just as I suspected," he mumbled under his breath. "No question about what happened."

Sam typed in other instructions and hit the enter button. Once again the employee file returned. He tapped in more directions to the computer and other information appeared on the screen.

"Yes! Exactly what I'm looking for!" Sam said too loudly. He noticed several employees looking at him. He smiled. "Sorry." He turned back to the machine. Punching the print button, he ran off a copy of the information. When the sheet came out, he folded it and stuck the data in his inner coat pocket. He turned the computer off and hurried back to Dale Beck's office.

"I've found what I needed," Sam told him. "But I must work on this overnight before I have any response."

Beck nodded. "I understand." He leaned back in the chair and crossed his arms over his massive chest. "I'll be here in the morning if you want to talk."

"Certainly." Sam reached out and shook his hand. "I can't tell you how much I appreciate your help." He stopped. "By the way, I consider this inquiry to be confidential. I'd prefer Freddy Martinez not know anything about my search."

"Certainly."

"See you tomorrow." Sam hurried out of Beck's office.

Basil and Jeff were waiting outside. "Gentlemen, we are pushing this good woman's closing time." He smiled at the secretary. "Don't want to detain this young lady."

"Oh, no problem," the secretary said.

"See you tomorrow—hopefully," Sam answered and walked out the door, trailed by Basil and Jeff. Using the elevators, the three men returned to the basement parking garage and got into their car.

"Take us back to the hotel," Sam told Jeff. "We've got some business to ponder tonight."

"Sure," Jeff said and steered the car toward the exit. "Think we'll be back here in the morning?"

Sam rubbed his chin and thought about the question. "Eventually," he finally said, "but I think we'll start the day with another chat with your boss, George Yeats."

37

At seven o'clock Sam met Basil in the hotel's restaurant to eat supper. As was usually the case, Abbas had arrived early and was already deep into a Washington newspaper.

"Finding anything worth reading?" Sam asked as he sat down opposite the Jordanian.

"Always," Abbas said. "Every newspaper has something important to tell me."

"And also puts a spin on the stories to deceive you," Sam countered. "I don't let the local political reporters throw me any curveballs."

Abbas pursed his lips and shrugged his shoulders. "Then how do you know what's happening in the world?"

"Have to pay extra-careful attention to the taxi drivers," Sam joked. "Makes me more alert."

"I take it that all this perceptiveness has produced some insights you've not shared with me yet."

Sam raised an eyebrow. "Think so? Well, I found my time in Dale Beck's computer room to be more than slightly helpful."

Abbas folded the newspaper and pushed it to one side. "What did you come up with?"

"Two things." Sam leaned over the table and spoke more quietly. "First, I ran the records on Freddy Martinez's employment in the Middle East and found that he was in Jordan when the decoder disks were both invented and stolen."

Basil's eyes narrowed. "Okay. What else?"

Sam nodded. "I also discovered Freddy was somewhere floating around the back streets of Amman when the bomb went off. Freddy was in Amman at the precise times the significant events took place. As a responsible FBI agent, he knew about or even studied the disastrous circumstances that took place when he was on duty. Yet he did not mention even one of these incidents to us."

Abbas didn't say anything but rubbed his chin. "And?"

"Then I went back over the street addresses that the FBI has on its data system and I found out something even more interesting. I checked the name Alvin Marshal to see what might come up in the street addresses and with the post office. The FBI has an Alvin Marshal listed at 1305 Corcoran Street in their records. Martinez simply didn't pass on to us the only street address that counted."

"You're suggesting that Freddy Martinez has something to do with this crime?"

"I find it hard to avoid that conclusion."

Abbas slouched back in the booth and folded his arms over

his chest. "Why would an agent of a major United States government agency get involved in stealing a DVD decoding device? You think he's helping the person who stole it? Taking a big payoff?"

"I'm not sure what's going on here, Basil. But I also think George Yeats has some hunches about this matter that he hasn't told me yet. We'll start with another chat with him in the morning."

Basil nodded his head mechanically. "The hole gets deeper the longer we look into it."

"Who said that? Socrates?"

"No." Basil grinned slyly. "I did."

As predictable as always, Jeff Meacham pulled up in the blue Chevrolet five minutes early. Abbas and Sloan were already waiting for him, standing on the curb. Sam instructed Jeff to return them to the CIA offices, and by nine o'clock they were back in agency headquarters.

"I'm going to talk with George by myself for a few minutes," Sam told Jeff and Basil. "Please wait for me outside in the secretary's office."

The two men agreed and the secretary rang Yeats. A minute later she sent Sam in.

"Good morning, George."

Yeats nodded. "I've been on the phone with Dale Beck this morning. He told me you used their computers. Before we start talking, I think you would find it helpful to update yourself on what's been happening with the Motion Picture Association of America. They're the people who started the racket about the

theft of the DVD decoder device. I believe the man who originally discovered the theft was an employee named Paul Miller,
a young guy with considerable computer abilities. You can call
him from my office." Yeats pushed a piece of paper with a
phone number written on it across his desk.

Sam glanced at his watch. "Good. Little early out there on
the West Coast right now. I'll call him at eleven o'clock."

———

Three hours later Paul Miller turned on his computer and prepared for another day's work at the Motion Picture Association
offices in Encino, California. Sandra Wheeler walked in and
leaned over the top of his cubicle. "I see Mr. Wonderful is
already at work this morning."

"Hey, Sandra, give me the respect that a senior officer in
this company deserves," he said with a tone of contrived
superiority.

The attractive young woman laughed. "Come on, Paulie boy.
We all know the truth."

"Listen, I'm the man in charge of correcting this DVD
problem. What more can I say?"

Sandra laughed flatly.

The telephone rang. Miller grabbed it and answered, "Paul
Miller here."

"This is Sam Sloan calling from the CIA in Washington,
D.C."

"Yes, sir!" Miller glanced importantly at Sandra. "The CIA?"

"I believe you're the person who does computer work for
the Motion Picture Association of America. We have been
working on the DVD decoder theft in Jordan."

"I am sure the association appreciates anything you've found, Mr. Sloan. You making progress?" Miller sat up even more erect in his chair.

"Yes," Sloan answered slowly, "but I'm also interested in what you are accomplishing in your response to this crisis. Has anything changed in the way DVDs are being recorded to prevent their being copied?"

"We're working on it right now. In the near future we will have a new system in place."

"In the near future?"

"Yes, we're working on a system that will prove harder to crack. The fact that you people are trying to shut down the DeCSS device should eventually dry up all major financial loss for the recording industry."

"I see," Sam answered thoughtfully. "Your conclusion is that much of the damage from this discovery has already been covered?"

"I wouldn't state it quite that positively," Miller answered. "But if you men keep doing your job, we're not looking at a sixty-four-million-dollar hickey anymore."

"Good. Thank you, Mr. Miller."

Paul pushed the phone closer to his ear. "Mr. Sloan, I want you to know we at the association are prepared to do anything that we can to help you. Please let me know if I can be of assistance in any possible way."

Sloan paused for a moment. "You're a specialist in computer work?"

"Yes, sir!" Miller answered. "I'm the best."

"You might be of help in another area," Sloan said slowly.

"Just let me know." Miller beamed. "I'm ready."

"My daughter, Cara, has been doing some research for me," Sloan explained. "Would it be possible for you to help her?"

"Absolutely!"

"Let me give you her telephone number in Colorado Springs and she can tell you how you might assist. I'll let her know that you'll be calling." Sam gave him the number.

"Excellent. You'll be hearing from me, Mr. Sloan."

Miller hung up and grinned at Sandra. "When I get finished working on this DeCSS problem, I'll probably be in one of those front offices upstairs. Sandra, you need to appreciate who you're talking to."

The young woman grinned. "Paulie boy, I do fully appreciate who you are."

38

Sam Sloan pushed back in his padded chair and stared across the desk at George Yeats. The CIA agent had on a gray sport coat with a darker gray sweater-vest underneath. His plain round face could have been that of the vendor at the grocery store or the man running the filling station down the street from Sloan's house. There was no sign of emotion whatsoever.

"I think you know more about this case than you're telling me," Sam said. "Quite a bit more."

"Probably," Yeats said dryly. "We're still evaluating those documents you brought us from the Corcoran Street apartment. You know, the letters and the lease agreement signed by this Alvin Marshal. We may not find anything, but there is a possibility that the paper the building manager gave you might match samples gathered from the J. Edgar Hoover Building over there on Pennsylvania Avenue."

"You already think that Martinez is involved in this crime in some way?"

Yeats nodded slowly.

"What way?"

"I'm not completely sure," Yeats answered candidly. "We have some information but not enough to put this problem together. The truth is that our concerns about Martinez began when he received the highly unusual assignment to work abroad. Our two agencies don't talk much except at the highest level, but something's not right about the Martinez situation. I hope you and your man Basil can help us."

"I can tell you that I have already talked with the tenants in the apartment building. No one, including the manager, has ever gotten a good look at the man claiming to be Alvin Marshal. The manager got a distant glimpse one time but was sure the man was wearing a wig. In other words, whoever this person is, he's covered his tracks well."

"We've got people watching the building."

Sam shook his head. "My bet would be that he won't come back."

Yeats picked up his pipe and lit it. "I think you're right, but one can never tell, Sloan." He blew a cloud of smoke in front of him. "We'll keep people watching, but I don't expect them to see anything. I imagine Martinez may have had some way to know that you checked it out yesterday. We're dealing with a most skillful person."

"Martinez didn't expect us to find the place," Sam said. "I know he removed the address or kept it off the list of names and places he gave me. Freddy certainly wouldn't have concluded that I'd run down the location in one day. If he's discovered that I have, then our man is more than upset."

"Hmm." Yeats puffed on his pipe and drummed on the top of his desk with a pen. "I've already checked out his work record and I know that Martinez was in Jordan when the thefts occurred, as well as the explosion. Why don't you go back over there and grill him on what he was doing in Amman during that time?"

Sloan nodded. "If nothing else, I can make the man quite uncomfortable. I think if you tell Dale Beck to hold Freddy so we can talk with him, your call will start the ball rolling."

George put the pipe back in the ashtray. "Don't forget that Freddy is a highly qualified agent, and he's good at this interrogation game."

"Sure." Sam smiled. "But maybe we can start a forest fire before the day's out. At the least, we'll pour a little gasoline around his desk."

———

The teacher of the first-hour computer class gave the class the day's assignments and started the students working; then he walked to the back of the room. "Cara," the lab instructor said, "you've already completed today's assignment, and you're ahead of the rest of the class. You will need to do something different today. Got anything in mind?"

"Don't worry. I've got a special project to research. I'd be delighted to work on this assignment during the next hour."

The lab instructor smiled. "I figured you'd come up with something. You always do. Fine. Go ahead and research your own project." He turned around and started walking back to the front of the room.

Jack Brown leaned over. "You've done it again. Snookered the head man."

Cara raised an eyebrow. "Come on, Jack. I was simply being honest."

"Yeah, yeah. I know." Jack winked. "Good show."

Cara smiled but felt uncomfortable. Jack was always playing an angle instead of just doing his work. She liked him as a boyfriend, but his flippant attitude bothered her.

"What's your project?" Jack whispered.

Cara gave him a distant, cool look. "What's yours? Aren't you supposed to be working on today's assignment?"

"Well, the truth is—"

"I want this talking to stop," the teacher said, looking straight at Jack. "You people need to get caught up with today's assignment. Cut out the noise."

Jack quit talking and immediately began adjusting his computer.

Cara stared straight ahead. She let her fingers rest lightly on the keys. *I need to help Dad find new information in his search for this Alvin Marshal creep.*

Up to this point, she'd been able to hack inside the Internet and come up with a name and an address. Apparently her findings had made a significant difference. Maybe she'd try another approach and come up with something unexpected and decisive. If it were only possible to find a new source of information! Cara started drumming on the plastic keys.

She considered bringing up the Columbia On-Line program again. Her previous attempts at hacking had given her a route to inside data. She thought through the series of numbers, signs, and data that could take her down hidden pathways. She quickly rolled past the school's network policy editor, which was meant to guard the Web. She clicked the program files, then Accessories, then Paint. After working for a few moments, Cara went back to the URL window and clicked on *Regedit.exe.*, then quickly moved on. She disabled the foolproof system that the school had installed to keep people from messing with the computer.

Cara kept thinking one thought. If she could find some way to get back inside the computer world of Mr. A.M., she might find important data now being transferred across the Internet. She needed only to find the right path.

39

SAM AND BASIL WALKED BRISKLY INTO DALE BECK'S OFFICE with Jeff following them. Freddy Martinez already stood by the window, looking out over the street indifferently. Beck immediately stood up. "Good morning, gentlemen."

Sam nodded but didn't smile. "Good to see you, Dale." He said nothing to Martinez. "We appreciate your allowing us to use your office. I assume we'll talk in here."

"Yes," Beck said. "I understand you made progress in your search yesterday."

"Definitely. Matters are unfolding well." Sam pointed to one of the chairs. "Please sit down, Freddy. We want to ask you some questions."

Martinez looked at Beck. "Is this your intent?" His voice conveyed nothing and his face was emotionless. "I'm following your orders?"

Beck nodded. "Of course."

Martinez sat down. His passive expression didn't change.

"Why don't you men sit in the other chairs," Sloan said and pointed around the room. "I'll sit here." He sat opposite Freddy. "I think we can begin at once."

Martinez looked at him but didn't say anything.

"I want to talk about your work record in Jordan," Sam began. "I'd like you to be more precise."

"In what way?" Martinez shrugged. "Be precise about what?"

"Can you account for your time each day during this period of employment?"

Martinez looked at Beck. "You have my daily record. The transcripts speak for themselves."

"You prepared that record alone, didn't you?" Sam pushed. "No one watched you complete the form?"

"Of course. Every FBI agent does the same."

"Then you could have lied about your use of time. Correct?"

Martinez grinned at Sam. "I have no reason to conceal anything. In my entire career I've never done anything even close to your suggestion. Why should I fabricate my record?"

"I'm not here to prove or disprove your account," Sam answered. "That's your job. I want clarification."

Martinez crossed his arms over his chest. "The record speaks for itself. Take a look." He smiled. "If you haven't already checked it."

Sam's expression didn't change. "I can do so if I choose. In the meantime, did you know about the theft of the DeCSS device and the explosion at the time these events occurred?"

Martinez unfolded his arms and twisted in the chair. "I don't recall being aware of those situations at that moment.

After all, they had nothing to do with the assignments that I was completing."

"In a country as small as Jordan, a city as tightly linked as Amman, you knew nothing of these happenings?"

"Who told you Jordan is small?" Freddy asked cynically. "I'd say you need to read your geography book."

"I've been there," Sam countered. "As I said, the country is relatively small, and I want to know why you knew nothing about the theft and the bombing."

"I did later."

"Later?" Sam raised an eyebrow. "How much later?"

"I can't say." Martinez suddenly smiled. "Maybe the next day, the day after. Such extraordinary events eventually surface— but you must remember that I was also traveling around the country. As you said, information gets around."

Sam leaned forward in his chair. "Is there anybody who can confirm your story?"

Martinez grinned as if he'd been waiting for the question. "As a matter of fact, I had an American associate working in and out of the office. He observed everything. Agent Alan Martin has flown around the Middle East far more than I have. Martin can validate my work record."

Sam blinked. Martinez's answer caught him by surprise. As Yeats had warned, Freddy had quickly proved to be a clever man.

"I don't keep up with Alan Martin's travels," Martinez continued, "but I'm sure that Mr. Beck can find him." Still smiling, Freddy turned toward the supervisor. "Anything else?"

Beck looked at Sloan.

Sloan rubbed his jaw nervously. "Regardless of what Alan Martin tells us, the fact remains that you were in close proximity to a theft and a bombing that killed people. And you didn't report this to us even when you knew we were investigating that situation."

"Look, Sloan." Martinez jabbed his finger at Sam. "I was also in relatively close proximity to bombings and killings in Israel at the same time. Closeness doesn't make me a *Hamas* terrorist. You're driving down the wrong street, and I suggest you start heading somewhere else."

Sam glanced at Abbas and Meacham. Both men wore a worried look. "I think that's all the questions we want to ask you at this moment. We'll be making further inquiries and get back with you later."

"Whatever makes you happy." Martinez stood up. "If you gentlemen are finished interrogating the interrogator, I'm going back to my office."

"Thank you." Sloan stood up. "We'll be in touch."

"You do that," Freddy quipped sarcastically and walked out of the room with quick strides.

"I'd like to speak with Mr. Beck alone," Sam told his associates. "I'll be out in a moment."

Abbas and Meacham left the room.

"That didn't go very well," Sam admitted.

"Sounds like Martinez has his bases covered," Dale said.

"Yes and no. We need to locate this Alan Martin and hear what he has to say. I didn't tell Martinez that I found the apartment hideout listed under the name of Alvin Marshal. I haven't told you that story either."

"What do you mean?"

Sloan quickly recapped his search of the 1305 Corcoran Street apartment. "You see, Freddy removed that one address from the computer system the FBI maintains. I checked it out on your computer yesterday."

"Why didn't you tell him?"

"I was willing to gamble that Freddy might try to go back to that apartment if he's our man. The CIA has the street covered and would catch Martinez if he tried."

"What if he doesn't?"

"He may have been able to determine that I've already found the site. I didn't feel like today was the right time to spring the trap door. I'm willing to let my gamble run for a while."

Dale Beck nodded. "Okay. You made me aware of what's happening, but you need to know we're all playing with fire. If Martinez is mixed up with the theft and the bombing, he's dangerous. On the other hand, if you've accused him unfairly, that's a big problem as well."

"I understand, but for the moment I'm willing to bet Freddy isn't innocent. What about locating Agent Alan Martin?"

Beck nodded. "I'll start working on that immediately. I'll find out where the man is and let you know what follows."

40

SLOAN, ABBAS, AND MEACHAM LEFT THE FBI HEADQUARTERS building on Pennsylvania Avenue and walked to a small street café. The three men sat down at a table not far from the avenue. Off in the distance they could see the Washington Monument. An endless parade of people marched down the street past their table. For several minutes the men sipped hot coffee and said nothing.

"Where do we go from here?" Basil Abbas finally asked, pushing the long strand of black hair out of his eyes.

"Great question," Meacham said.

"I'm stumped at the moment," Sloan said. "I suppose that Freddy outflanked me. When he dropped the name Alan Martin on us, he ran me up on a sandbar. I wasn't sure where to go next."

"The man's smart," Meacham said. "He came out of poverty and has risen up the ladder. Not many of the FBI people travel

around the world. That's usually CIA. I think it will prove difficult to figure out exactly what Martinez was doing in Jordan
unless Beck tells us."

Sloan crossed his arms tightly over his chest. "Something is
still missing from this puzzle. I've felt it for several days. All I
can see are fragmented pieces lying around on the table."

"Now we've got another name to deal with," Basil said, turning to Meacham. "Ever hear of Alan Martin?"

"No." Jeff shook his head.

"Maybe Yeats would know," Sam said. "At least he could
start a search for information."

"You don't trust Beck?" Abbas asked.

"I do," Sam said. "I just think the CIA might have a different angle that would make a difference."

"Exactly," Jeff added. "We have our own unique resources.
If Alan Martin is a real person, we should be able to provide
information on the man."

"Sounds like that's the next step," Basil said. "Let's see what
both the FBI and CIA can tell us about this person."

"I'll call Yeats," Meacham said, pulling a cellular phone out
of his pocket. "Let's see what he pulls up." Jeff stood and moved
to the curb where he could talk privately.

"You really think Martinez is an important part of this
problem, don't you?" Basil asked.

Sam nodded. "Sure do. I'd be willing to bet that he's going
to prove highly significant before this is over."

"But what's he doing?" Abbas pushed.

"I don't know, Basil. I can't believe that he stole the DeCSS
device and blew up a house for no other reason than to repro-
duce old movies."

"*If* he stole it," Abbas warned. "Remember that we haven't proved anything yet."

"Yeah." Sam nodded. "That's what's tripping me up." He stood. "I'm going inside to get another cup of coffee. I'll be right back."

At that moment a black car swung out of traffic, driving up in front of the sidewalk café. The windows were heavily tinted. The front passenger window was rolled down a couple of inches. As the car pulled over, the tires rubbed against the curb, making a high-pitched squealing noise.

Jeff moved quickly away from the curb. "Hey, watch—"

A blast of gunfire poured out of the window toward the small café. Meacham's body jerked back and forth as countless bullets hit his body. Within a second Jeff flew backward, nearly cut in two by the machine gun.

Behind the tinted window, the hidden assassin sprayed the entire area with bullets before whirling back into the street.

A waiter clung to the doorway for a moment and then toppled forward on his face. Several tables lay turned upside down on the cement, and men and women lay motionless around them. Glass was scattered up and down the street. Suddenly people were screaming and running in all directions. Basil was sprawled on the sidewalk.

"Help! Help!" some man called from inside the café.

"Police! Get the police!" a voice echoed from down the street.

"People have been killed!" a woman screamed. "God help us!"

Basil didn't move, trying to bring the world back into focus. The cold sidewalk pressed against his cheek as if the sting of the bullets hadn't yet broken through into his nervous system.

The solid metal tabletop with its wrought-iron legs lay on top of him.

"Basil? You alive?" Sam shouted from the door.

"I think so," Abbas whispered. "I don't know."

As Sam lifted the table, he asked, "You got hit?"

"I don't think—I don't know." Basil tried to sit up. "I believe the assassin missed me."

Sam stepped out and felt Abbas's chest. "Thank the Lord. I don't think the man got me either. Look at the hole in my pant leg! Two bullets nearly hit me."

Basil got to his feet. "Looks like I'm okay. The metal tabletop saved my life."

People were running into the café area. A policeman burst onto the scene. "Get an ambulance!" a man inside the store kept calling out.

The policeman barked into a walkie-talkie attached to his uniform. "Get emergency equip over here on Pennsylvania."

"Jeff?" Basil said. "Where's Jeff?"

Sam rushed toward the curb. "Oh, no!" he screamed. "He's been hit!"

Jeff Meacham had been shot at least twenty times. His cellular phone lay smashed in the street. His arm lay twisted at a strange angle. A pool of blood had already begun to form underneath him. His wide-open eyes stared straight ahead.

"Heaven help us," Sam groaned. "Jeff is dead." Then he thrust his hand into Jeff's torn pants pocket and grabbed the car keys. Off in the distance a police siren signaled the arrival of emergency vehicles. Sam grabbed Basil's arm and yanked him. "Come on," he demanded.

"What?"

"Follow me." Sam pulled Abbas toward the edge of the crowd forming around the atrocity. "We've got to get out of this place."

Abbas struggled as if his legs wouldn't move. The cries and shouts of people filled the air as Sloan pulled at his friend's arm, urging him to stay with him as he hurried down the street. At the end of the block, Sam stopped and held Basil against the building.

"Basil, are you all right?"

Abbas could feel his heart beating frantically and knew his mouth hung open. "I just don't know." He gasped for air.

"We've got to get out of the area. That attack was meant to kill all three of us. They got Jeff and we must assume they'll be back for us unless the assassin is convinced we're dead. We've got to vanish. The clock is running and we need to get back into that Chevrolet. Come on."

Basil took a deep breath and swallowed hard. "I think I'm struggling not to pass out."

"Don't talk right now." Sam pointed to the FBI building. "Run for the car."

41

THE BLUE CHEVROLET STILL SAT BENEATH THE J. EDGAR Hoover Federal Bureau of Investigation Building where Jeff had parked it. By the time Sloan and Abbas reached the car, the streets were filled with the sounds of sirens. Guards with weapons in hand were moving into place around the FBI building. People ran up and down the streets frantically. A sense of panic had descended over that part of Washington, D.C. Sam and Basil were equally distressed; they slammed the car doors and locked them.

Sloan caught his breath. "We've got to get out of here. I think we ought to drive straight back to CIA headquarters."

"Yes!" Basil exclaimed. "Let's get on with it." He rubbed his forehead with a handkerchief and kept puffing.

Sam turned on the car and started backing out. "I'll have

to take some back streets so we don't get tied up in the traffic jam that's developing on Pennsylvania."

Basil put his face in his hands. "You know," he said, then stopped and choked. "I dropped my napkin and bent over to pick it up when the shooting started. Someone must have knocked that table over on top of me."

"Yeah," Sam said and pulled out into E Street. "I can't grasp the fact that Jeff Meacham was just killed." He could only shake his head.

"He saved our lives, Sam. If he hadn't been standing there by the street, the assassin would have hit all of us who were sitting at those tables."

From watching Meacham drive, Sloan remembered enough streets to give him an idea of where to go. Without stopping for anything but stoplights, he raced through the city.

"Sam, I've been thinking about an aspect of this case that I haven't mentioned before. I thought it would sound paranoid. Now I wish I had."

"Go ahead."

Abbas gestured aimlessly. "The first time I heard the name Angelo Martinez I immediately realized that the name fit perfectly with the initials A.M. The only thing that we didn't get in Jordan from Yakoub Natshe was who he believed the initials stood for, because the explosion killed him and stopped all discussion."

Sloan nodded. "Yes, I thought the same thing and I didn't mention that fact either. But do you realize that Martinez only clouded the issue for us this morning? When he gave us the name Alan Martin, he threw another wrench in the machinery. Martin's initials fit A.M. equally well."

"I completely missed that one."

"We don't know who was shooting from that car. Angelo Martinez, Alan Martin, Atti Mossid, whoever! I'm not sure who exactly we're chasing," Sam said. "The only reason Martinez stays at the top of my list is because he removed that Corcoran address from the information he gave me. The truth is we're chasing a criminal who is chasing us. Not a healthy situation!"

"What if Freddy didn't delete the name? Maybe someone else did. How about this Alan Martin? Did you consider Dale Beck? We may be dealing with a person that we haven't even identified yet."

Sam shook his head. "I had never thought of such a possibility."

Basil looked out the window. Several times he muttered something in Arabic under his breath.

Sam kept speeding through the city. In forty-five minutes, they pulled up to the CIA's entry gate. This time the guards stopped them.

"We left this morning with Jeff Meacham," Sam said. "He's not with us now."

Instantly the military guard snapped his fingers and two soldiers came running to each side of the car. "What is your objective?"

"We're here to see George Yeats," Sam added.

"Just a moment." The guard stepped into the small observation house and made a phone call. After a minute he stepped back out. "These two men will accompany you to Mr. Yeats's office. Please allow them to sit in the backseat."

Sam pushed the button to unlock the doors and the two soldiers got in. No one said anything. Picking out the parking place Meacham had always used, Sam turned off the car and got out. As they had done every day, Basil and Sam found their way up to the anteroom where Yeats's secretary worked. The two soldiers stayed only a few steps behind them.

The secretary looked up immediately when they walked in. Her face was tense. "Thank you," she said to the soldiers. "We will take responsibility for these men from here." She signed the release form that the soldiers extended. The two soldiers nodded and left without saying a word.

"Mr. Yeats was hoping you'd come back here immediately. He is waiting for you right now. Please go in."

When Sam and Basil entered, George Yeats was standing behind his desk. Three other men stood around the room. Yeats looked at Sloan and Abbas like a general awaiting a report from the front battle line. "What happened?"

Sam gave a quick description of the shooting. "Tragically, Jeff Meacham is dead. We had to leave him on the sidewalk so we could get out of the area."

"That was the right thing to do," Yeats said. "Getting tangled up in a police report would only have increased our problems." He shook his head and looked at his desk sadly. "I can't believe Jeff is gone. What a good man."

"Everything happened so quickly, I didn't even get a glimpse of the car, except that it was black and looked like maybe a Mercedes."

"We think it was possibly from an embassy," Yeats said.

"You're kidding!" Sam's mouth dropped slightly.

Yeats shook his head. "That information is based on the fact that the driver apparently left the shooting and went to the Corcoran Street address. He ran into our people and there was more shooting before the man escaped, but our agents got a better look at the car."

Sam dropped into the leather chair in front of Yeats's desk and took a deep breath. "Good heavens! I can't believe the car went to Corcoran Street."

"At this time it appears that seven people were killed," Yeats continued. "I imagine the assassin left so fast he doesn't know whether you're dead or alive. Probably thinks that he's hit you. That's the way our men will report it."

Sam looked at the three strangers who were watching him. "I don't believe that Basil and I have met these gentlemen."

"They are our employees and you probably won't see them again after this meeting. It's easier not to mix names. Keeps everything clandestine." George sat down behind his desk. "We've only known about this shooting for about twenty minutes and are still in the process of formulating what to do next. We assumed you'd come back here . . . if you were still alive."

"Look," Sam said firmly. "We've found a problem that's larger than we thought. No one shoots down CIA officials as well as innocent citizens unless he is cornered. This situation is spinning out of control. Obviously we've stumbled onto something much more serious."

Yeats nodded. "Exactly. For the moment we will not speak of further details. I think we need to declare you two men as shot and dying." He raised an eyebrow. "Can your wife handle it as long as she knows you're actually alive?"

"We've been down this road once before. I will need to speak personally with her. If I explain the problem, she'll be okay. Not happy but understanding. She'll need to explain this problem to our daughter, but you can trust them."

"Okay, Sloan. You go out to my secretary's office and let your wife know the facts." He glanced at Basil. "Abbas, you okay? You look rather peaked."

"The killer shot an M16 assault rifle. I could tell. It was a deadly sound. I'm still feeling the effects."

"I understand," Yeats said. "We'd like to ask you questions while Sam calls his wife. We need a clearer picture of what happened. I'll go easier on you this time."

42

Sam punched in the number for Colorado Springs and waited. Vera wouldn't be thrilled about this unexpected turn of events. The phone rang several times.

"The All-City Detective Agency," a female voice answered.

"I need to speak with Vera Sloan," Sam said in an unusually low voice.

"Who may I say is calling?"

"It's confidential." Sam kept his voice low. "Just put me through."

"I see," the receptionist answered with hesitation. "Just a moment."

After a few seconds, Vera answered. She sounded professional and distant.

"Vera! It's me, Sam."

"Sam? Sam who?" Vera said sarcastically. "My goodness.

Nice of you to call. You must be having a hot time up there in Washington."

"Listen carefully. I may well be reported as shot or dead in tonight's news. Obviously I'm not."

"Sam!" Vera shifted abruptly to intense concern. "What in the world is happening?"

"I can't tell you right now, but I want you to know that Basil and I are okay. You can tell Cara confidentially but that's it. She must not tell anyone anything. Understand?"

Vera sighed. "I'll keep my mouth shut, but you must tell Cara yourself this evening. She'll want to hear your voice. I certainly wish that you'd come home."

"As soon as possible. I've got to run, but I'll call Cara tonight. I love you." Sam hung up. "Thank you," he told the secretary and returned to George Yeats's office.

When he walked in, Sam found Basil describing carefully what had happened at the sidewalk café. Sam sat down and listened. The three men with Yeats kept asking pointed questions. Sam said nothing. Basil was covering the details well.

"Anything you want to add, Sam?" Yeats asked.

"I was inside the café with my back turned, getting coffee, when the shooting started. I didn't see anything more than what Basil reported. A policeman was already there by the time we left."

"Okay." Yeats started pacing back and forth in front of his desk. "I think we should not communicate with the FBI for a period of time. We're not entirely sure who we can and can't trust over there. Dale Beck will panic when he hears about the shooting. I'll tell my secretary to report that I'm out of town and that will keep them guessing."

"I'll tell her right now," one of the unnamed men standing in Yeats's office said. "We'll keep you covered, sir."

"Good!" Yeats nodded for him to leave and the man hustled out.

"Sam, you and Basil are going to need to get out of town for a while," George continued. "We don't want you to go back to the hotel. Our people will pick up your luggage and accessories. To the best of our ability, we want to make it look like you are in the hospital, dead, whatever. You can stay in our facilities tonight. We keep extra rooms here on the grounds for such emergencies."

Sam nodded slowly.

"At this point we're not sure exactly who is our target," Yeats said. "We're going to have to let the dust settle for at least twenty-four hours—and it may take longer. I think that our culprit is floating out there right now, trying to grasp how much we know. We need to appear to be much more confident than we actually are."

"Then we might fly out by tomorrow morning?" Basil asked.

"Definitely. However, you should be prepared to leave at a moment's notice." Yeats walked around his desk and sat down. "We'll be watching all the doors around the city to see who walks through."

———

Time passed slowly during the next several hours. Shortly after four o'clock, George Yeats called the housing unit where Sam and Basil were waiting. "Sam, we're still not sure what's occurring, but we can't seem to locate either Freddy Martinez or Dale Beck. At this time, we do know that Alan Martin is in the

United States, but we haven't been able to get him on the telephone."

"Any leads on the assassin who did the shooting on Pennsylvania Avenue?"

"We have identified the car as belonging to the Turkmenistan Embassy but not the shooter," Yeats said. "Unfortunately, no one is answering any questions and the vehicle is now back inside their compound."

"Turkmenistan?" Sam scratched his head. "Isn't that country located next to Iran and Afghanistan?"

"You got it. They were once part of the Soviet Union and have now become an independent Muslim state."

Sam thought for a moment. "Why would they have any interest in shooting us?"

"I don't have the slightest idea," Yeats said. "Right now we're walking around in a funk. I'm being completely honest with you, Sam."

"Thank you, George. We'll be here waiting for any further instructions."

After Yeats hung up, Sloan turned to his partner. "Basil, you know anyone in that far-off country called Turkmenistan?"

"Turkmenistan? Heavens, no!"

Sam shook his head. "Neither do I, but Yeats believes the black car with the assassin came from their embassy."

"In Jordan we know about the country, though," Basil said thoughtfully. "They're a rather obscure Islamic community with a considerable amount of desert. The country abuts the Caspian Sea. I'm sure Turkmenistan has many citizens who would be sympathetic with Afghanistan and Iraq."

43

AN HOUR HAD PASSED SINCE GEORGE YEATS CALLED SAM, but nothing had occurred. Sloan sat by the telephone and Basil stared at the television.

Abbas looked at his watch. "Sam, it's nearly six o'clock and no more phone calls. I'm getting hungry."

"Sure. I understand, but I'm actually more tired than anything else. We've been through quite a demanding day. Why don't you go out and get something to eat? I'll stay here in case we get another phone call."

Abbas stood up. "Sounds like a good idea. I'll be back after I eat in that canteen they maintain for the night staff."

Sam waved. "Don't hurry. Looks like we've got all night before anything develops."

"Turn off the television?"

"Thank you, Basil. I'll sit here in the silence for a while. Quiet will do me some good."

"As you say." Abbas turned the television off and walked out.

Peace quickly settled around Sam. Since they had hit town, nothing but noise had filled his mind. Cars, engines, subways, people talking, and worst of all, gunshots—an endless array of sounds that buzzed around in his head like a swarm of bees. Every morning they had gotten up early and worked late with little time for meditative reflection between the constant running. The sheer quietness felt like the discovery of an oasis in a desert sandstorm.

Sam closed his eyes and instantly saw the body of Jeff Meacham lying on the sidewalk. He had not allowed himself to think about the shattering experience so far, but the moment had come to face the killings. With his eyes tightly closed, Sam could feel tears running down the sides of his face. He had gone from seeing Jeff as a spying intruder to knowing him as a self-sacrificing friend.

Sam remembered the many close calls that being a detective involved. He'd been shot at many times and had been involved in an exchange of gunfire with people like Charlie Boyles and Alfred Harris, but anyone's death always wrung him out and left him depressed. He loved life and believed that God valued humans above all things. The thought of someone being killed by a stray bullet or, even worse, by design, left Sam feeling empty.

He had no idea if Jeff Meacham had a wife, children, a family, but he assumed someone must have loved and cared about the man. As he thought about the terrible vacuum Meacham's death left in the world, Sam considered that he might write a note and ask Yeats to pass it on to whoever had been close to Jeff. He should express his and Basil's appreciation for Jeff's efforts and life.

Sam lowered his head into his hands and prayed. "Lord, bless this brave man's memory. We thank you for Jeff Meacham and his willingness to attempt to protect us. Please be with the people who cared about him and sustain them in their hour of grief. If there's a family with children, please protect them. I pray these things in Jesus' name. Amen."

Sam wiped his eyes and took a deep breath. His body sagged with heaviness. All those other people had also been killed by the assassin. Who were they and what would become of their families? The possible consequences of those deaths felt like a concrete block crushing him. As the minutes ticked by, the quietness of the empty room offered a healing salve of grace, covering the nagging, unanswered questions and giving Sam some consolation. What an unexpected and bizarre experience this entire trip to Washington had become! He leaned his head back against the chair, closed his eyes, and let the solitariness gather around him like a warm blanket.

Suddenly the telephone rang. Sam jumped. Without realizing it, he'd fallen asleep. His watch said he'd been napping for forty minutes.

"Sam, it's George Yeats."

"Good. Anything turn up yet?"

"We're still searching, and I probably won't call you back for some time. At this point it looks like both Dale Beck and Angelo Martinez are actually missing. In a few minutes, a courier will come to your door with pictures of Alan Martin. We've picked up half a dozen photos that will give you a clear picture of this man. No one will confirm anything, and we have no information on where Martin is at this time. We'll keep searching."

"Hmm. Looks like Basil and I ought to stay put."

"Wouldn't say that," Yeats said. "Whatever you do, it will be important to let us know where we can find you quickly."

"Okay. We'll let you know where we are going when we leave and wait for you to call us. Thank you, George."

Yeats hung up and Sam put the phone down. He thought for a moment and then called his own home on Twenty-third Street in Colorado Springs.

"Hi, kid. It's your old man," he said when Cara answered the phone.

"Dad! Mom said you got involved in another one of those terrible situations. I don't want you to get hurt."

"Well, Cara, you understand how police work goes. I'm okay. I wanted you to know that Basil and I are fine regardless of what you might hear on television tonight. We're alive and well."

"I want you to stay that way, Dad. You need to keep your nose out of the places where bad things happen."

"Keep praying for me, Cara. I need it every day. By the way, you're going to hear from a computer expert named Paul Miller. The man works with the Motion Picture Association, and I've asked him to help you with these projects. He'll call you and you can trust him."

"Good. I'll wait for his phone call. Dad, I've also got some information to tell you. The last couple of days, I've been working on the Internet, trying to come up with something more for you. I had to do a great deal of manipulating, but I came up with a surprising message just a bit ago."

Sam picked up a pencil and a piece of paper. "What did you find out?"

"I started hacking through the computer in my bedroom, trying to run down some communication either from Alvin Marshal or someone with the A.M. initials. Only about thirty minutes ago, I found this message from A.M. sent to somebody named Marwan Alnami. Didn't make any sense to me, but I got the contents."

"Marwan Alnami! Cara, tell me slowly and carefully what you picked up."

"A.M. sent out the following communication: 'Denver International. Friday. 3:30. Terminal B. Gate 23. That's all he said."

"Cara, I can't begin to tell you how significant this message is. Remember that you must tell no one except your mother what you've discovered. This will be our secret. Okay?"

"Sure, Dad."

"Thank you so much, dear. I'll be back in touch soon." Sam hung up and stared at the piece of paper on which he'd scribbled the information. Tomorrow he and Basil would be at the Denver airport well before 3:30. Whether A.M. turned out to be Freddy Martinez, Alan Martin, Dale Beck, or someone different, they would be prepared.

44

AT PRECISELY SEVEN O'CLOCK SAM AND BASIL WALKED into Dulles Airport. Within ten minutes their tickets had been processed and they had only to clear security. The extra time required to get through the metal detectors slowed them down, but in another fifteen minutes they were ready to hit the gate.

"I've been thinking about today's surveillance," Basil said. "Wouldn't it help to have Dick Simmons come up from Colorado Springs and back us up?"

Sam agreed. "We might run into a problem that we didn't expect, and Dick would be an asset. I'll call Yeats and you get Simmons on his cellular phone. Have him meet us at the International terminal."

Five minutes later both men returned to the front of gate twenty-five. Basil said, "I got him, but he was already on his way to Denver."

"At this hour of the morning?"

"By a strange quirk of fate, Simmons is expecting our old problem Charlie Boyles to try to board an airplane this afternoon. They hope to nail Boyles today."

"You're serious?"

"Yeah, Pretty Boy wants my help!"

"Now, that's rich, Basil. Only Simmons would come up with such a strange twist. You call him to help us, and he asks you to join his team."

"Looks like we're going to have an old-fashioned traffic jam at that airport this afternoon. We've got police and the crooks charging head-on."

"We'll see," Sam said cynically. "We can't give Simmons any assistance, because we've got our own fish to fry. He shouldn't need a hand anyway. I imagine he's bringing an army with him today. Should prove interesting."

"American Airlines flight 236 now boarding through gate twenty-five," the agent announced over the loudspeaker. "All passengers should have their boarding passes and photo IDs out."

"Looks like it's time for us to go," Sam said.

"'Stand prepared, for the hour at hand awaits you as the very calling of God!'" Basil quoted. "I believe Saint Simeon once said that."

"You do, huh? Since Simeon lived centuries before the age of airplanes, I'm sure he didn't have any idea that his quotation would refer to boarding an aircraft."

"Can't tell about those church fathers," Basil answered. "They were amazing men."

Three hours later American Airlines 236 flew into the Denver International Airport. The towering peaks of the Rockies loomed off to the west, on the other side of the bustling city of more than a million people. Passengers stood poised to rush out of the large jet and hurry into the crowded airport.

"You've got everything?" Sam asked.

"We've got to get our baggage because that's where the pistols are stored. I know we'll need them today," Basil whispered.

"Where are we supposed to meet Simmons?"

"In the baggage area. He's already here with the other police officers."

The passengers started marching down the aisle. In a couple of minutes the two detectives were in the large terminal, hurrying down the hall. They got onto the moving sidewalks for extra speed and hopped on the first train to take them to the baggage-claim area. Luggage carousel three proved to be close to the escalators that brought them downstairs. They lined up with the rest of the passengers.

"Don't move," a male voice said behind them. "I've got you covered."

"If I couldn't recognize Dick Simmons in a circus of clowns, I'd retire," Sam said.

"How do you know I'm not an assassin hired by the government to knock you off?"

"Your perfume smells like lilacs," Sam answered and turned around. "Has to be you."

"That was a low blow, Sloan."

Sam grinned. "Dick, you look as pretty as ever."

"That's getting extremely personal." Simmons didn't grin.

Abbas shook Simmons's hand. "You're chasing Boyles?"

"Yeah, we discovered this mobster actually went down to Buena Vista, hid out for a while, and then drove up to Fairplay. He came back to Denver on Highway 285. Using a fake driver's license, he got a ticket to fly to Dallas."

"Dick, you've obviously been a busy little boy, running this hood down."

"Harrison wouldn't be impressed, but it hasn't been as easy as it sounds."

"Never is, Dick." Sloan pulled his small suitcase off the conveyor belt. "Hindsight's always twenty-twenty. You've got extra people out here today?"

Dick nodded.

"We're watching the ticket counter as well as the gate. We won't grab Charlie Boyles until after he checks in with that fake ID. At least that's our plan. We're sure the man is dangerous, but he won't be armed by the time he's gone through the metal detectors."

"Good!" Sloan patted Simmons on the arm. "You'll be able to help us."

"Don't give me that! I've got my hands full with a guy who has already escaped twice."

"How'd you like to get in on a big international plot?" Sam jabbed him in the ribs. "Wouldn't that be exciting?"

"The last time I saw Charlie Boyles I was laying in a flower bed up there in Woodland Park with bullets flying around me. That was thrilling enough."

"Look, Simmons," Sam pushed, "we may truly need you or one of your men. This situation today could heat up."

"We've got airport police all over the place, and all you have to do is call me. I promise that I'll get people to where you are."

"I don't want anybody wearing a uniform," Sam answered.

"I understand. If you call, I'll send plainclothes people. Okay—just hit me on the cell phone."

"You got it," Sam said. "Now tell me where we can find a back room to get our weapons out of this baggage and start getting prepared for today's big confrontation."

45

SAM MADE ONE FINAL ADJUSTMENT, MAKING SURE HIS shoulder holster was properly straightened, then put his coat back on. "You ready?"

Abbas nodded. "As ready as I'll ever be."

Sloan pulled pictures of Alan Martin out of his pocket and handed them to Abbas. "Take a good look. Yeats sent them to me last night. You need to be prepared if this face shows up in the crowd. He could be the A.M. we're hunting."

Abbas studied the pictures for a moment. "Got it. I'll keep my eyes wide open."

Sam put the pictures back in his pocket. "I have an idea about what we should do. Each of the Denver terminals is connected by a tram system. I would expect our man to arrive on the train and get off. If memory serves me right, he'll have to come up a flight of escalator stairs to reach gate twenty-three.

One of us ought to be positioned by the exit of the tram and the other person should be watching the area around the gate."

Abbas nodded his head in agreement. "Sounds right to me. If the situation turns into a runaway problem, we call Simmons and ask for his men to back us up."

Sam nodded. "I'm not expecting much out of Dick personally, but we might need his people."

"I'll stay down by the tram," Basil volunteered. "You watch the gate."

Sam shrugged. "Sounds fine to me."

"What do you think will happen, Sam?"

Sloan shook his head. "I don't know, Basil. This chase has taken on so many twists and turns that I've run out of expectations. Maybe our target is going to hand off a copy of the DeCSS device. We'll have to wait and see."

The two men left their luggage in the police room and boarded the tram that would take them to terminal B. "We've got an hour," Sam said. "Should be plenty of time to get carefully placed."

When the tram stopped, Basil got off and moved to a far corner of the hallway, where he could watch the doors open and close without anybody noticing him. Sam took the escalator upstairs. In a small magazine shop, he picked up a newspaper and sat down at the edge of gate twenty-two, where he could observe everyone coming up the stairs as well as everything happening around the gate twenty-three area.

Sloan glanced at the newspaper and watched a small army of people going up and down the long corridor. It suddenly occurred to him that A.M. might not take the train at all but walk the long distance between terminals. If he did, Sam would still recognize him coming down the central corridor. Unless the person wasn't Alan Martin or Angelo Martinez—unless it was someone *they had never seen before.*

A sense of cold apprehension swept over Sam. What if the man came and went and he totally missed him? After all was planned, said, and done, they still had no idea who might show at gate twenty-three! Such a failure would do nothing but heap more disaster on top of Jeff Meacham's tragic death.

He glanced at his watch. It was now 3:20. For the first time Sam noticed an unusual Arab walking slowly down the corridor across from him. Well dressed in an expensive suit, the man was moving noticeably slower than everyone else hustling down the hall.

Could this man be Marwan Alnami? His tailor-made suit and silk tie contrasted with the clothing of 90 percent of the other passengers. The man wore a mustache and goatee and kept looking around as if expecting to see someone. He was short but stout with a thick back and arms. Near the end of the seat section, the Arab turned around and started back again. When he returned, Sam noticed that the man kept staring at the top of a trash can with a built-in tray collector placed next to a small pizza shop. Periodically people either threw their trash through a small wooden door or dropped off a service tray from the pizza café. No one paid any attention to the rectangular stand . . . except the Arab.

Sam watched the man wander down the hall and glanced at his own watch. Another five minutes had passed. If A.M. were true to form, he probably wouldn't walk down Terminal B until precisely 3:30. Sloan pushed the top of the newspaper up higher so that he was barely able to see over the edge.

Four and a half minutes later, Sam saw a familiar figure walking briskly down the hall. Here was the man they had chased all over the Internet and across the world. The puzzle was solved as Angelo "Freddy" Martinez walked toward him.

Never slowing his easy jaunt, Martinez reached over and dropped a small plastic box on top of the tray rack, a box the exact size of a DVD. Sam caught a glimpse of Basil Abbas following at the far end of the corridor, weaving his way in and out behind the large columns supporting the ceiling.

Martinez didn't seem to have any idea he was being watched. At the end of the next opening in the moving sidewalk, Freddy abruptly reversed himself, turned, and stepped on the conveyor belt, coming back the way he had just walked. Sam watched Basil disappear behind the large cement pier that braced the roof several gates back. Then he could see the slow-moving Arab walking toward Martinez as the moving belt carried him forward. When they passed each other, the men looked into each other's eyes but made no gesture.

In an instant Sam knew the man had to be Marwan Alnami. He watched the Arab walk over to the trashcan, and with one quick gesture, pick up the DVD box and slip it in his pocket. He kept walking.

Sam had already sized up the gates at that end of the terminal. No matter where he went, the Arab would have to turn around and come back, unless he tried to board an airplane. Since most of the gates listed flights toward the west, he probably wouldn't board them.

Martinez kept riding the conveyor belt toward the steps that would take him back down to the trams. Sam had slipped out of hiding and was walking in a crowd of people behind Freddy.

He waited until Alnami came back past him again and then fell in behind the man, staying fifteen feet away. The Arab started walking faster, moving quickly toward gate five, where the sign indicated a departing flight to Washington, D.C., leaving in twenty minutes. Sam picked up his pace.

"Your boarding pass and proof of identification," the agent standing by the entry gate said.

"Of course." The Arab reached in his pocket and handed her the card along with his passport. "My name is Marwan Alnami."

Instantly Sloan took three large steps and reached over, grabbing the passport. "I'm with the police," he said forcefully. "This man is under arrest."

The agent's mouth dropped. "What?"

Alnami whirled around. "Stop this!"

With his free hand, Sloan slapped a handcuff on Alnami's wrist. "Don't try to run," he warned. "You're surrounded."

"This is an insult!" the Arab answered in excellent English. "I am attached to the diplomatic staff of the country of Turkmenistan!"

The agent stepped back as if she feared getting struck by someone.

Sam blinked. Alnami's response was completely unexpected. "For the time being you are in my custody," he said. "You won't be flying on this airplane this afternoon."

"My passport explains my status," Alnami demanded. "Stop this nonsense!"

"Come with me and we'll discuss the problem."

The airline agent stared and said nothing.

Sam attached the other handcuff to his wrist. "We know what you were attempting to do."

"I demand to be released." Alnami yanked his arm back.

"Sorry." Sam didn't budge. "Come with me." He made a sharp heave, jerking the Arab toward him.

"You will pay for this!"

Sam studied the man's eyes. Although the Arab shouted like a general with an army behind him, his eyes were filled with fear. Reaching into Alnami's pocket, Sam pulled out the DVD box. "I think by the time we finish reviewing this movie, you'll be talking a different story."

Alnami stared at the box and swallowed hard. He clenched his jaw forcefully and stiffened.

"I thought that might turn your volume down," Sam said. "Excuse us, ma'am." Sloan nodded to the agent. "Go on about your business."

46

No matter how loud and hard Marwan Alnami protested, Sloan kept dragging him toward the airport tram. Part of the time, the man claiming to be a diplomat spoke English; at other moments, he shouted in some language Sam couldn't understand.

"I tell you that I have diplomatic immunity!" Alnami protested over and over.

"You've also got handcuffs on you," Sam answered, pulling the man down the hall. "I'd keep my voice down or you might find a gag in your mouth."

The Arab blinked several times as if trying to decide if Sam truly meant what he was saying. The man was obviously confused and frightened.

"Don't push your luck," Sam said. "I'd enjoy sticking my dirty handkerchief in your mouth."

Alnami quit protesting.

Sloan knew that Abbas had probably zeroed in on Martinez by now. The FBI agent would recognize Basil immediately, so the situation could have gotten sticky. But Sam felt certain that his partner would know what to do. If nothing else, he'd call Simmons.

The tram slowed for the stop in the main terminal. Sloan kept pulling Alnami along with him. They moved down the main hallway until they came to the police room where Sloan and Abbas had left their luggage. Sam pushed the buzzer and a policeman opened the door.

"Got an interesting case for you," Sam said. "I think you'll find this one on the noisy side."

"Okay," the cop said. "Put him in that chair over there, and let's see what he's got to say."

Sam unlocked the cuffs and pointed at the chair. "Sit down."

Alnami immediately started to protest again.

"I said," Sam repeated, *"sit down."*

The Arab threw up his hands and finally sat down.

"I want you to listen to all of this," Sam told the policeman. "I caught an FBI agent slipping this DVD to this man over there in terminal B."

"There is no law against my picking up a plastic disk from a garbage disposal," Alnami answered.

Sam looked at the disk for a moment. It appeared to be no more than a recording of *Shadowlands.* "Hmm." He stared at the label. The only difference was that the outside container wasn't covered with a cellophane wrapper. Obviously the box had been opened before Martinez dropped it on the trash stand.

"You got a DVD player in this room? A television?" Sam asked.

"Sure." The policeman pointed toward the other side of the room. "There's one against the wall."

"Excellent." Sam handed him the disk. "Let's take a look at what *Shadowlands* is like this afternoon." He watched Alnami.

The man's eyes widened and he looked even more fearful.

The policeman stuck the DVD in the player. He flipped on the television, and the title with the introduction to the movie came up on the screen. Background music swelled in rich, vibrant tones.

"Looks good." Sam smiled at Alnami. "I bet you'll enjoy this flick."

The man twisted anxiously in his chair and fidgeted uneasily.

After a couple of minutes the music stopped and electronic sounds buzzed over the speakers. The noise had a rhythmic movement. Alnami took a deep breath.

Sam kept watching the Arab's face. The strange sounds caused Alnami abruptly to relax. He exhaled slowly.

"Just as I thought." Sam walked across the room and flipped the television off. He smiled at the policeman. "Why don't you take a walk down the hall? I think I'm going to have a private talk with our friend Marwan. Don't hurry back."

The policeman grinned. "I understand. Knock on the door when you want me back in here."

"Sure."

The Arab rubbed his neck and swallowed hard. "I tell you that I'm a diplomat!"

The door closed behind the policeman. "Did I tell you that

I'm a sadist?" Sam responded, turning his back for a moment and making sure the safety was clamped down on his pistol. He walked around to the back of Alnami. "At this moment I don't care if your grandfather is the king of Saudi Arabia. You are mine, and I intend to have a nice, intense conversation with you. We're going to talk *my way*."

The Arab folded his hands in front of him, curling them tightly. "I am unconcerned if you threaten me."

"Really?" Sloan sat down in front of the man and placed his pistol behind him on the desk. "Do you realize that if your body was found in the alley behind this airport it might take days to identify you? In fact, you could be rendered completely unrecognizable."

Alnami looked frightened but didn't speak.

"I think that when I run this tape through my DeCSS decoding device, I'll hear a fascinating message sent by my old friend Freddy Martinez."

Alnami jerked as if he'd been hit by a charge of electricity. "You have a DeCSS disk?"

Sloan nodded. "They're not worth much now since the Motion Picture Association has changed how they are coding films to prevent duplication. I've been thinking about that for some time." He leaned over until his face was only inches from the Arab's. "But coding and decoding would certainly prove handy if you wanted to send secret messages around the world. Wouldn't it? I'd guess that Martinez sent you a humdinger of a message on this *Shadowlands* disc."

The Arab froze and squeezed his hands.

"Freddy's sent you some hot stuff, hasn't he?"

Alnami's jaw clenched and he stared straight ahead.

"I'll bet you know all about this exchange. Did you know spying can be a capital charge?"

Sloan stood up and walked around the Arab, watching the man carefully. Beads of sweat had already broken out on Alnami's forehead. The muscles on his temples, his jaw, and his neck stood out.

"Want to talk about it?" Sam asked in a kind, gentle voice. Before the Arab could answer, Sloan grabbed the gun and cocked it. "Or would you prefer me to blow your head off?"

Alnami jerked backward but Sam grabbed his tie and clenched it tightly, choking the Arab. "You may have diplomatic immunity, but at this moment it doesn't mean one single thing. You talk or you're dead."

"I . . . I . . . don't know anything," Alnami stammered. "I only work for the embassy. Not as a diplomat. A courier. Honest. I beg you." He held up his hands, pleading, "Don't kill me. I know nothing!" A trickle of sweat ran down the side of his face.

"Yes, you do," Sam insisted. "I can get the message off of the DVD. I want to know about Freddy's role in this operation."

"He spies for us. That is all I know."

"Why would he spy for you?" Sam growled.

"Because we transmit his messages on to Iraq," Alnami blurted out.

Sloan dropped back in his chair. "To Iraq?" he asked more in amazement than as a question.

Alnami nodded. "Yes."

"So, Freddy Martinez is actually spying for Iraq, and you're sending his message through?"

Alnami nodded again.

"But you know nothing of what's on this tape?"

"I swear by Allah! I am only here to pick up this material. Nothing more." The Arab looked terrified.

Sloan walked to the door and rapped on it. The policeman came in. "Our boy here's been talking some. I need to check on what's happening with my partner. Don't let him out of the room and be careful who you let in. I'll have some more cops show up before we're finished with him."

"I want to go," Alnami begged. "I should be released."

"Only when I'm sure we've emptied everything out of your thick head."

"But," the Arab protested, "I am—"

"Yeah, we know," Sloan said. "You've told us a thousand times. Like I say, don't let this man out of your sight."

Sam stepped out in the hallway and flipped open his cellular phone. To his surprise, he discovered that he'd accidentally turned the phone off. Sam quickly tapped in Abbas's number. No one answered. He dialed again but there was no response.

47

SLOAN TAPPED IN BASIL ABBAS'S CELLULAR NUMBER FOR the third time but no one answered. "He must be in a tight place," Sam said to himself. "I'll try Simmons." He punched in the number.

"Hello!" Dick Simmons barked.

"Hey, it's Sloan. I've been trying—"

"Sam!" Simmons cursed. "We've been trying to find you!"

"What's the matter?"

"Basil called me. Told me he was going into a rest room to make sure some guy named Freddy Martinez didn't exit by another door. He called for backup."

"Yes?"

"I sent two of my people over to terminal A, the rest rooms by gate thirty, and they found a crowd of people. Abbas was on the floor. Stabbed and smashed on the head. I'm over there right now."

"Oh, no!" Sam thought his heart had stopped. "I'll be there as quickly as I can run through this place."

"We've called for an ambulance, but Basil is in bad shape."

Sam started running. "I'm coming—I'll be there." He flipped the phone off and jumped on the escalator steps, taking two and three at a leap. "Excuse me," he told a lady as he slipped past. "Sorry," Sam said to a man he crowded against the metal wall of the escalator.

Without slowing down, Sam pressed his way to the front of the line waiting for the tram. "Police!" He held his badge up in the air and kept advancing. The moment the car arrived, Sam was on it.

Sloan leaned against the door and breathed a prayer for Abbas. Martinez must have seen Basil following him and cornered him in the bathroom. No telling what had occurred. The tram slowed and Sam bolted through the door.

With lengthy strides Sloan bounded up the escalator. Once on the top floor, he ran toward the rest room on the other side of gate thirty. A large crowd of people had gathered around the outside with police officers holding them back. Sam waved his badge as he pushed through the crowd.

Basil Abbas was sprawled on the floor, halfway out of one of the back stalls and drenched in blood. The front of his white shirt had been slashed and one of the policemen had already stuffed a cloth into the wound, attempting to slow the bleeding. Along the side of his head, a nasty gash was pouring blood over his ear and behind his head. The usual long strand of black hair lay over Basil's closed eyes and his mouth hung partly open.

Sam dropped to his knees. "Please tell me he's alive. Isn't he?" He looked desperately around at the policemen.

"Yeah," Dick Simmons said from behind him. "But Basil's hurt bad."

Sam whirled around. "You said an ambulance is coming?"

"They should be the people who move Basil," Dick said. "They'll be here momentarily."

Sam nodded. "Sure, that's the correct procedure." He looked around at the policemen again. "Anybody know what happened?"

Simmons patted him on the shoulder. "I'm sure the attacker recognized Basil and ducked in here to corner him. Looks like he jerked Basil into one of these stalls. My hunch is that the assailant stabbed him first and then clobbered Basil with something. Probably the man was carrying a black-jack, a sap of some kind. He obviously knew what he was doing."

Sam looked closely at the abdominal wound. "Looks like Basil turned slightly just before the guy stabbed him with the knife. The gash is more on his side."

"Definitely. If the assailant had hit him in the center of the abdomen, Basil would have probably bled to death before you arrived."

Sam stood up. "I'm sure Martinez is out of the terminal by now. Maybe the entire airport. He's an FBI agent and the man knows all the tricks in the book. The question is, where will he go from this airport?"

A medical crew rushed into the bathroom, pulling a stretcher behind them. Sam watched the men lift Basil's body onto the gurney. Abbas groaned but didn't regain consciousness. The emergency team worked on him for a minute and then hurried him out of the rest room.

"Got to get this man to the hospital quickly," the attendant said. "Fitzsimmons Medical Center is closest," he shouted over his shoulder at Sloan. "We'll be there."

"Thanks," Sam called after them. "I'll be right behind you."

"You going now?" Simmons asked.

Sam shook his head. "I've got a diplomatic employee from the Turkmenistan government locked up over in the main terminal's police room. He's claiming diplomatic immunity. We don't have any legal right to hold the man."

"Turkmenistan?" Simmons frowned. "Never heard of the place."

"It's next to Afghanistan and Iran."

Simmons shrugged. "The Denver police would run from holding anybody with diplomatic immunity."

Sloan started walking back and forth, thinking about what to do next. He stopped. "Did you capture Charlie Boyles?"

"We nailed him on the other side of the metal detectors." Simmons grinned. "It was like hooking a trout at one of those farm ponds where you pay for what you catch."

"And this time he didn't get off the hook?"

Simmons shook his head confidently. "We've got old Charlie in handcuffs and leg chains. The man is now on his way back to Colorado Springs, permanently out of business."

"That ought to make Chief Harrison sleep well tonight," Sam said. "I think what I need to do right now is call my CIA contact. Discovering what the boys in Washington, D.C., are saying about this situation would help."

Sam stepped to one side of the bathroom and tapped in the

number George Yeats had given him. He listened carefully as the phone rang.

"Yeats here."

"George! It's me. Sam Sloan."

"Sloan! I've been trying to get you all afternoon."

"I had my phone turned off, but we were right! Angelo Martinez showed up to hand off a message recorded on a DVD to some courier from the nation of Turkmenistan. He was using the DeCSS disk to send spy messages. Freddy proved to be our mole!"

"I know," Yeats said. "Let me assure you that Martinez is more dangerous than we ever postulated. I think Dale Beck figured out some of the details and unfortunately closed in on Freddy. Beck's body turned up about two hours ago. He'd been dead for at least twenty-four hours. We have no question that Martinez killed him shortly after the shootings at the sidewalk café."

"Looks like Freddy flew down here for the sole purpose of making the big handoff of the DVD at the Denver Airport. I'm not sure what the plan behind his coming is—he's obviously blown his cover."

"I would guess that action was always part of the plan. When you and Abbas showed up and started pushing the envelope, I think Martinez decided it was time to cash in his chips. My hunch is that Angelo will never return to Washington, D.C."

"I see," Sam said thoughtfully and then told Yeats about what had happened to Abbas.

"Dreadfully sorry to hear Basil got hit," Yeats responded, "but the attack fits our assailant. At this point, we have no question that Freddy shot up the Washington street café and had the fight with our agents stationed on Corcoran Street. The man's a killer. Don't let him get you cornered."

"Sorry to have to admit you're absolutely correct. I'm going over to the Fitzsimmons Medical Center to see that Basil receives nothing but the best care. I'll make sure my telephone stays turned on. I've still got the courier from Turkmenistan locked up in the police room here. I guess eventually we have to release him."

"I'm afraid so. We don't have many options with diplomats or people who carry immunity. Be careful, Sam," Yeats said. "We're dealing with a diabolical killer with the capacity to kill anybody, and I mean *anybody*."

"Yes, sir," Sam answered. "I'll be watching for the hatchet man." He hung up.

A recent conversation about *Six Degrees of Separation* came back to mind, and Sam remembered the theory that a maximum of only six people stood between him and any other person in the universe. If he knew the right combination of people, at this exact moment he could find Angelo Martinez. Only six!

48

Sam Sloan glanced nervously at his watch. It was five o'clock and the surgeons hadn't come out of the operating room yet. Some report should be issued on Basil Abbas's condition. Dick Simmons paced nervously about ten feet away. The hospital waiting room proved spacious, but the walls still seemed to press in on the men. Nobody wanted to admit it, but everyone had the same fears. It was possible that Abbas might not live.

Fitzsimmons Medical Center had provided them with every possible service, and the doctors had given Basil their instant attention. Nothing more could have been asked or expected. But Basil had been in surgery for an hour and time hung heavy in the waiting room.

"What do you think?" Simmons abruptly asked.

"I don't. I keep my mind off the possibilities," Sam lied.

"I called Chief Harrison in Colorado Springs and updated him about forty-five minutes ago. He'll convey an e-mail message to Jordan." Dick shook his head. "This isn't a good situation."

Sam looked out the window and wondered if Basil actually did work for the *Maukhabarat*. All the signs were there. He probably did report to the Jordanian secret service. What was the difference? All that mattered was Basil's survival.

"Night will come soon," Dick added. "I am prepared to sleep here if necessary."

"That's generous," Sam said. "Let's wait and see what they tell us before we make any plans."

"Okay." Simmons started pacing again.

Ten minutes later a doctor in medical scrubs came out of the operating room. Pulling a mask from his face, he walked toward the two detectives. "You're friends of Basil Abbas?"

"He's my partner," Sam said. "We all work for the Colorado Springs Police Department."

"Fine." The doctor smiled. "Looks like Mr. Abbas will be much better by the morning. We were able to get him sutured up and in good shape, and I think he'll be in excellent condition when he comes out from under the anesthetic."

"Can you tell us what you did to him?" Simmons asked.

"We opened up the wound to make sure no organs were punctured or severed. Abbas had some internal damage but nothing we couldn't repair. Fortunately, the knife missed any significant arteries, so there was no serious internal hemorrhaging. We cleaned out the abdominal area around the wound carefully and put him back together in good shape. We stitched the wound on his head. He'll need to take it easy for a couple of weeks, but our man will recover quickly. He's a lucky guy. You won't need to stay with him tonight, gentlemen. Our staff will pay careful attention. Go on home and get some rest."

Sam shook the doctor's hand. "Thank you, sir. Thank you very much indeed."

"That's why we're here." The doctor grinned. "We do our job and you men do yours. Makes the world spin better."

"We try," Sloan said. "Again, you have the deepest appreciation of the entire Colorado Springs police force."

"Thank you." The doctor turned and walked down the hall.

"Looks like matters have turned out about as well as possible," Sam concluded. "I suppose we can go back to Colorado Springs."

Simmons exhaled deeply. "What a relief! I really was afraid Basil might not make it."

Sam nodded his head. "That was always a fear. At least he'll live to fight another day."

Simmons picked up his coat and slipped it on. "I think I'll go back to the Springs too. You need a ride?"

"Afraid so. When we got up this morning, Basil and I weren't sure where this confrontation would take us today. We flew in but didn't rent an automobile. I didn't plan on ending up in a hospital."

"Ain't nothing like police work," Simmons said. "Certainly takes you to corners of the world you hadn't planned to visit. Fitzsimmons was one of them."

Sloan smiled. "Well, at the least, it will be good to go home tonight and see my family. We've been gone longer than I expected. Cara will be a happy girl."

Dick and Sam strolled out of the hospital, walking down

the steps toward the parking lot. Simmons unlocked the doors and the two men slipped inside.

"Got any idea where this Angelo Martinez is?" Simmons asked.

"Not the slightest. Maybe the guy jumped an airplane and is on his way out of the country."

"Not with the increased security at the airports these days. They'd have nabbed him quickly."

"Yeah. Probably." Sam sank back in his seat, thinking about the possibilities.

Simmons sped out of Denver, taking Interstate 25 home to Colorado Springs. For a long time no one spoke as the car silently cruised down the highway. Finally Dick said, "How was your trip to Washington, D.C.?"

"Challenging," Sam said. "We faced an uphill battle all the way."

Abruptly Sloan's cell phone rang. Sam flipped it on.

"Mr. Sloan?" a man asked.

"Who is this?" Sam answered.

"Paul Miller. Remember me? Paul Miller with the Motion Picture Association."

"Miller!" Sam pressed the phone against his ear. "Yes, certainly I remember you. Did you ever talk with my daughter?"

"Sure did, and I've been working on the leads Cara gave me. Her work saved me an enormous amount of time."

"Good. Were you able to help her?"

"Yes and no," Miller said. "I didn't come up with anything new for her search, but I did find out something I believe deserves your attention."

"Really?" Sam pressed the phone more closely against his ear. "What did you discover?"

"As we discussed earlier, I've been working on changing the security system for the way DVD movies are recorded on the disc to keep this DeCSS discovery from costing us a fortune."

"Yes," Sam said. "I remember."

"But I've also been involved in another project on the side," Miller continued. "Ever hear of the FBI's Magic Lantern technology?"

"No. No, I haven't."

"Rather fascinating because it's sort of a Trojan horse approach to breaking into anyone's computer. The work that Cara did made it easy for me to access Angelo Martinez's computer and use that system."

"Trojan horse?" Sam blinked several times. "I think you've lost me on this one. I know about computers, but I've never heard about one of those gadgets."

"The whole thing is new, but the idea is to get inside a suspect's computer and record the secret key the owner might be using to encrypt a message or a file."

"You can do that?"

"The legal questions are still up in the air, but I know how to operate over the Internet and get inside a hard drive. Yeah, once Angelo opened his e-mail, I was ready to settle in for the winter."

"Excellent, Paul. You've done well."

"Let my supervisors know you're pleased. G. Boone Jones would be glad to get a letter of commendation from you."

"What did you find out?"

Miller cleared his throat. "That's the point. I picked up a chance message that Martinez sent out today. Looks like he knows somebody in Mexico because that's where he was sending this information—to Juarez, Mexico."

"Juarez? You're kidding."

"No. Martinez sounds like he's heading south, but he's going to stop in Colorado Springs first. Isn't that where you live?"

"Yes." Sloan's voice became more intense. "I live in the Springs."

"Well, my Trojan horse came up with this message that I'll read to you. 'Must stop in Colorado Springs to end all eavesdropping. Going to cut off the big nose.' That's all he said, Mr. Sloan. I thought you might make something out of this."

Sloan stared out the window. "'Cut off the big nose'?"

"That's what Martinez encrypted inside another message sent in Spanish."

"Miller, I appreciate your discovery. Please call me immediately if anything else comes in."

"I certainly will. And my supervisor's name is G. Boone Jones. That's spelled G, period, B, O—"

"I got it. Thank you. We'll be in touch." Sloan flipped the phone off.

"What did you learn?" Simmons asked.

"I don't know." Sloan rubbed his mouth. "At best, a quite disturbing message."

49

For a long time Sam Sloan didn't say anything but stared out into the black night. Simmons entered Colorado Springs and started toward Twenty-third Street.

"You know," Sam said slowly, "the only eavesdropper on Martinez from Colorado Springs would have to be my daughter, Cara."

Simmons frowned. "What?"

"I know it's not correct procedure, Dick, but Cara is a very bright person and I had her help me with some computer work to save time."

"Computer work?" Simmons looked at Sam quizzically. "You know everything is confidential with the police department."

"Sure—and I didn't violate any of our secrets. I just had Cara run down material on who this A.M. character might be, and she helped me nail Angelo Martinez."

"You think Freddy could find Cara?"

"She ran him down, and Paul Miller in California told me a few minutes ago about a Trojan horse system that the FBI is now using to invade computers. Freddy's bright and ambitious. Sure, if she located him, I don't doubt Martinez could have uncovered Cara. I think you'd better speed up."

Simmons pushed the gas pedal down and flipped on his flashing lights. The car raced forward.

"No," Sam intervened. "Turn off the lights and don't hit the siren. We may need to coast around my house before we hit the panic button. Who knows what Martinez could be doing right now?"

Simmons flipped the switches off. "Okay, but I don't like the sound of any of this." He slowed the car as they moved up Twenty-third Street.

"When you get close to my house, take one of the side streets and let's go around the block a couple of times. We need to make sure the area is clean."

Simmons slowed and turned down Bijou Street to circle the block. "Don't see anything suspicious." He kept the car at a normal speed for the neighborhood.

Sam stared out the side window of the car. "Look!" He pointed down the alley. "I saw a man walking down the area behind our house."

Simmons pulled to the curb. "Are you sure?"

"Dick, park the car." Sloan reached for the door. "I'm going back to see what's happening from the front of our house. You go up the alley."

"You're sure it was a stranger?"

"No, the person could have been a neighbor setting out

trash. Maybe the individual is nobody, but we can't take any chances."

"Yeah." Simmons reached under his coat to unfasten his gun safety holding the pistol in the shoulder holster. "I'm ready."

"Move fast," Sam said and slipped out of the car door without making a sound. He darted up the side street and then turned toward his house. Sam slowed as he approached his driveway. He could see Vera's car sitting out front. Crouching near the bushes in front of his neighbor's house, Sam saw a light on in the kitchen and a glow from a bedroom light.

A crashing noise ripped through the peaceful night and Sam knew the kitchen door had been opened forcefully. He heard Vera shriek and a man demanded, "Don't move!"

Sam grabbed his pistol and ran for the house. He tried to steady his hand. He could feel his heart pumping blood like a jackhammer breaking concrete. He reached for the front door, hoping it was unlocked.

"Who are you?" Sam heard Vera shout.

Sloan turned the knob carefully. The door was unlocked.

"No, no!" the man in the kitchen said. "Wrong question. The question is who are you, Mrs. Big Nose?"

"What?" Vera sputtered.

"Don't toy with me." The intruder's voice was hard and demanding. "Been playing a little computer game with me, haven't you, Cara? Quite a hacker, huh?"

Sam froze. *Cara? The guy had to be Martinez, but why was he calling Vera by the wrong name?* Sloan slipped his finger closer to the trigger and prepared to leap in. *Got to stop him right now.*

"Cara Sloan?" Vera gasped.

"Yeah, I'm putting you out of the computer business."

Sam jumped into the kitchen with his gun pointed at Martinez. "Drop it!" he screamed. To Sam's surprise, in front of him stood a man wearing a black ski mask. He was standing about five feet away from Vera.

The masked man turned away from Vera. "Sloan?" He aimed his gun.

Vera grabbed the handle of the skillet she'd been frying hamburgers in and slung the steaming grease at the intruder. Sizzling oil splattered across the attacker's face. The man grabbed his eyes and his gun went off, sending a loud popping noise across the kitchen and lodging a bullet in the ceiling. Plaster exploded in all directions.

Suddenly Cara stepped out of the hallway door and swung a baseball bat, cracking the assailant across the top of the head. The attacker dropped to his knees and fell forward on the kitchen floor.

Cara stared at her father. "Dad? Where'd you come from?"

Sam could barely speak. He reached out and grabbed Vera, clutching her to his chest. "Thank God!" he panted.

Dick Simmons rushed in the back door. "Everybody all right?" he yelled.

"Barely," Sam said. He could feel Vera shaking as she clutched his coat. "Just barely."

"Never seen anything like it," Vera wheezed. "What in the world happened? This nut thought I was Cara!"

Cara rushed across the room and hugged her parents. "He thought you were me?"

"Yes," Sam said. "He picked up on your hacking into his computer, Cara. The crook must have thought the culprit was my wife, not my daughter."

The teenager gingerly tiptoed toward the man, reaching down and pulling the black mask off his face. Large red blotches had already formed around the man's eyes, with streaks running down his cheeks. His eyelids had started to swell. Angelo Martinez groaned but didn't move.

Cara leaned over and stared. "I've never seen this creep before!"

"Neither have I," Vera said. "I thought we were going to die."

"Cara, get the phone and call 911," Sam instructed. "Tell the operator you're Detective Sam Sloan's daughter and demand that they get a squad car out here instantly. This character on the floor is absolutely a killer!"

"Let me secure him." Simmons pulled Martinez up into a kitchen chair and handcuffed his hands behind the chair. "That ought to hold him." He looked at the man's gun on the floor. "This joker even brought a silencer with him."

Sam pushed back from his wife and walked across the kitchen. With swollen eyelids and bad burns on the side of his face, Angelo Martinez sat sullenly for a moment with his eyes closed. A large knot had raised on his head. Then he blinked several times and looked completely dazed.

"Martinez!" Sloan exploded. "Angelo Martinez! You idiot, thinking you were smarter than everyone else in the whole world, huh? Well, we caught you, didn't we?"

Angelo looked away and didn't speak.

Sam clenched his fists several times and then finally made his palms stay open. "Freddy," he said, "you've got a real sense of humor. You thought my daughter was my wife. And my kid whacked you with a baseball bat! Sorry, you lost on every count."

Martinez only stared at the floor with a stunned look on his face.

Sloan turned to Dick Simmons. "This is the FBI agent who stole the DeCSS disk, killed Yakoub Natshe, tried to bomb me, shot people on the street in Washington, stabbed Basil, and attempted to kill my family. I'd say he qualifies to be chained to a wall."

Simmons nodded. "We'll make sure Martinez can't wiggle by the time we drop him in a cell. You can bet on that fact. When the police arrive, we'll take him downtown and lock him up in the slammer. You did quite a job, Sam." He extended his hand. "Welcome home, Detective Sloan."

50

THE NEXT AFTERNOON SAM SLOAN REQUESTED THAT THE jailer bring Angelo Martinez into one of the police station's interrogation rooms. Sam watched through the observation mirror while a policeman put Martinez in a chair behind a small table and left him handcuffed. The officer walked out of the room, leaving the former FBI agent by himself.

Sam studied the strange man for a few minutes, observing his listless behavior. The defiant arrogance was gone. Grease burns had left ugly red blotches around his eyes and down the side of his face. Sam recognized the protruding bump where Cara hit the man. Martinez didn't look angry as much as sad and forlorn. His carefully formed plans had fallen down around him like an old roof. Whatever he might have thought a week ago, Martinez would now find it impossible to travel to

Juarez and freedom. He was trapped in a six-by-six-foot cell for the rest of his life.

Sam's original contempt for the corrupt man edged toward a sense of the ominous. Angelo was a bright fellow whose intellect was completely wasted. Sam shook his head and walked out of the observation area into the interrogation room.

Sloan sat down across from Martinez. "Good afternoon," he said professionally.

Martinez didn't answer but stared over Sloan's left shoulder, avoiding eye contact.

After a long pause, Sam said, "Matters don't look good, Angelo."

At the mention of the name Angelo, Martinez's abstract gaze shifted. He looked into Sloan's eyes but didn't speak.

"I'm sorry. Truly sorry you're here."

Martinez blinked several times but still didn't say anything.

Sam picked up the file on the table and glanced through it quickly. "You've been charged with grand theft and murder in the country of Jordan, as well as assault and battery on a police officer, as well as attempted murder against my own family. I believe that you will be charged with the murders of CIA employee Jeff Meacham and FBI agent Dale Beck, in addition to the deaths of the civilians gunned down at the sidewalk café on Pennsylvania Avenue. Heavy charges." Sam closed the file. "Of course, I have not yet mentioned the treason indictment for spying on behalf of the country of Iraq, as well as your personal attempt to kill me in Jordan."

Martinez's jaw tightened and he swallowed hard.

"I personally interrogated Marwan Alnami and he talked. Your contact gave me a description of the methods used to provide a conduit through his country for sending military information on to the Iraqis."

Angelo looked down at the table. His face sagged. He looked beaten.

"I should tell you that we used the DeCSS device I obtained from your Corcoran Street apartment and deciphered the message you encrypted on the movie tape. Your voice came through loud and clear."

Angelo slowly raised his head and stared at Sam Sloan. He puckered his lower lip and sneered. "You feel superior, don't you?"

"No." Sam shook his head. "I feel sad. You've squandered a life filled with opportunities for nothing more than a little extra money. You killed Yakoub Natshe to steal his discovery so you'd have an easier time transmitting your data on DVDs to the Iraqis. We know you've been sending our enemies military information for some time."

Angelo looked blank.

"I suppose the only question is whether the United States government will release you to the government of Jordan. If you are sent into that foreign land, I imagine you'll discover that the justice system of this country is infinitely more gracious than you ever imagined. For the bombing of the Natshe residence, I guess they'd shoot you on the spot as soon as you stepped into Jordan."

Martinez's head jerked slightly and he stared into Sloan's face. "You think they'll send me to Jordan?"

Sam pulled at his chin for a moment as if pondering the question. "I suppose it will depend on how you cooperate with the United States legal system."

"Um-hum," Angelo muttered. "Just what is it you want to know—in addition to this volume of data you've already compiled on me?"

"I'm not here as your enemy," Sam said, "although I must tell you that the deaths of Jeff Meacham and Dale Beck do weigh heavy on my mind."

"One more time," Martinez snapped. "What do you want to know?"

"Why in the world did you use the initials A.M. in your attack in Jordan?"

Angelo's eyes widened and he looked surprised. "I planned to drive straight through to El Paso tonight," he began, "after I finished this, uh, business in Colorado Springs. I thought I'd travel south and simply disappear somewhere in Mexico. Maybe I'd reemerge as a wealthy don in an elegant restaurant on the Rio de Janeiro waterfront, or possibly I'd settle in as a retired businessman living in Buenos Aires. Sounds good, doesn't it?"

Sam nodded his head. "Yeah. I understand."

"Do you?" Angelo barked. "You? A nice Anglo boy? I don't think so."

"I was raised in the slums of Chicago. Life was rough and I got whipped by the neighborhood boys of other nationalities with some frequency. Me, understand poverty? I grew up in it."

Angelo squinted at Sam with one eye partially open. "Chicago?"

"Immigrants had a difficult time of it. Jack Sloan, my father, came down from Canada during Depression times. We lived through everything Hispanics face today."

Martinez settled back in his chair and stared at Sloan. "So you want to know why I used the A.M. initials in Jordan? I suppose it was a little game with me, Sloan. You see, I always hated being called Freddy. The name came from that old Red Skelton parody of Freddy the Freeloader, a bum, a beggar, a leech—because I was the poor kid whose parents waded the Rio Grande to come north for a so-called handout. Of course, they worked themselves to death in this land of plenty. Every time I heard the name, I cringed. Do you understand?"

Sam nodded slowly. "I do."

"That name helped push this poor Mexican kid right out of the American economic system. I wanted to become a wealthy man without buckling under and becoming one of 'them.' Well, I didn't, and I used the name Freddy as a way of thumbing my nose at the police and security systems of the world. I answered to the name Freddy, but no one had any idea what was going on inside my head. The truth was that the initials were my way of saying that I had beat the system, the whole constabulary system around the world." He chuckled cynically.

Sam took a deep breath. "I wondered . . . and now I understand."

Martinez jerked his head defiantly. "Maybe you do and maybe you don't, *señor*." He spit on the floor.

Sam stood up slowly. "Angelo, you learned a great deal about catching crooks, using computers, making explosives, and you've been a very clever man. But unfortunately the world isn't put together so that cleverness always wins." He started walking toward the door. "The Bible has something important to say to people who consider themselves more intelligent than the rest of society. The book of Ecclesiastes says that 'wisdom is better than weapons of war; but one sinner destroys much good.'"

Martinez looked puzzled. "What?"

"No matter how intelligent a person thinks he might be, if he is decadent, his best-conceived actions come back like a boomerang in the face. Sorry, Angelo. Using the initials A.M. was actually what brought you down."

Martinez's mouth dropped slightly.

Sam closed the door behind him and walked silently down the hall.

51

A week after Sam Sloan's interrogation of Angelo Martinez, the Sloan family drove to Basil Abbas's apartment. He'd been home only a few days, and Sam wanted to make sure Basil was as good as he sounded over the telephone. He knocked on the door.

"Just a moment," Basil called out.

The Sloans could hear him unlocking the bolts. It sounded like Abbas had five locks on the door frame.

"Yes?" Basil said, allowing the door to crack open only an eighth of an inch.

"Expecting terrorists to strike?" Sam said.

"Sam!" Abbas swung the door wide open. He was wearing a long robe over his pajamas. "Welcome!"

Sloan grinned. "My, my, but don't you look like the man of leisure."

"Vera!" Basil hugged Sam's wife. "And you brought the little one!" He kissed Cara on the cheek. "Except that she isn't little anymore."

"We wanted to make sure you were truly doing okay," Vera said and extended a pot of soup, "and be certain that you're getting a good lunch every day."

"Good heavens!" Basil clasped his hands together. "The Bible says, 'Blessed are the poor,' and here you are making me rich!"

"Hardly," Cara said and handed Basil a loaf of bread, "but here's something especially nutritious to eat with your soup."

"Bless you, child." Basil took the bread and hobbled over to a table, placing it on the tablecloth. "I actually feel better than I look. Just can't straighten up like I wish I could."

"Look, Basil. I saw you on that rest-room floor in Denver." Sam glanced around the apartment. "You were in serious condition."

"Just a few scratches."

Sam noticed the furnishings were sparse but the living room walls were lined with full bookcases. "You've got quite a library here, Basil."

"A few books," Basil said modestly. "Come in and sit down."

Cara looked attentively at the shelves. "Basil, you've got more books in this one room than most people gather in a lifetime."

Abbas looked up and down the shelves. "I do read all the time. You'll notice that there's no television in this room either. I don't allow anything to cause my mind to go stagnant."

"Have to commend you for that," Sam said.

"I do believe there's no limit to what we can grasp," Basil said. "The more I learn, the more I know of the wonder of the world and the glory of God."

"That's what I told Cara weeks ago," Vera said. "The more we learn, the greater is our potential to come close to God."

"Yes!" Basil raised his finger in the air like a professor lecturing. "Absolutely correct! I believe we were able to solve this murder because we used all the resources that intelligence made available to us. After all, Cara, your knowledge of the computer broke this crime wide open."

"Excellent, Basil," Vera said. "That's a good rationale for why God allowed these inventions to come into existence. Scientific discovery, intelligence, learning, Scripture, the search for the truth—they all fit together. God desires truth from us. The book of Proverbs tells us to acquire wisdom and understanding."

"Spoken like one of the church fathers." Basil patted Vera on the hand. "An intelligent woman!" He pointed around the room. "Please sit down."

The Sloan family spread out across the small living room, sitting in different chairs. "They kept you longer than the doctors indicated they might," Sam said. "You know Freddy nearly killed you."

"Apparently killing was something of a hobby with this man," Basil answered dryly. "I give thanks to God that he only sliced me. A couple of inches to the center, and I would have truly had a problem."

"We're grateful you called Dick Simmons when you did," Vera said. "That one action probably saved your life."

"You know, I haven't heard much about this case since I went into the hospital." Basil pushed the long strand of black hair out of his eyes. "Has Martinez talked yet?"

Sam shook his head. "Freddy's shut up tighter than a rusted car door, but we've put all of the pieces together. Martinez tried to unload fairly significant military secrets on DVDs the Iraqis. We don't know how much he peddled, but appa ently he sold significant information."

"I guess Dale Beck's death alone would hang the man." Bas shook his head.

"Yes," Sam agreed. "Simmons also has Charlie Boyles in ja Strange how the chase ended. Remember we talked about th movie *Six Degrees of Separation?* The idea of the film was that v are separated from everyone else in the entire world by only s people. Line up the right six individuals and you can find an body." Sam laughed. "We started out chasing someone wit the initials A.M., and it certainly took less than six people find Angelo Martinez. It looks like this case is wrapped up."

Basil winked at Cara. "Think so, Cara? Think it's all done?

"Well . . . before this problem in Jordan started, I worried if could do enough to get my parents to see me as an adult. I gue I felt inadequate and not very capable, but as things have turne out, I was able to do far more with my computer than even thought possible. And"—Cara stopped and looked at her fath with one eyebrow raised,—"I kept *all of it secret.* I didn't even te Jack. Got that?" She pointed her finger accusingly at her fathe

"Oh, a toughie!" Sam laughed. "Well, it's hard to admit, b my little girl is far from little anymore."

"Absolutely," Basil added. "I'd guess that Cara and Vera we sisters if I didn't know better."

"Know better?" Sam rolled his eyes. "At the least, this tim you didn't lay a quote on us from some long-dead saint. That an improvement."

"Really?" Basil said. "I was about to note what Augustin once said about sisters . . ."

About the Author

ROBERT L. WISE, Ph.D., IS THE AUTHOR OF TWENTY-SIX published books, and also writes for numerous magazines and journals, including *Christianity Today, Leadership*, and the *Christian Herald*. He is a bishop in the communion of Evangelical Episcopal Churches. He collaborated on the national best-selling Millennium series, which includes *The Third Millennium, The Fourth Millennium,* and *Beyond the Millennium*, and is the author of *Be Not Afraid, Spiritual Abundance,* and the Sam and Vera Sloan Mystery series.

DON'T MISS THESE OTHER BOOKS IN THE SAM AND VERA SLOAN MYSTERY SERIES

The Empty Coffin

This first book in the Sam and Vera Sloan Mystery Series introduces a Christian detective and his wife who live their faith in the rough and sometimes brutal world of crime solving.

The daily work of a policeman can push an officer into the most debased side of life. Sam Sloan struggles to stay faithful to his Christian ideals while solving brutal murders and heinous crimes. *The Empty Coffin* finds Detective Sloan and his wife, Vera, faced with the greatest challenge of their lives. In addition to solving a difficult case, this tough cop still tries to live out his faith with honesty and conviction. The problems Sam faces at work create tension at home. As the Sloans struggle to keep their marriage together, the couple evolve into a crime-fighting force, working together on difficult cases that baffle the police. Sloan's hard-nosed detective work, coupled with his faith and humility, brings an unusual solution to a murder case in which there is no corpse!

ISBN: 0-7852-6687-9 • Paperback